Mr 101

Z. R. Ghani

First published 2016
by Rowanvale Books Ltd
Imperial House
Trade Street Lane
Cardiff
CF10 5DT
www.rowanvalebooks.com

A CIP catalogue record for this book is available from the British Library.
ISBN: 978-1-910607-51-0

To my English/Creative Writing teachers:

Ann Oakley
John O'Shea
Colin Edwards
Ian Breckon

One's Battle

On Titan, one of Saturn's unrivalled collections of moons, a mighty horse stood, whiter than the coldest Antarctic snow. His complexion was ghostly as a veil, and like icing sugar dusting on chocolate fudge he began cruising along Titan's surface. Leaving hints of glistening crystals in his path like a rosy-cheeked flower girl detailing the path of the betrothed, on he went, while the persistent thought of innocence sent a tear to his eyes. He observed the sun from a distance, a speckle of a raindrop resting upon the smoky petals of a phantom rose. Titan's sands shivered at the horse's heartbeat and he carried on without reflection, releasing heavenly frost from his nostrils. At his hooves begged a generous lake, calm and brilliantly blue wherever the light offered its majesty; where light was obstructed the methane ocean was a livid sapphire. The horse dipped his head and took a sip from the liquid, drinking to his satisfaction. When his thirst was quenched and enough was enough he lifted his gaze, humble as apple crumble. It was barely a second later that the liquid turned to poison within him, causing him to collapse and convulse, the acid seething from inside, salting his sacred flesh with fire. He neighed frantically, heaving and kicking with his hooves. The emptiness about him echoed his cries. Eventually, the horse collapsed to the ground with a low thud, still managing to breathe faintly.

Mr 101, in his idle occupation of Titan-gazing from the discomfort of his living room had just about absorbed this miracle with the help of a glass of wine and a modest telescope, which up to this present time he had believed to be an object of pseudo-machinery. With the expected release of a burp bearing the stench of alcohol, he waved the object about, shaking, stroking and finally putting it back in its velvet-lined antique box.

1. *A star cannot, by itself, realise its own beauty without first falling to experience the throes and joys of life.*

Mr 101 despised the sun. He had decidedly cut the 'dollop of worthlessness' from his life one morning after realising he wanted to dedicate his life to eradicating his fears and not live — and perhaps die — the way he was conditioned to by society, by nature, by his own subconscious. He lived to carry out his errands, one of which was to continue on living. As long as he was living and not plotting his own demise, he could achieve his goals. Seated on his Turkish-imported 'saffra', he voyaged between the lines of books, diving head-first into the realms of puzzles, mysterious items banned or unheard-of and theories incurred by anonymous men who, in their lonesome retirement, built a repertoire of excuses and explanations to harness an understanding for their unruly lives. At the same time, he gave orders to his 'Higher Self' (or as a few would call it, his 'Drunken Self') to build a small church for attending to his Sunday duties, along with ninety-six bedrooms, a living area, two Chocolate Rooms and a Running Room. The remainder of his days were assigned to rest. He spent one hundred and one sunless days in dire solitude and contemplation before his occasional sleep eluded him completely.

2. *The brighter the light before you, the darker the shadow behind you.*

His skin crawled at the mere thought of sleeping now so that he couldn't do it, no matter how long he lingered in bed. He cleansed his mind and that was enough. Enough was enough to keep someone calm and satisfied. Happiness was not exactly a desired emotion; he believed it to be a mysterious concept, one that he was much too superior to understand. He was determined to remain unhappy and there would be no dark corners to it; it would be no clearer than the light of day... or perhaps that was the worst association to make. What was meant was that it would be no clearer than the clearest crystal under the observation of electric light. Though, it was the contribution of excessive electric light which made him delusional, as if he was much more intoxicated on red wine than usual, so he lit candles instead. Of course, wine was the only liquid he consumed or ever approached without the feeling of disdain. And what did the neighbours say about him living in complete darkness? Well, there wasn't anyone else — apart from those who would trespass his realm as a symbolic transition from one dimension to another. The house earned a remarkable reputation among mystics and was a landmark to those who knew of its existence.

His chosen home was on one of the many islands near Cornwall — it doesn't matter which. He was its only known inhabitant, having ferreted himself out from the real world for a jolly good waste of time, along with the dense forestry of cedar trees and an untamed garden of huddled hyacinths and wildlings bordering the house. The building itself took a strange form, displaying the fascinating relationship between skin and bones. One could not argue that it was a fine piece of architecture — controversial by all means of modern interpretation. There was not a single living soul who'd decoded the layers of mystery or ever dared to replicate this artefact of fantasy, it was certainly against the laws of health and safety. Upon entry, one could expect nothing but the normal decor of an English country house; large banisters with thick marble stairs piled upon a chequered floor. But this farcical setting ended there, for with one glance upward, far beyond the monumental chandelier which held a mirror-like resemblance to Medusa's menacing head, an infinite number of stairs twirled and twisted in diverging displays in all directions. They formed abnormal spirals and writhed, elongating more than seemed necessary like cigarette smoke. Some led to doors; others led to nowhere. It was as if someone, most likely the owner of this awful house, had accidently kicked paradise into purgatory resulting in a gushing radiance with equally abysmal phantasmagoria without a seal or stopper put in place to stop it from spreading.

3. *In the beginning there was nothing, and in the end you must expect nothing less. But while you're suspended in between, do your utmost to make it something.*

Every doorknob was a curled fist enclosed in a leather glove; it would unfurl ceremoniously when a creature came to the landing. The visitor would then have to shake the gloved hand to be admitted. This was done to welcome them in and seal the agreement that whatever would be experienced within was not to be blamed upon the room itself but the traveller's curiosity and imagination.

Some visitors claim to have heard the Medusa chandelier speak to them and demand the reason for intruding this mysterious place. But this was perhaps their imagination speaking. And often when the word 'perhaps' was used, 'definitely' was meant.

***

Sometimes, to escape inexplicable thoughts, Mr 101 would sit and stare across to his velveteen black curtains or his 'guards', and would contemplate the vast subject of beauty; how it withers with time, how it temporarily heals the soul and then devours itself. Those poor women, born beautiful, grow to die in the eyes of society. But he had no need to worry; a bachelor remained young, always. On other occasions, he would try to work out the best way to help someone by satisfying his own insatiable desire for the human flesh... But the fact remained that there was little he could do to save the world where he stood. He could hardly pluck up the courage to save himself. His scalp, to be more precise, was almost rid of all its hair and this played incessantly on his mind like a scratched record. He then wished he'd pointed out the refuge of his marbles before he'd lost them, so that he could aspire to relocate them one day. One day, having caught his distorted reflection in a wine glass, he made haste to alter his appearance by combing back the patch with an ivory-boned comb and his saliva. The result would have been effective if it hadn't been for gravity, which would flick his fringe back to its comfortable position. And yet it cannot be ignored that flawless beauty still resided in his features.

So, nervously reaching for the wooden drawers, he removed a container of face paints which were on the verge of solidifying. As he drew back the lid, nostalgia from the circus travelled into his nostrils and effused in the atmosphere — but he was a performer no more.

Could the din of the grand parades come knocking on the door of silence at that very moment?

He withdrew the contents and smothered his face with the white fudgy substance, spreading the paste in all directions, not missing a single inch of naked skin. When this was done, he curled his eyelashes with the small amount of mascara that he had saved from a meeting of one of his many lady friends. He kept it like gold, cherishing the notion that one day he may pluck up the courage to return to it. The black smudged onto his batting lids and when he tried to rub it off, it smudged even more. The whiteness of his face did not aid the flaw but rather accentuated this error. He then smothered his lips in black lip-gloss which afterwards resembled a butterfly's shadow. Altogether, with his eyelashes clotted in black, black potent lips, black pupils, black suit, he was the darkest existence since the new moon on a backdrop of a white universe. He returned the acknowledgement with a wry smile and nodded at the mirror. He was on the edge of a 'thank you' when he realised there was nobody there. Then he left the room for another occupation until the coming evening.

It was the lavish evenings that invited the hope of excitement and led him to stray off his thoughtful path. Coaches stuffed full of female fancies would arrive to entertain him, sometimes in masks which he enjoyed, sometimes not — but never the matter! Prior to entry, the imagination could only underestimate the unreligious liberality that whisked away any prepared prudence or rehearsed reticence. Logic dictated nothing, and the normal was nothing more than a functioning tail to the enormous 'paranormal'. The studied mind was tested, made a mockery of, theoretically flattened into a coin and dropped into the stirrup-cup of the obsolete for later analysis. And this supposed coin joined and jingled with many others long forgotten. The hall of Room Two held Beauty's attar of roses, myrrh and incense. Its floors would lie under an array of feet all night, desperate in its desires to be trampled on in the next occasion. The ladies suited the regal baroque furnishings and added glimmer to the delicate chandeliers in waiting for Mr 101's chocolate. All in all, in one all-consuming conclusion, it was a sight giving the thumbs-up for offensive gestures. The dismal notions came with an even more dismal price: his guests came and never left. Their souls just about managed to leave with them. His home and hyacinth-plenty garden was the meretricious joy and secret pain of him and from it Mr 101 could never escape. The cedar trees barred the house from peering beyond the crowds of female gatherers and the resurrected hyacinth flowers from the planet's yearly ritual: spring. How cruel a season!

On rare occasions, Mr 101 dwelled on the possibility of perhaps reforming his habits, somehow shifting his addiction to another and another until he would come full circle on himself — or at least until there would be not even a single germ of labour to be fought over and he could relax and stretch his legs properly. In Room Two, he caressed his warm mug of mulled wine; jasmine petals slept under the almost scarlet liquid. The warmth made his index finger twitch uncomfortably and he thought of how unnecessary it was for his fleshy twigs to tingle at the mere sign of heat. It was certainly a rare sight to catch Mr 101 with a hot beverage; he preferred his daily intake from a wine bottle, which was more convenient, needing no preparation at all.

Soon he'd be old enough to be excavated, he thought, and have a number of scholars shine a light on his deeds and argue over how relevant he was in the depiction of the modern society in an age of austerity.

It was on one of these ponderous dusks (he was not counting) he spent in complaint with the divine over his destiny, when an unexpected rapping came from the main entrance of the house. This was quite extraordinary to him seeing as his lady friends would always come through the small back door. He thought the sound held the likeness of someone accidentally knocking Satan's backside with a brief kiss — yet he had never witnessed such a thing or even been brave enough to eavesdrop on such an encounter, so perhaps the familiarity corresponded to a nearby future event. He glanced at his reflection for a moment to confirm he was presentable — or at least not too despicable to sign for the wretched parcel if it was the postman — and pitter-pattered his way down his fine set of ivory marble stairs, his footsteps light as organised raindrops following a graceful pattern. The desperate rapping came once more and he noticed by the ravaging sound that the quiet dusk had evolved into a most hellish night; his house was under siege by torrential rain. When he came to the landing he noticed a crop of unopened letters and parcels on his chessboard floor. He kicked them aside as he reached for the wooden door.

Unfortunately for Mr 101, it was not a postman or any other irrelevant workman, but an old acquaintance that arrived drenched in rain despite his frail umbrella, which was continuously hopping with liquid bullets. What shook the master of the house to his near premature death was the presence of a meek young girl. She stood next to the man, wearing an olive green dress and stockings, just about stretched up to her knees, and cockroach-mangled shoes. He looked down at her in horror. To him, her eyes were reminiscent of the dead and her face bore no emotion — just a blank canvas, an unopened drawer, an unreadable note.

Mr 101 then glanced at the trembling man, crouched and holding his umbrella seemingly for dear life. He held a briefcase in his other hand. It was the master of the house who started the conversation, as he had already sensed Walter's nerves like a siren going off in a silent hall.

'What can I do for you, *dear* friend?' He presented a fake

smile and stretched out his hand, praying that it would not be met by Walter's wet handshake.

Walter's hands were full enough, so instead he thrust the girl forward with his briefcase, and stuttered, 'I... well, my Daffodil here needs a place to stay while I'm gone. It's a business trip, you see, it's very urgent, sir. I beg of you, look after my Daffodil. I have no one else —'

'What about her mother? One can hardly exist without a mother,' Mr 101 asked, not allowing his eyes to stray from the girl.

Daffodil gazed up at him. Whatever she made of this strange man, it was nothing special, not yet.

'She is... unwell. She is not fit —'

'No, I couldn't possibly. Well, maybe I can if I try. *Yes*,' said Mr 101, maintaining his gaze on those telling eyes of total despair.

'What? So you're saying that... you...'

'This sort of place will leave a stain on your child's... already stained stockings.'

4. *Everything we feel is fabricated from the splashes of chemical imbalances and a host of internal anomalies.*

Walter's hands trembled like a dancer's swan-feathered fan. 'Yes, but I am desperate more than anything else. You're the only one I know. Just promise me you'll keep her from —' He was abruptly cut off as the building received a sadistic whipping of violent thunder, as if it was a malevolent wife who'd spoken out of turn and was undergoing her overdue comeuppance.

'I'm not promising anything.' Mr 101 turned his gaze from them and took to analysing the floor littered with envelopes and spits of rain.

'Right. Well, Daffodil knows I'll only be gone a couple of months, don't you? Alright now, be a strong girl.' Walter's smile to his daughter was as brisk as a slap.

Having been fooled by the smile, Daffodil leant over to embrace her father but in return he shielded himself with the briefcase and gave her another swift smile and, without an ounce of hesitation, disappeared into a blanket of rain. The door slammed shut behind Walter; something clicked to indicate the activation of a lock and made the walls respond with a haunting echo. Daffodil slipped inside delicately. Without a package or luggage of any sort, she hesitantly took a step closer to Mr 101 who was now standing on the landing, frozen and staring straight into her sunken eyes. His mind was partially preoccupied by the notion that he might soon start gnashing into the main course of his life — whatever that meant. He observed her olive dress absorbing the white light of the gazing chandelier.

Daffodil lifted her eyes from him; beyond the terrifying face of Medusa she saw a miraculous series of spiralling stairs. She encountered webs spun in concrete and marble that escalated to the heavens, only a few of its silk threads leading to doors.

'Where will I sleep tonight?' she asked.

But Mr 101 had long disappeared without a trace or sound in this house of infinite passages.

In the middle of this chaos, there was a sinister part of me who knew my life would never be the same again.

The Lady in the Mirror

Daffodil, in her discomfort and grief, spent the night resting on a dusty flight of stairs next to a doorway which held no door or destination, but simply a black hole. After Mr 101 had disappeared, she'd spent a good hour or so searching for him, knocking on a few doors but receiving no reply. She had thought she'd heard something from behind a wall that, to a knowledgeable ear, would have sounded like something not far off an elegy being recited.

> 5. *Let the glimmering landscape fade. Leave it all to darkness and to me.*

After having travelled since early morning and crossing the ocean, she had found herself to be uselessly fatigued; her legs were worn rubber. She'd collapsed onto the floor and had immediately fell into a wholesome sleep — apart from momentarily awakening to the sound of the incessant scratching of either a pen drifting along the horizon of paper or fingernails scraping allergic skin. In her dreams, the walls were the composites of doors that could be shifted like tiles with the intention of the mind.

***

The next morning Daffodil was woken by the sound of clapping thunder and the dancing of rain to be faced with Mr 101, standing closer to her than he'd ever been and observing her with a wealth of curiosity. His face was no whiter than chalk. She got up immediately.

'What in the world possessed you to sleep on the stairs?' His fingers were trembling.

Daffodil stared at Mr 101 with no idea what to say. She continued to stare instead.

'What makes this situation more absurd is that you were resting just on the brink of your bedroom. Look closely, will you?' he continued.

When Daffodil neared Mr 101 she saw, as before, a black hole. Yet as she took a few steps closer, she began to realise that it was not a hole but in fact a velvet curtain covering a hole in the floor which, when drawn, looked down into a reasonably sized bedroom. To enter, one had to pluck up the courage to drop ten feet to land on a double bed. This bed was so springy that when Daffodil first took a leap she bounced back up through the hole to land next to Mr 101 as if she were magnetically attracted to him. But Mr 101, who was not amused, pushed her back down to her bed.

The bedroom consisted of a bed, a floor and a window. The walls were black and cold. Its simplicity should've been almost offensive to a child. Even a minimalist would have demanded more than this, in both content and character. However, Daffodil was grateful — even excited — about the prospect of not having to sleep on the stairs again.

'Dear me,' Mr 101 said, staring down at her as she shot up and down from the mattress, her hair almost brushing the ceiling. 'You do have a strange imagination, but if that's the way you are then that's the way I must accept you. Now, come here this instant; I must inform you about this house —'

'AAARGH!' cried Daffodil, hardly able to contain her excitement.

'Come back here, before you hurt yourself!' growled Mr 101.

When Daffodil bounced back to him, he hastily shut the curtains in anger exclaiming, 'Do I look like I'm a suitable guardian?'

Daffodil stared at him, swallowing her own thick saliva. Breakfast would be nice, she thought, and then her mind returned to his question. But he was much too quick for her.

'Your father is not *here*, so let me make this clear to you. Everything you do must be thought of much in advance and be executed with immense care. For example,' he said, pointing a long-nailed finger resembling a shark's tooth at her nose, 'you must not go gallivanting through any old doors, for there will be consequences! You can go in there, there, there, there, there, there and there!' He pointed in different directions to the doors which read the numbers zero, one, one, two, three, five, eight and the last, thirteen.

But as far as Daffodil could see, there were no other doors than the ones he pointed out, so she simply nodded. She positioned herself to dive back into her room, but Mr 101 grabbed her by the collar and pulled her.

'One last thing,' he said. 'I have *people*, or shall I say *women*, who come to visit me every evening after the sun is clearly gone from the sky so you must make sure that you are in bed by the time they get here. When the weather is nice, you may go outside. Don't ever bother me, I am always busy. If you need anything, don't ask for it. Look after yourself now. Goodbye!' and with that he left her for Room Two.

6. *I prefer Saturn's rings to wedding rings.*

That tumultuous night, Daffodil could not find herself comfortable enough to sleep; a tall, shadow-like tree was continuously thrashing against her frail glass window, as if holding a scourge. The rain viciously spat at it. She found herself unable to recall when the curtains had actually opened, for she certainly wasn't the culprit. Chaos was in her mind as one who is possessed with the most unwavering fright. She raised the bed sheet up to her eyes, but didn't cover them; if anything happened, she wanted to bear witness. Here, she was forced to participate in this show as a member of an audience, whatever it was about. In the very end, would she have the strength to raise her hands together?

Much later, beneath the floorboards came the sounds of approaching carriages, then later still the sound of forced laughter that seemed to stem from discomfort. The fluttering of oriental fans, sweeping of heavy dresses, the jangling of chandeliers, the toasting of wine glasses, the kissing on mirrors, the shuffling of hairs and other thuds on doors, walls and corridors — or so Daffodil imagined. The sounds caused her bed to jitter and shiver, so she was inclined to rest on the floor. Like a baby unborn, she curled and covered her ears and eventually drifted off.

In her sleep, Daffodil's breath was restless. Painful and joyful cries arrived sporadically, echoing within her mind as if it were an empty hall. She received momentary images of the eternal labyrinthine stairs, swooning forever like smoke which had failed to fade away, impossibly solidified under the dome-like roof. She saw doors. Doors — everywhere she turned there were doors, and each one was slightly opened. The door which lingered in the dream was the biggest one of all and was white, effusing the scent of new paint: clinical and acidic.

The knocker was absent so Daffodil shook its gloved hand to enter. It was fleshy and warm. The room was astounding — not in size, for it was small enough to be a broom cupboard, but in content. The walls on all sides were mirrored and the floor was tiled, alternating in a mystifying red and yellow mosaic pattern. They played with her eyes when she looked at them directly, giving her the sensation of being on a merry-go-round. Daffodil's reflection was missing on the mirrors, making her doubt that they were mirrors at all and that she was there in the first place.

On the floor on the other side of the empty reflection, she noticed a small object she could not quite see. She went down on all fours so as to acquaint herself better and adjust her focus. It seemed this little object was a miniscule human being: a woman in fact, wrapped in white garments. Her body was multiplied by her many reflections, producing the illusion that there were millions of her, symmetrical to her position. She slept on her side on the floor, snoring. When Daffodil moved closer to her, the lady woke with a low scream and millions of versions of herself jumped to their feet as she did. Daffodil remained in her position, observing this curious creature who was clearly holding an empty bird's nest in her arms.

'You! Get me out of here!' The creature's voice was muffled behind the layer of glass which separated them.

'How?' muttered Daffodil, her head close to the glass so she could hear the lady's voice.

She looked about her, searching for something to help her release the woman. As if out of nowhere, handles emerged from the mirrors and Daffodil, following her instinct, grabbed onto them and they stuck to her grasp as if invisible ropes tightened them. The lady waited with a look of curiosity on her face. It was obvious that the workings of this room were as much of a mystery to her as they were to Daffodil.

Daffodil, unable to free herself from the handles, struggled and found herself to be in control of the mirrors. She was able to manoeuvre the walls like the captain of an aeroplane. Whenever the mirrored walls moved the lady stayed still, so Daffodil was able to move the door towards where the lady stood. So if she had thought correctly, when she opened the door the lady would be on the other side. Having done so, her hands slipped from the metal handles of the mirrors and they, in their imagined existence, disappeared in an instant. She now stared breathlessly at the large door, which opened. She was bewildered when she saw the lady grown to the normal size of a human being. She was fitted in a tight corset of immense white, but her skirt was an enlarged birdcage that encased a young twittering bird. The lady produced a genuine smile and walked gracefully through one of the doors which were plastered on the wall, her sleek auburn coils stirring in the wind.

Daffodil stayed seated on the floor when it swallowed her back to reality with the full force of gravity. Without realising, she was back on her bed, bouncing away.

7. *The diversion from good takes on an impractical journey which at one point turns in on itself and directs us to believe in the infinite forces of the divine.*

Time seemed tight-footed in Mr 101's house; it seemed to take breaks in between hours and inhale wholesome breaths at the termination of a half hour. Having no particular business with time itself, Daffodil carried on springing up and down from her bed. She was perfectly amused with her hobby, hopping like a deer through hedges and tree bark, until a hand grabbed her leg. The hand dragged her through the feather-filled mattress and pulled her further into the floorboards, where she was flung to the living room floor by Mr 101, who was standing on an immensely long ladder that was leaning over the ceiling.

'You're disturbing me,' he bellowed with disgust, glaring at her, his lips smothered in black goo.

Daffodil gave him a look that iron would give to gold.

'Why don't you read a book?' he growled.

Daffodil got up nervously and quickly snatched the closest book to her on the walled mahogany bookshelf. It was a yellow bound book without a title. She sat on the floor not far from Mr 101 who, having climbed down from the ladder, threw himself onto his infamous saffra, opened a small diary from his trouser pocket and began writing. Now and then, he would shoot a look askance at Daffodil who was faced with immense difficulty with the text of her book. Some of the words were faded and paragraphs were vigorously annotated or simply blacked out by Mr 101's excisions.

'I see that you are not *reading* the book,' said Mr 101.

Suddenly, he received a revolutionary idea and began scribbling with delirium-rooted intent; the pen scuttled across the pages as a rabbit shuffles the earth to make itself a new home. He shot a glance at Daffodil, who was speechless.

'Well, why aren't you reading the book?'

'It's difficult and there are no pictures.'

'*No*. Why would there be? Grown-up books don't have pictures in them,' he stated, starting to doodle in his diary.

'Why can't grown-up books have pictures in them?' Daffodil replied resolutely. Talking to Mr 101 was like prodding an angry tiger with a wooden shaft: he could simply snap at any minute. Knowing this excited her further.

'I don't know. Probably the same reason why your father doesn't love you, ha ha!' he guffawed, seeming rather impressed with himself, and returned to formalising his previous theory.

This comment did not sit well in Daffodil's mind; indeed, it was doing the waltz, alone, dressed in its Sunday best. She certainly thought it a careless retort for her question — and her father *did* love her, otherwise he wouldn't have promised to come back. Daffodil's eyes flitted through the pages as her mind dug itself out of the present into the burrow of the past, until she was re-living last night's adventure. She believed the woman could have been a ghost; it was definitely not a dream. So what exactly could it have been?

It did not take long for Mr 101 to become uninterested as he felt the book he'd recently begun to read had a reverse effect, in that it was reading his own mind. So he left Daffodil to her pretend reading, heading for the Chocolate Rooms. Before his guests arrived that night, he thought about his earlier comment to Daffodil and made the effort to write it down with an implausible excerpt; something from the back of his mind had just been made useful from the new circumstance.

8. *'Flour of Daffodil is a cure for madness.'*

Fears

Two tables of stone were placed beside one another in Room 0, which reeked of dried flowers to the point of driving one to the doorstep of insanity. They weren't draped in supple linen as in preparation for a supper, but neither did they appear like an unburied body. These tables bore the only appearance of togetherness in the house, and on their surface was encrypted the fears one could adopt in Mr 101's house. One stated the common term used to define the fear while the other informed, to the intruder in Room 0, its most honest definition. These were (in alphabetical order):

Amathophobia: *Fear of dust*
Anthophobia: *Fear of flowers*
Apiphobia: *Fear of bees*
Dishabiliophobia: *Fear of undressing in front of someone*
Domatophobia101: *Fear of being in a house with Mr 101*
Equinophobia: *Fear of horses*
Ichthyophobia: *Fear of fish*
Mottephobia: *Fear of moths*
Nostophobia: *Fear of returning home*
Ornithophobia: *Fear of birds*

If Daffodil had shaken the gloved hand of the room's door and entered, she would have been compelled to slide her forefinger on the tables' damp surfaces and raised it to her nose. Her nose, like a rabbit's, would have fidgeted in the air. Then, the lingering scent of a rotting bride's bouquet would have sent her soaring beyond the threshold of sanity — or at least to another strange doorstep. But she didn't.

9. *She's the one, I'm the few.*

The Genesis of Stairs

No-one can say how long this piece of silk thread was as it descended from a dark, reversed well in the universe. This well was a weak vessel, a trumpet of glass, sounding out stars and spectacular rocks. By accident, by chance and by the will to cause mischief all at once, it had fallen from the hands of someone who could knit magic from simple strings, such as noose ropes and fishing threads. On its spiralling voyage downward, the string withdrew a cunning riddle to the atmosphere that wiped away all its reasons for existing. And as it bulged and swelled from the symptom of ego, the thread became a branch of cirrus which a sanguine musician, in awe, captured.

This instrumentalist (expectant and never innocent) was also a wanderer, a veteran on all the verses of the universe and the just-about-believable breviaries. Before this, he'd awaited considerable book-lengths for a sign, meandered blind-cornered tunnels and tightropes before twirling satin-like in the air. Being inside this universe made him feel like a seed, thus muted and waiting to unfurl with the potential to inspire and heal through reveal. He was devotion incarnate, but held a yearning to be its nemesis: distraction. When he felt like sleeping, he would play his harmonica out of tune to awaken the switched-off stars that would keep him company. They would hum awake, the rhyme of rime, opening like eyes to let fall the sun-snow from their eyelids.

As soon as the cirrus came into his realm, he treated it as his second harmonica. As if previously acquainted with this object, he played it expertly in tune, stretching and coiling the cloud in length, blowing the white substance like dust on an untouched surface that interplayed with light and shadow. He was its candyfloss machine without the nostalgia. In any case, the steps were forming from the work of his hands. By finally dropping it in a well of water, it solidified as in the production of glass but lacked the potential to smash into pieces. How could he tell then that his creation would eventually become a slave to feet, a seat to uncomfortable arses, carpet-muffled and planked? It was important that he detached himself from this venture, to undertake another conundrum so someone else could take the blame or acclaim as the inventor of stairs.

The Chocolate Rooms

'Welcome to the Chocolate Rooms'. There was once a sign erected in gold, carved with these words and nailed to the secret door situated under a flight of stairs. Now the sign, along with the pleasantries intended was nowhere to be found. To elaborate; no-one was welcome to intrude upon the main subject of Mr 101's pride as they'd been before, for his growing fear that the rooms, that had made him sought after and manifested envy from those lucky few who knew about him, were under threat. Also, there'd been too much gold in the house that it was soon becoming an inverted sun. Now, access was almost impossible to anyone with the exception of the one who made it so. The Chocolate Rooms' door (riddled with locks), once pushed with great effort on the owner's part, led to a hypnosis-inducing spiralling staircase which only Mr 101 could journey down and terminate. Every step of this strange staircase was a tale of trickery like watching a magician at an exhausting play with his cards. Once complete, the last rung unfurled two huge chambers designed and built to look like two links of a chain. Each one was as enticing as the next, purposefully made to look like a mouth; the first room acted as the bottom of the mouth, the latter was the roof of it.

Overall, the construction had the vastness of a cathedral matched with the claustrophobia of a genie's lamp and the intimacy of a boutique hotel. Lofty walls of crimson rained down from a small ceiling and arched over the procession of giant mixers and ten feet long ovens. Coolers hissed on sparkling chequered floors where sweetmeats, wonderments in brilliant colours and cloisters of sugary treats flowed on conveyor belts. Everything provoked the taste buds and was magnificently satisfying, even to Mr 101 who never ate any of his own creations; just looking at them pleased him. After travelling along the conveyor belts, the sweets ended up in the mouths of large sacks. When each sack was filled, an empty one was replaced automatically on the hour, and so this ritual continued until hundreds of bags were piled in the corner like giant cubes of marshmallow.

Will there be enough chocolate to feed his ladies for tonight's event? Mr 101 was counting their heads in his head while admiring the striped fountain of melted chocolate deliciously blended with peanut butter from the distance. Then he turned his head to the strawberry and cherry slices pirouetting in their own pulverised jammy juices, confined into giant gold-lidded jars, and dollops of custards spurting out of randomly placed copper pipes landing in hollowed out pastry. With inflated pride, Mr 101 looked upon his red velvet walls cemented with red liquorice twisting ropes. Far below that the red velvet cupcakes topped with butter-cream frosting parading out of the oven that would later end up in an appreciative mouth profusely rouged.

The ingredients for the making of these little wonders came from the second room of the two, whose ceiling rose much higher to fit in a fine piece of machinery which resembled a fairground Ferris wheel. It was made of wrought iron to make it sturdy, and decorated with blinding neon lights of all colours. The lights made Mr 101 smile, which is what he'd come down here to do in private. The seats were replaced by large bulbs of translucently-shelled eggs which cracked the ingredients upon reaching the floor into a cart that sped on its own accord (as most of Mr 101's machinery did) to the first room. There they would empty themselves into shining copper cement mixers that would spin the batter for cakes, chocolate and a dozen other things that make the mouth curve into a smile.

The object of rife gossip, and second only to the Medusa chandelier in its ability to intensify any atmosphere, was the very chandelier seemingly in a struggle above Mr 101's head. It ignited a thousand colours from its chains of infinite crystals, at that moment giving Mr 101 a headpiece of light which looked as if it was layering bridal lace on his dark patch of hair. He used the chandelier's rainbow prisms to reflect on the oven trays positioned directly below on the floor to create edible rainbow strips. Apart from that, it was not needed for anything else — although Mr 101 knew it could be used for much more. Attached perilously to the small 'screw-top' hexagon ceiling, nothing — especially not something as trivial as science — could explain why the chandelier would swing ceaselessly from side to side, taking a risk on its fine little crystals which could, if it came any closer to the wall, smash into pieces. Its behaviour was that of a comet restricted by a noose, yet Mr 101 paid not even a single glance to the monument which harrowed above his head and sent a spring breeze to his untameable fringe. Spring: a cruel season indeed! It could be inferred that the chandelier sought to destroy this mechanical establishment, in turn ending its own miraculous co-existence with the house. But it's unwise to assume that objects have a purpose, not even if this object began to act on its own accord. In his mind, Mr 101 conveniently assumed that it was a playground toy discarded from the heavens and conveniently landed itself here and was somehow captured by the ceiling. Because things had a way of appearing without a logical cause in his house, he saw it fit to reify the strangeness and give them an explanation — even if it was contrived from imagination, and especially if it was absurd. Most often the truths behind serious questions *are* ridiculous.

Mr 101 took a few paces here and there, checking if all was running smoothly without a fracture in sight, not fussing too much as he knew that his system and structure was nearly fool-proof. In the midst of all of this temptation, Mr 101 could not bring himself to pursue even a single item of edible goodness. He was saving his empty stomach for later. Soon, the noise and sight of it all began to suffocate him rather than flatter his ego, so he left The Chocolate Rooms for Room 101.

One on One

It was yet another turbulent night for Daffodil, who twisted and turned on her springy mattress like a worm in the rain. Sweat grew and swelled from her pores.

In her dreams, once again, she was sucked into a scene where long, dark corridors' walls were plastered with doors. Somehow throughout this unnerving journey, she intrinsically knew where she was heading. As she continued on, breathing irregularly, she found a door with the number 100 nailed on its varnished surface. A silver smudge of moonlight came from somewhere, although there was hardly ever a window devoid of a curtain in the house. Could it have been Mr 101's face reflecting on the door? No. Looking over her shoulder, she saw the dark corridor snaking infinitely. She gently shook the hands of the door and let herself in. Her bare feet met the weirdly warm wooden planks as she observed the space around her; the stuffiness and the smell of sweat told her she was in a shoe closet. Railings after railings lined the walls, yet they were empty save for a pair of stilettos at the far end of the room which confirmed the shoe closet's purpose. The shoes were platforms with high, slim heels elegantly covered in dark satin where the motif of a white horse was repeated in a pattern. A tag was tied like a tiny noose around the heel. The scruffy hand-written note read:

Genuine Ginny Chew. Worn by: Madeleine. Died: 01/01. Cause of death: Mr 101. Note: Must Recycle.

A green recycling logo was printed on the bottom to emphasise the recyclability of the tag.

Daffodil dropped the shoes immediately but they didn't make a sound after hitting the floor — or perhaps Daffodil was much too disturbed to pay attention. She stared about her in desperation, but all that could be seen were naked white walls and an infinite amount of railings. Was Mr 101 a murderer? Surely she should not be surprised at such information? And who was the lady she rescued from the mirrors? As the questions began to tumble over each other in her mind, she made a run for it. However, in her haste she toppled out of the doorway and into the arms of Mr 101, who was steadily making his way to Room 101 to actualise his procrastination. Having not realised what he'd done until after a few moments, he hastily dropped her on the marbled stairs in disbelief of having touched her.

Then it dawned on Daffodil that what she'd just experienced was not a dream. She must have sleepwalked — or perhaps dreams and reality were one and the same under this roof...

10. *I'm sure when the time comes to learn the one truth, we'll either snigger at it or look down and wonder disappointingly, 'is that it?!'*

Daffodil looked up at Mr 101; the strength to get back on her feet was non-existent in this instant, as she'd wasted all her energy on being petrified. She also felt awkward in his presence, much like a zebra in the midst of a pride of hungry lions — only much worse. Having entertained his guests all night, Mr 101's make-up had loosened and grown crusty; the flesh of his lips emerged from the dark shadows of his lip-gloss, appearing as blistered petals of a once red rose.

'What in the bloody —?!' he cried angrily, wiping his dry hands on his trousers.

Daffodil took a nervous breath and stuttered, 'I was, I —'

'Well...you shouldn't have! I haven't got all day to sit around and chat with you. The sun must be out, so go outside and stay away from me!'

Daffodil nodded frantically.

'And take this...You might want to make use of it,' he

hissed, handing her a bruised pear as he walked away.

He had encountered the fruit on the floor of the Chocolate Rooms that very morning, having probably been placed there by an uninvited visitor. For Daffodil, this was the only hint of food she had laid her eyes on for days. She scoffed the fruit as fast as she could, saving a couple of seeds in her mouth which she threw on the soggy garden lawn along with its tainted core as soon as she was outside.

The garden was certainly impressive, offering a necessary realistic relief from the extreme eccentricity of the house. Among the untamed verdure of weeds which sprouted in instances bloomed the early colonists, including the tall blue-throated hyacinths which poked their curious heads above the green crowds, introducing welcoming bursts of colour. The flighty bees circled petal after petal, unknowingly collecting pollen upon their backs in their amusing youthful naivety. Daffodil felt as if she was swimming in the sun's oceanic blue light; the plants synchronised with the dream-like quality of the moment. A wild hare appeared and peeped from a gathering of overgrown lawn, munching away on an afternoon snack. Dandelion seeds were plucked free by the fingers of the wind and created imaginary spirals in the air like Sufis without gravity. The incredible mass of cedar trees close by held out their branches like longing outstretched hands. The unfathomable lurked beyond them.

11. *I am opening myself up to her one petal at a time, the scoundrel that I am.*

The coastal waves beckoned her to the island's escarpment. It was surprising how the house could block out the sound of the ocean entirely as if purposely wearing ear plugs. One would never realise they were close to the ocean; after a while, they would easily forget even the mere existence of it and then they come to know nothing but the house itself.

The waves bravely leapt unto solid rock where they dispersed into sprays that hissed, merging into the unseen air. This process was repeated as if nature was at work, like axe men tearing down a large bark. The waves continued to heave and hiss; sometimes the odd plastic evidence of a long gone Friday night would join the tides on their endless mission of destroying the land.

Having flown for many miles, a strange flock of birds arrived cawing, circling the blue-grey sky which seemed to borrow the grey shade of a whale's back. They settled on their chosen destination: a rocky outcrop not too far from the island where Daffodil stood quietly observing. Thousands of white specks dotted the translucent sky above, blocking out the previous serenity. Some soared closer to Daffodil so she could make out the spot of golden sunshine which burnished their heads, their bodies being lily-white save for the hint of charcoal smudge on their wings. One plunged into the icy water, hungry for prey but only managing to grab the remnants of a broken beer can with its long pointed beak. Without hope, the creature flapped its wet wings to the nearest spot of rock and rested among thousands of others. The birds made a pearl-encrusted brooch from the lofty piece of rock.

The sun dived from the whale's back eventually; the sky marked Ra's temporary departure to the underworld with a purple hued protest. Its exertions were in vain, for a few moments later the purple was reduced to night with only a mental patient, the Moon, for it to redeem. Adding to this, the winds turned chilly and the darkness merged all things visible to one entity of black. The waves still catapulted their might upon the rocks in their eternal quest to erode the land while the birds cried and cawed in conversation, their voices echoing in the air. Daffodil looked at the house behind her and noticed a slight fidgeting of the curtains.

When she returned to the house, Daffodil saw a flicker of light reflecting in one of the doors like sunrays on a knife blade. Ascending the stairs, she saw Mr 101 fixing a light bulb belonging to a rather peculiar praxinoscope. Another glimmer of light came from the candles surrounding him, adding an oriental hue to the yellow wallpapered room carefully painted with cream coloured roses. Little did she know the yellow pigment of the wallpaper was made by

Mr 101's use of a crucial ingredient: pig's urine, which he'd attained from a distant dweller of the cedar forest a long time ago.

Having hung his silk blazer on his chair, Mr 101 was hard at work fixing an antique. He'd obtained this particular article in a swap for an authentic peacock feathered fan that once belonged to one of his many lady friends. He took the entire piece apart, examining each aspect of the object so that if it ever broke he would be able to fix it in no time at all. That was a clever little philosophy (or uncalled-for gibberish) he'd picked up in one of his leather bound books titled: *Don't Wait Until it's Broke to Fix it.* So, after exercising this newly adopted principle, he stared at the object as if seeing it anew, then sighed.

'I know you're there little girl, there's no use hiding from me. I can feel the walls breathing on my skin; each step you take is like unblocking a pore. Come and sit here, make yourself uncomfortable. Come now or you'll make me nervous!' He kicked out an armchair from under the table.

Daffodil crept into the room, almost tiptoeing to her chair. Mr 101 twirled the wheel of the praxinoscope and the mirror within spun round, projecting the silhouette of a galloping horse. The light was no match to the black print of the horse — if anything, the plain white background emerged to the foreground. Like an expanding star, it was slowly swallowing the horse, thinning its outline, but the creature persisted in racing in this cyclical strip. The light was too much, too strong; the poor creature was no match for such power but still he carried on battling with the light. Mr 101 spun the object, fervent in his approach. He wanted to see this. He had waited much too long. He was in the position of control and for him there was no better place to be. The horse, after much adversity, eventually tripped on a blank space of white, falling flat. Uttering a sigh of relief, Mr 101 stopped spinning the praxinoscope. Staring into Daffodil's eyes, he began to chuckle, revealing the large tombstones in his mouth. She had never felt more uncomfortable. His laughter was brief; Mr 101's joy was one as fragile as the flame of a candle flickering closest to him.

'Well, did you have a good day?' Mr 101 asked impatiently, glaring at Daffodil above the angelic light of the lamp.

Before Daffodil could begin to think of an answer he brought out another question like an envelope filled with explosives. He had a talent of doing so as to make the recipient wish to maim him in some way or another.

'Did you admire my gannets? But now tell me how the sun is.'

Daffodil felt a sweat begin to break from her forehead; having nowhere else to look but into the pit of Mr 101's eyes, she replied without thinking. 'Yellow...and bright?'

His eyebrows furrowed in mock confusion.

'*Right.* Tell me, is this lamp which sits before your eyes not bright and yellow enough?'

The girl said nothing, she momentarily glanced at the wall and realised that the flowers, so carefully painted, were distorted into human faces that had pearls for eyes. Mr 101 proceeded with the conversation.

'Your dress,' he began, eyeing up her clothes, 'looks like the dirty stuff that comes out of my nose in the morning, and your eyes weigh heavy on me like lead.'

A tear formed on the sill of Daffodil's eye, but before it could leap over and provide further ammo for Mr 101's use, she surreptitiously brushed it away.

'You see me?' he continued, having not noticed the sorrow his words had inflicted. 'I can afford this entire island, the island of the gannets and this beautiful object which sits before us, are you listening? Your father cannot even afford you a pretty dress. What I mean to ask is: how desperate must someone be to come to me for help? *Me.* Do you know who I am? The things I do...the obscenities which take place in this house is not fit for a child, it is enough to sever your halo. Not even in my worst nightmare could I have ever hoped a child would enter this building...hmm... now leave me.'

Daffodil glanced back before she left Mr 101 to see his face buried in his hands.

12. *We injure ourselves in injuring others.*

***

In one of the empires of in-between consisting of merely ocean and night, bleaker than black, the horse was an island stranded and pinned to the water. He was fading poetry on a poster, now undecipherable save for a word or two. Corpses in his periphery offended his now degenerating sense of smell, but the horse persisted on floating like a tender hope. For as long as he could last, he juggled the prospect of becoming immortal and the fear of being carelessly scratched out by a gold coin then swept away for no-one to see. If he so desired, he could destroy all but love — though he was hardly infallible. He was unstable, deserving better. He kept his eyes closed to cancel out the risk of witnessing anymore violence forced upon all but him. He'd lost his knight in the battle, the fourth horseman, the only warrior he knew who could maim without a sword. The neighbouring moons swelled, glowing like lamps to keep him company, the smallest ones the size of pearls — ever so precious — that the oceans harvest.

One drop, then two, until finally raindrops descended at the same pace as autumn leaves. They caressed his wounds and slowly zipped them shut in a fading blush. The sound was a song of woe. He continued with his pondering as he died again to live again for the attainment of a dream. An echoing sigh from the starry night pressed against his eyes; he kept them closed as an image of a piano's anatomy came to bring him solace — a piano that was falling from a considerable height and would inevitably come to crash. The pins were loosening, a drama was unfolding, the lines were blurring, a century blinked, and at that moment he recalled the psalms, lost it again to find it again; the painless option of fleeting death looming. His eyelids lifted, undressing those eyes of inconsiderable blue.

Saturnus, I cry in the daytime and the night seasons;
And
Silence is all I've ever been...

Wordsworth

Once again the night was chilly and unsettling, sending Daffodil into an irritable mood. The everlasting whining of trees forced her to burst open her eyes and leap out of her bed; she dared not dream again. Her bare feet touched the sheet of ice which was the wooden floor. The light of the ghostly moon leaked through the window, although very much hampered by the leaves and branches. A cry was heard from a room close by. A storm was breaking out of its chains; the clouds spun into action while a flicker of candlelight momentarily danced under her door before vanishing. The carpet muffled the sounds of footsteps, but they were heard nonetheless. Relentlessly, a hoard of clouds traversed the sky, loosening and spreading like spilt ink; the rain was falling in haste. The drops fed the trees and the earth as they greedily guzzled the moisture.

Daffodil peered out of the window. A small tree was in the process of growing where Daffodil had carelessly thrown her seeds that very morning. The sprout urged itself from the ground, unfurling and curling rapidly into life, extending its branches as if in the midst of a great yawn; it unfolded its leaves and grew pears that hung like lightbulbs on the branches. Daffodil watched, lost in thrills and elation for having been given the chance to witness this magic, while the storm fast-forwarded the growth of the tree. Thunder arrived ceremoniously and roared with a blaze of magnificent light.

Behind the light of the moon was its darker face where Mr 101 yearned to be, for his nightmares had just begun. And as he sat in Room 101, he felt a slight spasm on his index finger where his pen rested for the moment, in between another commentary on Ridiculism.

The madness he branded as Ridiculism was no Bedlam-insanity, no; it was not so simple a concept, but a much-needed dolorifuge to ease away the grit from experience. Simply put, this mad way of thinking was kept as a rare area, a show-garden that doesn't stop in its spontaneous bouts of retching with life. And Mr 101 would happily sit on his bench and admire, meditate, even dip his feet in the stagnant pool of fears he took to be the cleanest chute in the world.

> 13. *They started shaping diamonds differently after the 1930s, perhaps they should have done the same with women.*

***

In the morning, Daffodil rushed outside to see the tree. Without Mr 101's consent, she pulled the large door open and ran out freely onto the verdant path to the pear tree. It gleamed in a golden splendour in the sunlight that was as sporadic as a false promise. Daffodil couldn't tear her eyes away from the tree; there was certainly something artificial about its appearance that made it seem like a mockery of what a tree should be, or like a plausible symbol of a joke. Pears hung heavily on their branches and were coated in attractive olive-green, with a hint of a rosy blush on their curves. Daffodil reached out for the pear closest to her and didn't hesitate in biting through the barrier of skin which dissolved into her mouth with a juicy crunch. Not satisfied with just one, she had another and another, not minding her glutton a single bit. One pear took a plunge unexpectedly and rolled to her feet as she was eating. In her joyful state, she picked it off the ground and begun to undress it with a series of crunches, revealing its ivory flesh. As it churned in the interiors of her crimson mouth, she began to realise that she was chewing more than just a fruit, but rather an amalgamation of fruity flesh and something with a more wooden texture. Removing it from her mouth, she discovered that it was a chewed-up note and hastily unfolded it. Her knees sank as she read the blurred words from who she believed to be from her father: *'Be strong now, my Daffodil.'*

Before she had the chance to read it twice, three times or even a million times over as she would have done, a stubborn gust picked up the wet piece of paper and wrenched it from Daffodil's hands. Looking up, she realised that the clouds had covered the sky, returning it to its usual grey demeanour. How fickle the weather was nowadays! The hollow pear fell from her clutch and was immediately blemished by the dirt.

'My dear girl...'

Daffodil gasped at the sound of such a serene voice; it was not her father's as she had expected. When she turned to investigate, she caught sight of the strangest man she had ever seen.

His eyes were the brightest of blue of which only the heavenliest summer sky could be the envy of, and they were miraculously freckled like precious sparrow's eggs. The dense hay of hair which wavered upon his head was streaked in shades of honey. The seldom breeze he attracted tickled his loose linen shirt and brushed his hair slightly. When he spoke, his voice was quiet and in rhythm with the wind, and the leaves rustled excitedly to such extraordinary company. A chirruping sparrow took accommodation in the densest webbing of the tree, having grown tired of frolicking on the man's broad shoulder.

'...you must make haste to leave this unhealthy environment.'

Daffodil stared at him in shock having hardly heard what he said. However, there was an air of safety and security in his presence that made her remain on the spot, stapled to the ground. He held an authority in his posture and voice that was undeniably justified, even when one had no idea what there was to be justified. Having this feeling of comfort and being not at all inclined to go back to the house, Daffodil stayed with this mysterious man under the tree.

'What's your name? If I may ask,' enquired Daffodil, after a lengthy silence.

'Well, if it concerns you so much, my name is Wordsworth. You may not call me anything but that,' he said in a soft but stern manner. 'And you are Daffodil, who is currently lodging at this house.'

'Yes I am indeed, how did you know that?'

Wordsworth's crystal glares were searching. 'I caught sight of you when you arrived with your father; he called you Daffodil. The skies were raging that night. I myself took refuge in a cave, without fire or any source of light, and prayed for the sun in the morning which never came. However, my faith stayed with me and here we are today, in the sun's full bloom conversing under an unusually formed tree.'

The sun was coming and going that day, but at least it was present. It seems that silence sprang up between them once more, but strangely it felt more comforting than tense. Daffodil caught a faint sniff of honey borne upon the warm breeze.

'I miss my dad. I wish he hadn't left me here,' said Daffodil, sadly peering down at the wild daisies near her feet.

Wordsworth winced at Daffodil's statement and began fiddling with his loose shirt, not losing an inch of his acquired dignity. The mystery he exuded was unmatched, sensed by the child who watched him from what felt like a world away. He leant against the tree for support, staring down at his knee-high boots in complete solitude and sadness. Taking a deep breath of the west wind which filled his nostrils, he began to speak words of hope and encouragement.

'My dear girl, your father remains with you. Have you no faith? Take this,' he said, removing a wooden cross from his trouser pocket and placed it in Daffodil's left palm. A red rose embraced the cross with its mighty thorns.

'Keep it with you and be cautious. You do not know the dangers which await you here. There's so much that takes place here that is enough to send angels on a permanent voyage far, far away from here. If you fail to follow my guidance you *will* be lost. Let me make it clearer to you, Daffodil: run! Run as fast as your little legs can carry you, away from that house. The man who built it feels no remorse and has no conscience.'

As he spoke, the clouds began to gather, wiping away the seldom sun which had been eavesdropping on their conversation. The air became icy in a matter of seconds and the overgrown weeds hissed as it did so.

The sun wasn't the only eavesdropper to their conversation: Mr 101 held a magnolia trumpet to the wall with his long fingers, revelling in his animosity. Mr 101, who was never afraid to laugh at others lower than his infinite status, guffawed, then commented on the situation for his walls to hear. This monologue was fast paced and full of expletives; when finished, Mr 101 furiously spat on the floor.

Little did he know that at that very moment Wordsworth was looking with disgust at his festering house, a star dancing in one of his sky-blue eyes. He regarded the building as an infectious laugh that would take assiduous work to be sobered; a grotesque face staring into the blank expression of nature. His eyes suddenly turned sullen at the thought. Wordsworth eventually ambled from the scene with his feathery companion, and disappeared into the crowds of cedar to his dwelling.

Far across the distance, beyond the mossy cedar trees, neighed a white horse, showering himself in ecstasy as he was reborn yet again. He disappeared soon after, undiscovered.

Wordsworth's Dwelling

The earth brings life
to a shelter under sunlight,
near where black trumpets
and daisies grow on forest soil;
twigs interlace in tresses
and twills for walls that twine
with thyme flowers,
milkweed and baby's breath.
They breathe out sprays of gold,
old-romance to the peanut sprout,
and cress-furred roof as rough
stones and wildlings heap below
the arches of cedar, on top
of where a sparrow and a white
moth, that have come from
a gathering of forget-me-nots,
begin to dance.

One Ball

A day, night, hour, or perhaps a second later, Daffodil followed Mr 101 to Room Two, the living room. While Mr 101 bustled around, Daffodil observed the room in which she found herself. The room was currently populated with beaten sofas, a neglected piano on the far side and a small clock whose hands seemed to follow the pace of the phasing moon. The furniture was decidedly bright, and so inevitably clashed with the effortless rococo ornaments with its awkward geometric shapes and cluttered adjoining of lines. Dim lighting effused from bleeding candles that were located randomly around them. Daffodil's knees dug into the planks of wood as she knelt down to face Mr 101. He did not mention his motives, but began to breathe deeply as if he was restraining clouds of fury.

> 14. *This world is a cruel place: the only one which dangles your desires like bait before your starving eyes but gives you nothing until you've given up something precious to sacrifice.*

Behind the curtains, the rain tiptoed on the glass windows while the walls sucked in the chill of the outside air. Mr 101 hastily pulled over the already closed velvet curtains and kneeled on the floor facing Daffodil, the table acting as a barrier between them. Confused, Daffodil remained, still awaiting a magnificent show. She thought Mr 101 was very much like the magic trick where the magician pulls an endless stream of handkerchiefs under his sleeve. In short, he was forever anticipating a resolution to the chaos he started without ever finding it.

He placed three transparent drinking glasses in a line. Daffodil could see a small ball, incarcerated inside the middle glass, as clearly as she'd seen Wordsworth's eyes earlier. Mr 101 silently and swiftly shuffled the glasses, and after he was satisfied with his exertions he stopped and lifted his head.

'Which one holds the ball? You are not allowed to pick the glass in which you see the ball.' Mr 101 looked at her with the eagerness of a predator, hoping she would be wise in her actions for once and pick one of glasses which was empty. 'Take a little longer — you know I love to wait.'

Daffodil's hand slowly travelled towards the glass with the ball inside when Mr 101 seized her wrist and blessed it with a backhanded blow. 'Not that one.'

'Why not?!' demanded Daffodil, nursing her little hand, soft as her bed.

'Why not? She asks, why not? Look...here you have your goal, it is shown behind the glass' — here he pointed at the ball — 'but I will forever prevent you from reaching it, so *choose again.*'

Having been punished once, Daffodil was reluctant to try again but she did so to avoid his stare upon her which was cold enough to freeze the sun. She was fed up. Like a leaping cat, her hand darted to the nearest empty glass and returned to her lap in a matter of milliseconds. She sat there trembling with fear but Mr 101 was in a world of his own; he seemed satisfied with her choice. He eventually breathed a sigh and lifted the seemingly empty glass. A small ball identical to the other one rolled from the cup towards Daffodil, like a skull summoned to the sewers. To the child, even if the world had come to end it would not have even mattered. It was the most astounding event she had ever feasted her eyes upon; the ordinary drinking glass was now worth more than any crystal in the universe. For a minute, she sat there in complete paralysis and for that very moment, Mr 101 was a man of miracles.

As she picked up the ball, Mr 101 advised her to be careful. As soon as he did so the building cackled with the incessant knocking on the back door, signalling the arrival of his lady friends and comrades.

He lit a cigarette quickly and straightened his smoking jacket to answer the door, leaving the girl in the company of fading smoke and the useless clock whose face appeared to smirk in its display of the time. The ball nestled in her hand, as if it were a golden egg.

> 15. *Nothing should be taken away from you if it is rightfully yours and if such a thing is threatened, be ready to fight for it back.*

An Evening in Room Two

Mr 101's 'women' arrived, flooding his kingdom in small phalanxes, fluttering the essential extensions of their hands: their Venetian feather fans. They were draped in hand-embroidered cloths and Middle Eastern silks, their faces painted in precision to make out colours that were never there on their plain faces. Outfits made of passionate reds and soothing blues, their shoes complimented and subdued, until they resembled a Klimt composition. Rigid was the perfumed air that melted Mr 101's cigarettes fumes in an unfair battle. They whispered, stared and cackled.

Some of them had undergone surgery to have multi-layered eyelids that aided them to lose weight. Of course, this meant that great effort had to be made in order to blink: first they would shut their eyes and then they were forced to wait while the rest of the layers of eyelids blinked in succession. The average amount of eyelids per woman was ten, but some exceeded this to more than twenty. These were the ones that held an emaciated complexion and fainted before the night was over; blinking, for them, required the same level of effort as climbing a long set of very steep stairs, hence it quickly increased the number of calories they burnt.

Of course the women spoke obsessively to mask any assumption of fear; they were the twinkle-bells of gossip and other such energy-mongering vices that lead the lives of many to chilling contempt. They stated many words that were nothing but nonsense, the flapping of wings, simply to try to inject a little life into the architectural corpse of a room. Their auras lingered with heady perfumes, and if Mr 101 had the care to transform these scents into bricks he would have surely built another house by now, in the vicinity of this one, or a prison to keep all of the women in the world inside. For the women, normality couldn't stand it here; only the frightening could overthrow the frightening. Their old lives of longevity seemed like an imagined state before the tangible, excitable brevity of Mr 101's domain. So the wine poured from the fountains of bottles and they gulped down every drop as if time itself would run out on them, just as they were starting to add meaning to their lives. Sooner or later, the room was a sea of heads; some of the women smiled showing tombstones for teeth, others searched for the exit with protruding eyes, while others still simply reclined on a nearby wall, succumbing to boredom. Not a single object could be considered uninteresting for observation, yet most were judged as being useless due to the observer's fear to investigate further. If an object could not distract by chanting a deathless persuasion, it was discarded, buried somewhere dangerous and unapproachable by Mr 101. For this reason, everything in the room that could be seen with the naked eye sparkled with its own unique frequency, was profusely adorned with a magnificent throw or had been gone under a surgical level of etching that forced it to depict a forgotten folklore, given an extra purpose and surely surpassed the ordinary. Being much too engaged in their own terrible affairs, the women failed to notice even little Daffodil who had retreated to sit on the floor next to the stained sofa — partly to hide and partly because she felt undeserving of the sofa.

16. *The drive inside me has grown old, yet I'm still young.*

As was his custom, Mr 101 was on his saffra, salient as a commandment, saintly as a Chinese proverb, rather enjoying the ribald scenery. His seat was his Sufism, a retreat which transported him to metaphysical beliefs, notions and paradoxes. He combined all these components to create an altogether pointless elixir. Wasn't it an epoch ago when he plucked out the furniture from a room inside his mind which he branded 'a roomy room for Rumi'? This room or segment was where he forced himself to behave conservatively and ruminated senselessly upon untouched ideas to learn the A,

B and seas of mysteries. The room's second and last purpose was that of a tenuous waiting room which prepares its visitor for the obvious — but its walls could come down by a mere incongruent appearance of a gnat. By attending this room frequently in his mind he was able to influence his peers in his house into asking themselves in privacy, 'How could I describe this enclosure to anyone, when it is something that is nothing at all?' It must be noted that the notion of 'as above, so below' took flight in several strange ways in this location in relation to Mr 101's mind and his house; of course, one of those ways was by flying.

In a cosy niche, he sat like an orthochromatic voyeur, meditating silently on something he had perused earlier that day on the subject of patience. He took a draw off his cigarette and closed his eyes; the smoke enhaloed his moonlight face. It was then that a vision came to him. He saw the opening of a drawer with nothing in it, not anymore...

17. *At whose hands do we perish the most: life's or death's?*

The girls, his pawns, moved to and fro upon the Macrophotographic mirror of his eyes when he chose to open them again. He wasn't intimated because they weren't beautiful in the abnormal way, just as every candle flame more or less looked the same. His eyelids consumed them with a giant leap in the procession of a blink. As it did so he momentarily caught a glimpse of many microscopic germs that were his desires mutilating in undecipherable forms. Taking a deep breath, his lips sucked in a dose of nicotine. He breathed quite normally, especially when he heard the arrival of the unrepentant storm, for he was used to these natural atrocities by now. But his fingers were in a subtle state of agitation; they crawled the air as if boneless and playing an invisible harp. Beneath the layers of the blemished walls in his heart, he wished the night would run smoothly like the untying of a satin bow. *It would be perilous to waste the night,* he thought, *the underestimation of time is the greatest error of all*. It was with his bare dedicated hands he constructed the foundations of this building, with his own intricate fingers he tapped the tiles on the floor while the cement was still wet. Like the golden orb weaver he spun the stairs relentlessly in precise stages using a technique which previously only the spider had ever known. *But please, enough of this nonsense. Who was it going to be tonight? Who will stay until after midnight —*

His thoughts were interrupted by the entrance of two of his closest colleagues. They were formally dressed for the occasion, in black tuxedos and polished shoes like Mr 101. However, their appearance differed in the sense that while one held the air of arrogance in his obesity, with one of his arms elongated and armoured, the other stood tall, a reserved man whose small eyes harboured the same mystery and sorrow that the eyes of one who had acquired knowledge usually held.

The latter greeted Mr 101 with a casual nod and graced him with a tremendous gift of a rare antique music box that was immaculately constructed with mahogany. With hidden gratitude, Mr 101 accepted the gift and gave Mr Wordsworth — as was the man's name — a queer look, running his fingers on the lid of the object, where the outline of a horse was carved deftly, even by Mr 101's high standards. Having opened the magnificent piece of ancient machinery, he placed the box on his Art Deco table. He walked to the side of the room, and then from one of his many mahogany shelves he brought out a record and placed it on the box which began to spin and play serenely like a coprophagic beetle caught on its back. There was a glass entrapment inside the box where miniature eccentrically dressed youngsters danced in rhythm to Mr 101's bizarre interpretation of what music should be. To him, it was the most magnificent sound; he would sometimes reincarnate his love for Death Metal Opera when the birds were singing or when the telephone would ring. However, he was itching to tear the object apart, just in case it broke and he would have no idea as to how to fix it — though he was reticent to lose face at such a crucial time of the night.

In the corner, Mr Wordsworth seemed to understand

his anxieties and gestured him to take a seat on his beaten saffra. Mr Wormwood, the mechanically armed gentleman, was making mental notes on which girl he preferred the most, his robotic hand twitching in annoying clinks.

The men huddled in the dark, beginning a topic to start one of their never-ending discussions. Sometimes a desperate young lady would glance nervously over to them, concealing her face behind the lace fan and lose herself in a conversation to the nearest object standing next to her. She would be lucky if it had a heartbeat.

One of the girls grew impatient and tired after beating all her eyelids senseless. She opened her fan in a fluster. The former theatrical prop was more than just something used to send her loose fringe in a flutter like a wind-blown curtain to give a horrid view of a large forehead. It could be transformed into a bench. The pleated fan was extended by her meticulous fingers, curving the instrument into a full circle. When the spine was unscrewed, it gave way to a supportive wooden screen which functioned as both its backrest and legs when extended fully. Its intricate carvings attempted to copy the designs of Art Nouveau. Much to Mr 101's dismay, it did so too well and if the ladies were not so important to him or contributed to his Ridiculist career, he would have done a good job of sending all their fans into the fire whether they could be transformed into chairs or not!

The chair was an object created for the purpose of rest, as if it was its own Sunday. This could not be denied, as uncomfortable as the fan-chair was, but for the ladies it was symbolic in balancing the status of both genders. They felt like queens on their thrones, but one always had to find the correct time to make use of it and this was an immensely arduous task. To be specific, a crowded room could, at most, allow two fan-chairs to be opened at once. If a third were to be opened, one would risk setting Room Two in a blaze, what with all the candles that were lighted. It was as if electricity never existed.

'The weather is not very nice these days,' she began.

She was sitting in the middle of the crowd who was now

beginning to notice her.

'No, the weather is utterly disgusting! My feet were indisposed to touch the ground tonight so I waited until the water dried up, I tell you it was so cold in that crowded little carriage, I could've *died*!' cried another, who was sporting an outrageous hairstyle.

'The weather, oh the weather, what a shame!' fretted the other and soon enough they all began to talk about the weather.

The moon resembled a bullet hole in the sky that night as the men in the corner began their own series of small talk.

'Speak to me, Mr Wordsworth,' sighed Mr 101. 'Tell me about the failure of literature —'

'Mr Wordsworth?!' spat Mr Wormwood — the man with the mechanical arm. 'He never says a thing worth knowin'! These days he never speaks a word, what's wrong wiv ya? Growin' a heart or summink'?'

'Shut up, Wormwood,' said Mr 101 calmly. His words enslaved and entangled like an unforgiving snake. 'I was speaking to Mr Wordsworth.'

Mr Wormwood growled and drained his glass of red liquid with his metal hand, which nearly smashed the glass into pieces.

'You tell me, 101,' croaked Mr Wordsworth. 'These days I can hardly tell the difference between what is good or bad and as for literature, that thing went to the dogs a very long time ago.'

'The truth caresses my ears very gently, dear sir!' said Mr 101, clapping his hands. Although his glares were icy, from his oral sphere words of wisdom did make their presence known. 'It seems originality has truly made haste for a general sorry state of things. I mean, one author will come up with some sort of a creative concept and everybody follows in the same rhythm. For example, there was a fantastic novel I read some time ago named 'The Piano' then not so long after a little creep comes out with 'The Piano Musician' and straight away I hear of 'A Piano Tuner' and so on and so on...'

The last words of Mr 101 drowned into an ocean of

silence and nothing was heard but the shuffle of dresses and whisperings from the girls. The small group of men, on the other hand, entered a state of reverie. Mr Wordsworth stared into space encumbered in sadness while Mr Wormwood observed his glass over and over and again like a child with a rattle. Mr 101 also entered this blissful state of nothing. It was Mr Wormwood's lack of patience which broke the untamed meditation.

18. *Never let your desires run free, you can never know where they'll lead you, astray is just the start.*

'So...you're still calling yerself one or one, are ya?'

Mr Wordsworth's eyes glimmered at the question as he was suddenly awakened from another bout of contemplation.

'Is there a problem? Can't you muster the tenacity to be gentle?' snapped Mr 101.

'Dunno 'bout the ovver two but no. No problem,' guffawed the man who was nothing short of being a monster. 'But why one or one? Surely the only option you have is being one? Why can't you just be the one? Stupid innit?'

For the first time since the guests arrived that night Mr 101 glanced at Daffodil who was still sitting, curled on the floor. His eyes spoke to her in these words, 'This is what my life entails: night in, night out.'

Mr Wordsworth could not contain himself much longer as he had noticed Daffodil for quite some time.

'What is a child doing here, 101? Surely this is just a tad incongruous?' he stated in a fury wrapped in sarcasm.

'Walter's scum...' began Mr 101 before a glass was heard smashing on the floor as Mr Wormwood saw the child for the first time. He was truly aghast. He muttered undecipherable words under his breath, clearly shocked and excited by her presence.

'Is she real? Is she edible?'

He was now up like a toddler and started making his way to Daffodil when Mr 101 blocked him, starting to regain his previous anger. All the other women in the room had ceased their conversation and huddled like an audience watching.

However the fluttering of the fans continued, in hope that one of the men could still be hypnotised by it even though they were blatantly engaged. One of the closest woman, with her best dramatic skills, fainted but quickly stood up when she realised no one had paid attention to her.

'Keep away from her!'

Mr Wordsworth was trying his hardest to pull Mr Wormwood away from the girl but like an excited dog he was no challenge to his strength. Mr 101 was forced to momentarily step out of the room to fetch a horse tranquilising drug he kept in a secret stash. He returned swiftly, holding a small needle like a pen and darted the injection into Mr Wormwood's flesh. He sunk into the sofa like the *Titanic*. Mr Wordsworth sat next to him in disgust.

Mr 101, still clutching the injection, waved it about like a flag and stood in front of Daffodil, his arms gravitating towards the ceiling and to his audience he exclaimed, 'Ladies! This girl here is nobody's business and neither is she for sale! Leave her alone, all of you!'

He then left the room and no sooner than later the party was in full flow again. The girls continued to talk rapidly. Mr Wordsworth sat silently in the corner fidgeting with his cuffs. Mr Wormwood's body lay unconscious as a fish caught sailing on a boat. Daffodil felt safe enough to approach the former; she sat down at his feet and asked him a question which had been bothering her all night.

'Why do you look different to how you did in the morning?'

Mr Wordsworth's face changed in confusion, his eyes darker than ever, 'Whatever do you mean? We have never met until now. Do not allow these walls to play with your mind.'

'But I met a man named Wordsworth under the pear tree today and he told me to run away, far away from here. Was it not you?'

Mr Wordsworth was in shock but he had a great skill of hiding it, like the magician who locks his assistant in his suitcase and when he opens it, his assistant vanishes. To the audience it's fascinating; they gasp like children, their hands clasp to their open jaws but to the magician, he has lost a rather useful companion.

'Why... Why, you were fantasising, I believe... Enough of that now.'

'Please —'

'Do not speak to me. I am *Mr* Wordsworth. There's nothing else to it.'

'But I saw him.'

At that precise moment Mr 101 entered with a grin plastered on his face (it was rather forced and disturbing) pulling a large cloth bag. The ladies all looked at one another, some gasped, others purposefully dropped their fans, some even cried in joy. When Mr 101 unloaded the bag to reveal a heap of chocolate rabbits wrapped in glimmering golden foil, edible rainbow strips and custard tarts, it was not hard to see why. Without shame, the crowd got on their knees and begun to gnaw and hammer down the pile like wild beasts. No sooner had they began to do so, their pampered faces slowly became soiled in chocolate as they carelessly smeared the melting sweetness on them.

Mr 101 looked menacingly at Daffodil, pointing. 'You! Bed.'

Without needing to be told again, Daffodil heavy footedly trotted towards the door. Glancing back, she saw the forged happiness upon Mr 101's face as he watched the girls devouring chocolate.

'Ha Ha!' He laughed. 'The party has just begun, my friends! Have some more!'

19. *I have no tears, nothing but laughter. And I shall become possessed and frighten others with it. I have become mad and careless.*

Room 101

When Daffodil left the party, she had slipped by accident into Room 101 but she was slow to realise this. The door clicked shut behind her and an automatic light bulb which resembled a glass pear was switched on to reveal the interiors. The walls were pale and reeked of paint, and the slapdash brush marks seemed to wipe the skin of the wall beneath it. The dusty floor shivered to the sound of Death Metal Opera and screaming ladies. The room itself bore a formal resemblance to an office where a table slouched in the corner, and from where she stood she could see that Mr 101's recognisable leather-bound diary was on the table. The only windows in the dank room were Daffodil's own slanted eyes that were seeking something to digest. It had been days since she had anything to eat but pears.

She walked towards the table, hardly making a sound. Its companion, the chair, waited patiently to be sat upon but Daffodil paid no attention. She noticed what seemed to be a very formal looking dressing table standing against the wall, and after opening the drawer Daffodil discovered it was lined with cedar wood. The walls of its interiors showed rabbits running, leaping over logs and resting, all carved in the greatest of detail, while the bottom was lined with the finest magician black velour.

She peered inside, avoiding the whiff of rotten flesh which the drawer transpired and it seemed to end in a void. There was nothing but a piece of a torn photograph which Daffodil picked up and observed but saw only a dark window which was on the corner of the photo. It seemed as if she were staring at her own pair of empty eyes which were only just a fragment of her body but nevertheless important. She stored the fragment into her dress pocket where the cross Wordsworth had given her had now turned into ashes. All about the room she searched for a clock but it seemed time did not exist in such a space of confinement. She sat on the uncomfortable chair which had an awkwardly slouched back, and began perusing through Mr 101's diary as if her hands were hungry and begging to be fed.

'Curious, is it not, this new face which lurks about my rooms, taking different pleasures off each one? I cannot sleep having her laughter and groans in my empty hall. I cannot weep knowing my reservoirs are empty of emotions. I can only creep in the night when my white face traces her scent on the walls. The vines on my Persian rugs lead me to her bed. But instead she ridicules me, insinuating her desire for miracles. She knows my past but I don't know hers. Why is she in my house?'

It seemed Mr 101 had spent his days sketching roughly all the things he saw with his eyes, putting words together and making them dance on the page. He documented his days and feelings about things which were abstract to Daffodil. Words she had not heard of, ideas which were bizarre at the very least. Even the page numbers lacked chronology. Who could have guessed that one was next to ninety-nine? He made fun of himself on the current page but the next would feature the most putrid dejection. There was certainly no doubt to his confusion; his words were his refuge and retribution. Defeatist remarks such as 'If I was a good person I would have died young' was one of the many and moulded themselves into one large question mark in Daffodil's mind. He complained endlessly about Daffodil's dress as being 'snot-coloured' and her father 'a money-hungry donkey of a man!' They resembled the scribbles of a child written in haste, anger and the desperation which was assigned to inspiration.

'Some say that our powerful emotions should be

dismissed, that happiness and sadness should mean nothing to us as the sunshine and rain and that these things fade away just the same as our weather system. But allow me to say this, does not the rain which plucks itself from the raincloud descend upon the intent to spill itself upon our skin and fall down to fornicate with the earth whereupon a seed is born?'

'Everyone knows about the clown who persuades you to lean forward towards the flower on his breast pocket so that he is able to spray you with another cold burst of reality-'

'I'm not sure whether it's the year of the horse or the year of the idiot, I don't think it makes much of a difference...or does it?'

The silence in the room was disturbed by the continuing screaming of many women, as if they were experiencing the fear of a merry-go-round that was spinning much too fast. For Daffodil it was like an alarming school bell so she quickly found her feet and hastily left the room. She fell into bed shortly after.

***

Daffodil blossomed the next day, caressing the photograph segment; she yearned to find the other missing pieces of the puzzle. The only way, she knew, was to find Room 101 again, or wait until it found her.

A window, a dark window on the side of the photograph, probably went unnoticed to the individual who took the shot — but to Daffodil this was her treasure. A window, something she stared into and saw nothing. Four black squares, grids of a void, nothing, that's all there was no matter how many times she stared at it. In a house where even the walls breathed and sniggered, there was finally hope. There was hope in the shape of a void. A photograph could not be anything but a photograph. Its glossy skin shone like a licked lollipop. The smell was of burnt paper, but it was nowhere near burnt. This is the universal scent of photographs but she sniffed it nonetheless.

The Perfume Door

Poppies, pearlstools,
scarlets, chanterelles,
corals and florals
were velvets to hold
on The Perfume Door—
a hearty sliver of garden
on the wall, a replica
of another existence
which Nothing could open.
Fungi and floral oddities
poured their fragrances
in the deadened corridor
to make dream and steam
of anyone that passed,
and at last inhaled them
to their instant death.
The deceased existed
only to linger and recall
the memory of a heartbeat.

Consequence

Ochre was the light which pierced the previous bullet-hole in the endless blank sky the day when Daffodil laid underneath the pear tree, after having satisfied her hunger from its fruits again. The clouds were beginning to crowd above but Wordsworth was admiring the sun, clutching a pear in the nest of his palm as his sparrow hopped on his broad shoulder. This was their usual meeting place whenever the sun shone, so before it disappeared again Daffodil felt the need to raise her question.

'I met a man called Mr Wordsworth last night in the house; he looked nothing like you and he shouted at me when I called him your name without the 'Mr'. Are you related to him?'

Wordsworth with his calm exterior hid his desire to guffaw out of the pure feeling of shock. His blue oceans widened in a frame of heavenly white, like when a blue whale opens its great orifice to consume the many little crustaceans of the open sea, slams it shut and plummets, smashing the waves in an imposing landing. Wordsworth's eyes performed the same notion with his fleshy-rimmed eyelids whenever he blinked.

'My dear flower of brevity, do not enquire upon what you already know. I am no friend or acquaintance of that man you speak of, Mr 101, and neither am I familiar with Mr Wordsworth. Surely there are some who mimic me and achieve success through imitations only.'

Daffodil sighed, looking scornfully at the house and nodded at Wordsworth's words although not understanding him fully. She felt safe in his serene aura.

'I don't like staying there, Wordsworth. Why can't I stay with you?'

Wordsworth turned his gaze to Daffodil, sensing the coming of rain which would take her indoors. He spoke once more before he faded through the myriads of cedar trees.

'Although I sense your hate for the earth, my skylark, it is on land that you rest and find peace. The skies are limitless and in no way secure for a homely gendered girl as yourself.'

Then, as was expected, the rain began to pour like a generous fountain telling Daffodil Mr 101 would be lost in his reading in Room Two or scribbling his usual fantastical nonsense. A strike of thunder later, she was home.

***

After the evaporation of sweat, chocolate and tears, Mr 101 descended the stairs with fluidity, as if riding on a piano's back. In the darkness-bearing hallway, he was on his knees playing with the floor like it was a human-sized sliding tile game. He was arranging the black squares in the motif of a flower as Daffodil walked past, taking care not to arouse his attention. He had previously worked on arranging the tiles to the motif of a circle, a door and a key.

It appeared to be an amusing game to Daffodil but she held no notion that to Mr 101, this game was one of the most obstructive riddles of his life. Having laid each brick and tile of this house, painted every corner, he still did not possess all its knowledge and he did not understand how this predicament could have fallen upon him like a piano from a colossal height. Writing a manual would have helped him but he thought he'd appreciate the challenge of not being bossed around by his own writing, and if that was not the issue, he would have most definitely lost it. Of course this was the perfect place to lose things. Had he not lost his all his senses under this roof?

There were mysteries and answers hidden beneath the floors, things related to his past that couldn't be grasped because they were wisps of smoke, events which were unfolding with precious time like petals of a flower in the spring, the ghastly spring.

20. *Perhaps all I'm looking for is the God in everyone.*

A fed up Mr 101 rushed up the stairs past Daffodil and slammed the door of Room Two behind him, perhaps for a few drops of wine after a long twenty minutes of hard work. Daffodil took this opportunity to return to Room 101.

When she entered, the door of Room 101 slammed shut behind her, just as it had done before, as if it too was starting to get into a new sort of routine. The strange emetophilic light filled the room with a sickly orange brightness. She opened the drawer once more and admired the carved rabbits while the stench of dead bodies pricked her nose. But she did her best to avoid it because she was on a mission. True to expectation, she found another piece of the puzzle: another piece of a torn photograph. It shone black like a keen crow's eyes perched on a tree, but much darker. Other than that, it showed nothing that could raise suspicion. Disappointed with her find, Daffodil slid the segment into her dress pocket. She observed the room about her; there was a deathly chill that embraced her. The black diary of Mr 101 was there opened flat on the table like a dead bird that was cursed with square wings. Reading its contents, she realised the writing was much more orderly and readable. She sat on the hunched red chair indulging in the master's oratories.

21. *None of us are sane enough to safely imply that the next person is less deranged than we are.*

Below some obscure codes, Mr 101 had written a formal letter. Daffodil was shocked to find that it was addressed to her.

Dear ~~Daffodil~~, ~~Girl~~, Thing,

I am writing to complain about your snotty dress. It revolts every fragment of my existence, please find another one. In a wardrobe would be a suitable place. You must find another while you wait for your final day. Let me state this clearer: you will die after I have taken 101 lives. You will barely exist. Pray to your father now and beg him to come back. We'll see if he can budge the mighty legs of fate. You should have never entered my forbidden room. Don't be sad, now; we must all depart.

And who is this strange woman I have never seen or known before?

A silent fire alarm seemed to have been triggered as a sense of dread filled Daffodil's insides and her stomach lurched uncomfortably as she let the information of her coming death sink in. She turned to see the door half closed and escaped the suffocating room only to enter the shoe cupboard which now had two more pairs of shoes than before. Death was something she had never thought about before. Every pair of shoes, sandals and slippers made her realise every step she took on the thorny path of her dreaded fate. The new arrivals of shoes were overtly decorated with glitter and embroidered in tangled flowers. A clock from afar ticked like an insect of the night resting on a bosom of a flower.

***

Ignoring the pleas of sleep that night, Daffodil drifted from one prohibited room to another, deliberately avoiding the ones she was advised to enter. Darkness played circles around her eyes but her pupils retained the light. The rain rattled on and she danced to their music like an untrained ballerina in the levitating hallways. No doubt, she was curious and dreamt of the impossibilities, seeking black diamonds and black hearts and other things she had seen in her dreams. In every forbidden room lived the red; red hearts and red diamonds but with Mr 101's lip gloss (there was always one rolling about) she painted them black and everything she painted drank her poison wilfully.

Mr 101 in the meantime was feeding the paper with ink, knowing and sighing at the girl's predictability.

Daffodil was now enamoured with this world where the harlequin (a stranger she met in one of the endless corridors) was the national heritage, hibernating in the winter to make art and juggling symbols of life with his skilful hands. But now that it was spring, he sprouted from all the corners performing tricks of an abstract nature with his hands. When his anger shifted from his stomach to his mind, he pressed his finger firmly against the walls' petals that never grew back but hung like loose curtains against dripping windows. Uncertainty certainly followed his existence. There were many lost souls who followed his guidance under the shadowy roof, performing and juggling life like himself. Daffodil, too, joined the phalanx at times of wonder between doors and the harlequin rewarded her with poetry and tales. And at the very end of the night, he would rest and sing lullabies in his sleep; the words marching out like soldiers on a battle plain while his distorted troops dwelled and danced in the silhouette of the silver-glassed window.

He was there and then he wasn't, his ghost flickered on and off like light bulbs.

By midday he was off again, leaving a ribbon of blood behind him so that Daffodil would always know where he was. Day by day the numbers in his troops increased; their injuries were largely disturbing as the numbers grew.

The woman who Daffodil rescued from the room of mirrors sometimes would watch her from a loosening crevice on the wall. The harlequin did not accept her within the circle of comrades and in turn she did not look for his attention. Her attention was directed elsewhere. Her purpose of existence dwelt with Mr 101 whom she haunted and called for every night in one of the many bedrooms, tormenting him about the past he couldn't remember. And she laughed, sometimes cried and sometimes asked silly questions.

Daffodil at times followed her and hid under a bed and watched her flirting with the reflection in the mirror. Her caged skirt scraped the wooden dusty floor like fingernails against a fleshy back. Back and forth she went from wall to wall; *kkssshh* retorted the floor when she did. KSSHHHH it complained again until she resumed at a satisfying spot in front of the mirror. She observed herself once more, unsatisfied. She sighed. On the floor she found a rolling black bottle of lip gloss and scribbled on the mirror: 101.

Sometimes Mr 101 would join her in the writing of the number 101 on the mirror. She would then cherish the brevity of his companionship. At times she would pester him about the night he'd lost all wisdom. But he could not remember. When the pressure became too much to handle, he clutched his cane firmly and beat her with all the force that was left inside of him and she sat and cried with every blow. Daffodil watched from under the bed, all she ever saw were two pairs of legs, one pair behind the other. She shut her eyes to every blow and flinched.

Daffodil listened, sometimes from behind the walls of Room 101 in her daily routine of snatching the remnants of a photograph. And each day she read a paragraph or so from the master's diary, sipping one word at a time but never able to digest them. Mr 101 made no mistake in reminding her of her final fate. At the bottom of each carelessly scribbled paragraph was written: '*Don't forget, little snot, you will die after ninety-nine deaths!*' and so on as if he was enjoying this rather puzzling game where only he could win. Perhaps it was a matter of savouring the best till last.

He also made sure to remind her in other ways. From all the deaths, he procured the blood which remained from the victim's corpse and he painted on the white walls, big and dripping with liquid iron, '1', '2', '3'. Three sacrifices were made and more was to come until the final number, '101'. On most occasions when he consumed all the blood for his own gluttony, black lip-gloss was used instead. That dripped too like blood and he paid it a compliment with a wet smile and flicked the tiny brush over his shoulder, for he now owned stacks of lip-glosses in his drawers.

There was a seldom time when Daffodil and Mr 101 shared a mutual friendship with one another. They were rarely on the balcony stargazing, mostly at Titan on Mr 101's gigantic steel-coated telescope. He showed her the stars through the tunnels of the telescope. In return she felt the closeness, his warmth and heard the music of their orchestra. That's when Mr 101 whispered the secrets in her ears. The arcane knowledge about the musical spheres and life and how they were no less different to one another. She gazed into his eyes; a smaller telescope and there, too, were stars and music.

And after departing Room Two one night, Daffodil sank right back into the room of shoes. The number of shoes had increased and she was reminded of her limited time in the house and garden. The causes of death on the tags were always 'Mr 101' in his own hand which Daffodil had become accustomed to because of her frequent intrusion into his journal.

***

Mr 101 left the Chocolate Rooms prematurely and headed for the bedrooms in his normal dream-like manner. All the rooms were dark, save for the moonlight which brought about a blue glow.

He stripped all the beds, one after the other. His unkempt nails ravaged the fleshy cotton and in return it slipped off the mattress like when his hands would slide down from forehead to chin as he washed his face. That was certainly a while ago, when his memories were clear like the waters gushing from the spring. The spring — what a terrible season!

In huge snowballs, the sheets were taken one by one to the landing beneath the colossal chandelier and stuffed inside the cupboard under the stairs. It took five or six rounds to be completed, each one as exhausting as the next. He made a decision to not make the beds again as they would get dirty again.

He sat on the cold tiled floor underneath the golden chandelier; he prayed that the giant head would fall on his own. This fantasy prevailed with some others a little more absurd but normality and abnormality normally sank inside the same boat. He then added a full stop to all the wandering visions with this statement: 'I have to read all my obstacles as blessings.' And it had been written down somewhere, somewhere along with other notes that sank in the same boat underneath the floor tiles.

He spent many nights before the ladies' arrival at work on the tiled floors to encrypt the symbol to open the floor until his knees were sore and his body had pumped enough sweat. The sweat bubbles drank the light of the moon and for moments he shone like a crystal of the deepest blue. Daffodil watched him from behind the banisters. She did so every night, knowing that when she was not watching him, he was watching her.

22. *What you lose in this life, you gain in the other.*

The Egg of a Sparrow

23. *As my health deteriorates before my eyes, so does my sense of being, and I begin to wonder why I had started this. My eyelids weigh heavier than a star at its last stages.*

As the days go slipping by, I begin to draw more and more attention to the dust that occurs around me, the dust that takes rest into the most impossible of spaces. I feel I must proclaim my disgust for these occurrences, those useless particles that must only exist to remind me of age and time. My poor furniture, my hair, my chair above all victimised by the interference of dust!

And there's nothing I hate more than dust. Well, perhaps I hate tassels a little more, but I'm unsure. They come in all shapes and sizes for the purpose of delightful draping and finishing of a twisted rope. But I see no use for them. I shall make sure to snip them out as I see them for they are without purpose, none whatsoever! Unless I enlarge them and treat them as brooms, but then I will have too many brooms for someone who never cleans and why is that? The house can clean itself, that's why!

PS: You will die in ninety days, make the most of these testing times.

After reading this, Daffodil collected her daily segment of a photograph in Room 101. The whole picture was starting to come together now; she almost had every part of the left side where she could see a window and the branch of a tree. As she left the room which held a stale air, a sunlit corridor greeted her with an open window at the far end. She recognised Wordsworth's sparrow with a sense of guilt; it had been a while since she visited him and was unsure whether spending time with him would benefit her mission. He claimed to despise all creatures within these walls, but wasn't she one of them?

Holding her doubts, Daffodil approached the bird which tweeted for her attention. There was a note attached to its twig-like legs. The note was scribbled carelessly with charcoal, 'Have the strength to escape your comfortable prison, child.'

She met Wordsworth under the pear tree that day. The sun produced a dazzling contrast to the drab interiors of the house and Daffodil felt a new lease of life in her breath. She brushed past the bee-gemmed hyacinths and the prematurely premorse daffodils on her journey to the tree. Wordsworth had not altered in the slightest; he was Palladian in presence, permanently withholding an unstained innocence.

His nest-like palm blossomed to reveal two sparrow eggs. They were blue and freckled, just like his eyes.

'Take one,' he smiled and Daffodil quickly pinched an egg and stored it in her pocket. 'I suggest you boil it before you eat it.'

He stared at Daffodil who remained still, looking back like a black ocean in resemblance of an obsidian mirror. She glanced back at the house in an act of desperation and then lied that she saw a silhouette of some kind behind the glass window that she took to be Mr 101. Of course there was none, not in Wordsworth's eyes, but she sought an excuse for her escape. He did not show his disappointment when he let her go.

When she entered the house, Mr 101 was on his knees shifting tiles. There was an obvious desperation marked on his face and this was one of the seldom things he did not mind showing, not even if he could help it. The lady in the skeletal skirt was half watching, half lost in a daydream, arms and fingers crossed, making an attempt to hide herself under a shadow. As Daffodil walked past, Mr 101 began sniffing the air as if it held out an aroma. He shot a glance at Daffodil.

'Egg of sparrow!' he cried, lifting his head. 'That! Give it to me!'

'No, don't!' shouted the lady, having already approached the scene.

In his surprise, Mr 101 quickly grabbed the lady's throat and threw her onto the nearest slime-infested wall. She laughed manically in her struggle while Mr 101 sneered at her, clenching his fingers tighter around her throat.

'I'm going to kill you...' said Mr 101. His whisper, as always, was louder than a shout.

'I can kill myself thank you very much, you know that!' sniggered the lady, half in jest, half in something unexplainable through words such as these. Mr 101 could not bear to look into her eyes so he reluctantly set her free from her slimy cage.

Daffodil observed with sunken eyes. She did not need asking twice and handed the egg to Mr 101, who observed it under the chandelier that brought out more shadow than light. However, he did not return it after observation but merely wished her goodnight in his unsentimental way, although it was clearly a spring afternoon. What a terrible season spring truly is.

The Removal of a Ring

Before Mr 101's rendezvous arrived that night, he was caught in a long-lasting reverie.

If all Earth and universe are illusions then the same can be applied to the eleven heavens, therefore illusions are inescapable and not necessarily negative in existence.

Mr 101 was sitting reading his newly bound book: *Why the Moon Is More Than Just A Pretty Ornament* by Hŭda Helnoes. The sparrow's egg slept serenely in its cup in the dimly lit living room like a cursed pearl in the mouth of an oyster. It held the same appearance as Mr 101's head on his steady shoulders behind the clamour of philharmonic Death Metal Opera.

After reading a few chapters which brought him no satisfaction whatsoever, he flapped his napkin in the air which was for a moment the wings of a dove in flight, and with the decorum of a gentleman he'd learnt from books, stuffed the latter part of the fabric in his collar so he could be suitably prepared for this experience. He took a deep breath for it had been almost a lifetime since he was in the company of a sparrow's egg and the memory was long lost under tiled floors, and what more he had made a solemn promise not to ever enjoy foods other than vomit and human flesh but yet here he was, at the dinner table with a noose-like napkin around his neck ready to plunge back into the real world if there ever was one.

'Somewhere within my ribs,
Lies a garden I will never see.'

After the napkin was flung to the side and the sparrow's egg steered well clear of, Mr 101 found himself in Room 101. His hands firmly covered his eyes in a display of despair; he'd exhausted himself of making the hard look easy — at least for now. Should idleness be blamed for depression and idleness alone? For he could not think of any other symptom that could excite such a dreary phase, not even memory loss, or dire solitude or an incredible appetite for flesh or a subtle fear of dust that had yet to fully form. The journal's blank pages twitched before him like a soul aflame, waiting for the chill of a wind to render its return to normality. To be precise, Mr 101 wished to begin writing but couldn't think of a single topic. His chair creaked slightly as he adjusted himself. Arching his back, he leant forward, burying his head in his arms. Then he took out his fingers and began rubbing the scratch marks on the table made by unknown fingernails. He looked up. The marks followed the same patterns as the ones on his back. His heavy eyes caught the only drawer of the table. Clearly, he was oblivious to what was inside as he placed his hand on the knob that was exquisitely carved into a labyrinth. The stubborn drawer did not reveal its contents; it seemed to be locked. He began to pull at it in a vigorous manner. To him, it was preposterous that he could not work something that was his and doesn't remember locking. He became agitated and once or twice kicked the legs of the table, but this only enraged him further.

'*Argh!*' The pain sunk in and he was less than happy.

The wall banged in consequence to the table being dragged from one corner to the next. Without being conscious of it, he was using the table legs to score the floor to the pattern on his back. The journal slid off the table and landed with a slap on the floor, closing itself simultaneously. Mr 101 was not going to give this up. He grabbed the handle again and was starting to tug at it as if it were a rope attached to a raging bull. It would not open no matter what measure of force was applied. The table seemed to have its own reflex as white grease miraculously began to ooze from the handle so that Mr 101's hand could slip off easily.

Soon, Mr 101 left the room, leaving it in disarray. It was to be another day (or night) wasted to struggle.

Daffodil would stroll in Room 101 the next day and remove a fragment of a photograph from the same drawer as easily as it was to pluck a pear from a tree.

***

Once the creases of the day had at last been ironed out by the night, another one of Mr 101's immoral parties was in progress. The night was rich and thick with black, blindly devoting a good twelve hours of worship to the insane silver rock that was the moon. In Room Two, Mr 101 was caught unwillingly in a throng of heavily perfumed girls, pouring out the last remnants of whiskey into his glass. If he had the choice, he would have rather dipped his head into Daffodil's dress but he didn't. He looked around for her but she wasn't there. Instead he caught a few glimmers of rubies hanging from the ladies' necks and the torn out pieces of their chatter. Although the house was his, he would have liked more than anything to harness the beast that it had become. Instead there were visitors upon visitors upon visitors like the dew that spoils the original beauty of a rose. And the dew had to be left there because the moon was its purveyor, and the moon was always correct, always the absorbing mirror for the blinding light of the sun...

He was impartial to the chaos of the room, although he was at the heart of its honey-combing. In the midst of the garish groups of multi-layered eyed women, was one quiet kempt woman. She had one pair of eyelids and this was generally accepted as she was not over-weight. Her empire-lined dress was so simple that it was almost blasphemous under Mr 101's roof — blasphemy against blasphemy. Would the rebellion ever end? He hardly noticed it — or even her in her entirety. It was her left hand that her wine glass wore as an amulet, which caught his attention the most. The ring she wore in her middle finger caught his eyes; the shine flirted with his vision, refracting a sparkle at a time, lambent and kind. It reminded him of a star he was once fond of for giving light and life to the world. Somehow his heart raced with the harnessing of the memory as he looked at the bearer of the ring. It would be a mistake to say that Mr 101 was anything but a detester of women, but when he saw her, the worst he could do was to serve her with a nod in greeting. The two of them were still as women drifted all about them like chalices of fate he didn't want to accidently have spill on him.

After placing her wineglass on a nearby table, the woman who Mr 101 felt like he was well acquainted with touched her ring to remove it. He was intensely focused. All sounds were muffled. A fright overtook him. Holding himself in abeyance, shivers began to whisper as they dispersed up his spine and he oozed with expectation. He had written about this act in his first revolutionary Ridiculist discussion. He even began to recite it from the Ridiculist abscess that existed in his mind. He remembered the sound of scribbling with his quill as the words spilled out.

> *The removal of a precious ring from a Ridiculist before another attentive colleague is the greatest mark of respect. One must not forget that a reflection is the highest symbol of compassion; if something can reflect it has the capacity to give, especially if the reflection is light. In this case the Ridiculist in performance is giving the giving. Therefore the brighter the jewel the better! For the former's part it is the loss of control, the surrender for another. Remember my pious Ridiculists, the ring must be in the middle finger as it is a symbol of Saturn...*

As Mr 101 rested his gaze on her feminine hands, he envisioned himself as a magician's assistant lying flat on his back on a velvet-lined propped-up box while a magician passed a hoop through his body to confirm to an audience that Mr 101 was in fact hovering. The audience, in his imagination, was in awe not knowing that light was what made the trick. Later they would brand the magician as a special being, one with supreme powers that could manipulate, vitiate nature according to his taste.

He imagined they would Chinese whisper his career to an unsurpassable height, that only the stars could touch. Though it was the prop and the laws of reality that'd created the illusion.

'Twenty-three,' Mr 101 whispered in her ear when the act was over.

The ring toppled as it escaped her finger and addressed the floor in a most underwhelming clink compared to the magnitude of the situation. Senseless sounds from the crowds surged back into the two Ridiculists' hemispheres, but by then they had both already fallen into exploring the depths of each other's eyes to even take the least bit of notice. The woman swooned into the master's arms shortly after without any further strength left in her, perhaps having finally shaken life off her shoulders.

***

On the way to the shoe cupboard, Daffodil swept past walls after walls of number twenty-threes dripping thickly with blood like her own final fate slowly journeying to meet her. The pungent reek of iron she was used to but the sight of blood always made her dwell on the numerous amounts of women that were sacrificed. It also spoke of her death, there were twenty-three deaths and there was not long to go until one hundred and one, and the numbers now seemed to increase with every black-blooming night.

The cold wooden floor met her feet as she entered the room and the frosty air greeted her as usual. She wondered if the room acted as a refrigerator to preserve the shoes. And there were many this time, black lace heels to velvety kitten ones, each were hung next to the other. In a solitary corner Daffodil spotted a pair of diamond slippers which coated itself in a colourful prism reflecting the morbid light.

She removed the tag and inserted her tiny feet into the shoes. She enjoyed being elevated by the heels, and trotted around the room enjoying the 'click-clack' sound the pair made, being sure to savour the moment.

When she left the shoe cupboard she entered Room

Two almost immediately. The room shone with ladies who wore gems and encrusted rubies on their dress with matching lips. Mr 101, too, was trying on the new cosmetic product which he had been informed lasted for more than eighty-four hours once applied; it remained longer than a burden or like a hallucinogenic drug you wished you had never ingested. Death Metal Opera spun like the waves of a magician's wand, stirring the air with corrupt influence. The candles flickered, the wax lunged from the flames like persistent martyrs over rocky cliffs.

When the ladies walked (and they did so a number of times with great effort), they scraped the wooden ground with their gem-collected, lace loaded dresses and pointed heeled stilettos. Daffodil wondered which pairs she would spot tomorrow in the shoe cupboard. It was now a game she thought. She had nothing else to ponder about, not even her coming death brought her satisfaction. Or she could dilute time with her best friend, the harlequin, who was still attempting to teach her how to speak backwards and make the furniture dance by singing in a twisted little lullaby and standing on the tip of her toes until she could eventually levitate for a millisecond.

After having smothered his lips with 'forbidden rouge' as it was labelled on the package, Mr 101 retreated to the window with his small telescope and observed the stars. Mr Wormwood and Mr Wordsworth were among the piled up beads of heads which surrounded them with overt flirtation and attention.

Daffodil struggled past the crowds and finally reached Mr 101 who lifted her onto his beloved saffra and handed her a strange telescope with ancient markings over its gilded coating. The clouds on the moon were like a leaning shadow blocking its throat from screaming, 'The moon is more than just an ornament!'

Peering into the strange instrument, she saw millions of tiny stars of all colours she could never have imagined. She drifted past the moon, Sirius, Mars, Jupiter, and Saturn until finally the view settled into a chocolate coloured planet which sweated blue gas. She gasped — the image was so clear and her vision tricked her into thinking she was nearer to the planet than she really was, but she only realised this when Mr 101's voice beckoned her back down to reality.

'It's Titan,' he muttered, gazing down to her with his rouge glimmering.

'Tighten,' she confirmed, stunned and still staring at the giant orb.

'No, I believe it's Titan,' he said, shortly.

'Oh, *Titan*,' she replied, after a pause and slowly removed the telescope from her eye and returned it to Mr 101. It was only when she looked into Mr 101's eyes she realised there was no real difference between the shape of Titan and his eyes; the two were perfectly round and infinitely radiated mystery.

'I believe it must be a giant globe made entirely of milk chocolate and marshmallows, but the problem is there is no other being who shares my belief so it can never be proven true.'

'I believe you,' replied Daffodil, looking up at him, but words could not be arranged to express the intensity of appreciation which had built up inside Mr 101, so he remained silent.

He decided that when he had moments on his own, he would find a weapon to subjugate his emotions or perhaps he would rummage through his many Ridiculist books to satisfy him with a philosophical quote. Both actions seemed to hold an equal bearing.

Moments later he was gone swiftly through the door and returned pulling the heavy sack of chocolate he fetched from the Chocolate Rooms and, as predicted, it was welcomed by screams and a handful of fainting spells which recovered quickly by the lack of attention paid by their peers.

The Horse Continuing on His Journey

The ghostly horse's lupine breath, which, prior to this, preceded him through every single stormy condition on Titan, was now transmitted into a different dimension and brought hope for its pre-biotic molecules. All his particles intact, the white horse was caught in a blank state on a dissection table until the arrival of light on metal hoofs. His angels had predestined his arrival and sprinkled the seemingly endless path with love like falling cherry blossoms. They unwrapped his fur coating as it was once a celestial gift, to start work on his clockwork anatomy. They applied a wholesome amount of honey to help the lagging of his cogs. Like the flowers attracted the gem of bees, his heart collected the red of rubies and in his veins were rich valleys of gold. From his carcass, bees emerged, self-created, and flew about in a craze as if they were hands desperately attempting to wipe away the scene at their demise. Soon they'd set-off in a line to their fastidious, fatiguing work of honey-making. The angels repaired the broken horse, breathing life and a pre-destined death unto him and sucked out the storms from his battlefields. From that instance, he deserved the sun. Before finishing the ordeal, they removed Guilt, Fear and Pain, blowing them away like coconut flakes.

A Game of Losing

Daffodil found herself in a semi-dark room where she was led in by curious noises and the harlequin himself whose smile persuaded her to prolong the damage of her rebellion. She wasn't one to fight against him whose company she valued the most, as she took him to be the most genuine of all. He told her to 'be brave and fruitful' before he vanished into the darkness with one glimmer of a sequin on his costume fading last. Then the light of the dusty chandeliers intensified to display what was contained in this room. Daffodil stood motionless by the door which was slowly beginning to close behind her without a sound. To distract herself from thoughts of escaping, she thought about what the harlequin had just told her, she didn't know exactly what he meant but it sounded delicious. With this on her mind she took to observing the room more closely.

The space was longer than it was wide, and many confession booths lined the walls allowing a disorderly path to form in between. It was evident that the compartments were all occupied, despite the grapevines that were interwoven through their decorative wooden damask filigree in an attempt to mask whatever was inside. If it were possible to sew a structure with wood rather than fine threads then perhaps these beautiful monuments would be the products of such hard work. It was no wonder that Daffodil stood agape at such magnificence that was beautiful as much as it was sinister. At first, she thought the grapes were dusty but the smell and a closer observation revealed that they were, in fact, in the process of rotting.

Inside the booth something made the sound of wood

being sanded down. Occasionally the candlelight from within flickered and the deft move of a hand or two could be seen. And then she heard a pleasurable 'Mmm'.

She leant in closer preparing her eyes to focus in great detail.

The interior was well lit in a cosy, lambent fashion — despite its outward appearance to the casual observer — and the wall that divided the priest and the sinner had perhaps been knocked down or not been made for this particular confessional as it was present. Daffodil spotted two men. They seemed to be intensely focused on the game of chess which was in procession. Even if they'd sensed Daffodil's peering in, they would have continued playing because as hard as it may be to believe, they had only one chance — one chance to lose. As the rules stated next to them:

- *Only one game per existence*
- *Whoever loses can eat all the players*
- *If you win, you can have my condolences, but you may taste a player at your peril.*

Mr 101

Daffodil furrowed her eyebrows at the rules, reading them once, twice, but still not quite understanding a single rule. There was a long pause before a player made his move. Each one was quick and abrupt as if signing an important contract.

She checked another booth and another game had just begun. Both players held their composures to one another not revealing their true feelings of anxiety. The chess game was at a crucial point where a pawn had to be killed or the game could not go on. Although it was not a specified rule, Daffodil guessed that the game should always be finished. One of the players indignantly killed a pawn and the latter quickly stuffed his loss into his mouth with an 'Mmmmm!'

In the past, players had dubbed this experience 'worth travelling light years for'. This unmatched taste seemed to serenade on the tongue, this psychedelic entrancement that only Mr 101 could provide was worth its weight in gold and comets of ruby gardens. It was an intense sensation that was begotten from none other, asking, pleading to the point of ordering for the soul to surrender. Is it any wonder this game was a subject for discrimination?

These creatures had crossed dimensions to cap, for some time anyway, a pious living in order to waste it on this decadent experience. It was not forced upon them. As the saying goes 'you can't force a horse to drink', the creature comes to the trough at its own appeal. But it brought joy if not delight. It was excess to a sky-scraping point of ignorance. This was a fine example of avoiding the will to subject oneself to pittance. In its most concentrated essence, this game was about losing to gain. The most basic of all human principals, when one gained another lost. However, the player in the throes of indulgence did not realise this — only the one who doesn't taste the sweet nectar can learn what an awful occupation this was, and then he must spend the rest of his time lamenting on his previous life until he is back to normal and no longer impotent.

There were secrets, strategies and books written on the subject of losing this game. By all means, one should be much experienced in losing to gain the most irresistible taste and also in acquiring eminent rank and excellence of soul.

Daffodil crept away from close observation as her eyes were beginning to throb. The smell of rotting grapes was beginning to make her hungry stomach churn, so much so, that she plucked one of the juicy heads. When the taste of mould had dissipated, she was surprised to find that the flavour of a rotten grape was rather sweet. And so she had another until she had eaten all the grapes on that particular confessional. By that time, the game had finished and the last utterance of pleasure was heard. The player who won had a face which bore the sign of utter dejection and stepped out. Upon seeing Daffodil, his expression changed, uplifted like the sun springing up from the sky. Spring! What is the use of spring?!

'Would you like to join me for a game?' he asked her.

Before a reply could be formulated from Daffodil's stained lips, the harlequin appeared from a ribbon of smoke. He smiled at Daffodil in a sly manner then placed his forefinger to his lips to advise Daffodil to not speak a single word.

Meanwhile, Mr 101 was in the Chocolate Rooms watching chess pieces being pumped out of ovens. His mind was elsewhere, thinking how each room of the house was a strand of hair that he wished to pull out of the scalp, leaving him with bare floors. It was in his power to perform such rogue ruses but he was dubious as to whether, after such an intensive operation, the house would progressively end up in the same state again. The wind may blow the petals away but there's nothing to say that the plant may not grow another of the same flower.

A Memory

24. *At times, in your hopelessness you venture into the outside world searching for normality; the behavioural patterns of others cause you to imitate them. This results in something similar to inner peace. Dearest martyred paper of my own delirious thoughts, no matter how hard I push my stubborn self I always seem to fall behind as if I were not truly in control of the being that is 'I'.*

Back in his golden days of youth, Mr 101 was an illusionist. Flowers flourished from his fingers, steadfast and upwards when he spoke the magic words, like one who sprung up from their bed during a terrible nightmare. Except these flowers bounced with life and have never been sleep-deprived. They were born from the vase of his palms for the eyes of his sweetheart, his woman whose face he didn't recognise. The bees had been hungered by the sight of them from behind stained glass windows. Watching him they threw themselves upon the glass, but it was a futile feat as a child throwing pebbles into a lake hoping that they would float.

Mr 101's love never stayed afloat, just like that pebble; it sunk to the core of the earth where living organisms fail to survive.

The Harlequin's Death

The thunderstorm moaned like the sound of a weighty wooden chair being dragged through the parlour's already scarred surface of the floor. Mr 101 took this thriving opportunity to turn up the volume of Death Metal Opera playing on his music box. The little people inside the glassy interior danced with their plastered smile upon a blank face. He dragged another puff of smoke from his cigarette that had been lit from a while ago; if one was watching from an opposite view, one would witness something like a ghost being gobbled up.

Yes, the last puff had and always would be the worse one of all. The smoke then was eventually expelled from his nostrils and joined the invisible moving particles in the air. It was rather hypnotic, the overlapping motions of smoke. It slithered like an exotic dancer from an eastern land and eventually dispersed and disappeared.

Mr 101's right eye twitched then. He knew that such a phenomena could only be elicited when someone was looking through a peculiar book from a particular shelf, and ran their fingers over the word 'eroticism' on its second page. He only hoped it wasn't Daffodil up to no good, but the rational part of him, which also happened to be the smallest part of him, knew it was her.

Before he could think of reacting, he thought about the song he was listening to and how appreciative he was to have it on so he could pretend not to care. Music had always made Mr 101 go silent.

Of the slivery fumes from my heart's desire,
I own every plume of the birds I admire.

He nodded slowly to these lyrics and was rather lost in the intentional meaninglessness of it all, in the middle of creation and perfection inheriting both with each tide of breath. The singer's voice was much like the growl of a possessed child, but to him it was a gentle whisper. The bass guitars pounded the drums of his ears and the dreamy melody brought him to the most profound part of the seas. He was in a similar state to that of a sea creature drifting past a sinking pebble that had been chucked by a child on a nearby shore, roaming into the tenebrous portals of the water, beyond the gates of laws and misconception.

25. *Sometimes I wonder whether the ocean wishes to lie upon the sand. I question the water's acceptance to the medium of oscillating energy which causes its crash upon the jagged rocks.*

At the precise moment of having nearly drifted into the void, the harlequin appeared before him observing the room in the most punctilious manner but ignoring Mr 101 at every cost. His eyes were no bigger than two boiled eggs having been given to nursery children to scribble over for pupils and hastily fitted back into the sockets. Mr 101 sensed, if not smelt, him upon his arrival. What a surprising occasion this was! These two had never intentionally tried to be in the same room together and if such an event occurred one would surely walk out on the other and completely ignore the situation and any start for a discussion.

The harlequin's observer, having already given a sigh or two from intense dismay of his untimed appearance, opened his eyelids slowly and gave the harlequin a questioning look which he received with an invisible prod.

'Out of my sight, spondee,' said Mr 101, sighing out grey fumes.

'Spongy? I can be spongy, especially when I'm being sat on...' Noticing the disagreeing look on Mr 101's face, the harlequin decided to change the subject in haste. 'Th-the main reason for my visit —'

'You can drown in the sewers, 'quin,' Mr 101 retorted.

And with that he closed his eyes and hoped that would make the pestilent creature return to his little hole. The uncomfortable quiet of the room told him that the harlequin had not budged and he drew back his white lids once more.

What Mr 101 failed to notice was the dilemma facing the harlequin, who had forgotten his title and was arguing with himself whether to address him as his highness or lowness. His opinion of Mr 101 was as low as anything but after having not been acquainted with him for such a long period of time, he was unsure whether he was a close enough acquaintance (not in proximity) to insult the owner of his shelter. His nerves had gotten the better of him and he began to perform an informal dance he called 'The Galumph'. His arms, tentacle-like, flopped about him like a strange squid and his legs dangled like worms; altogether it was an unsatisfying performance to say the very least. Fortunately, this mockery lasted no more than a few minutes until he was severely out of breath and gasping on the scarred floor.

Mr 101 stood up from the uncomforting sight of anything touching the skin of joy and celebration. Why couldn't this creature of subordinate Ridiculism savour the embarrassing moment for a time when he was not in a meditative state?

He was about to utter a blasphemous statement but relented, and instead muttered the following, 'Why do you disturb me from my...' Unfortunately he could not find himself to finish the particular phrase and said forcefully, 'Now would be a good time to interrupt me you...'

'Well yes, your lowness!' The harlequin jumped to his feet. 'Well, the reason why I'm here in front of you, a little overdressed if I may add, is because — now listen — I couldn't help but overhearing that exquisite piece of opera you were serenading to —'

'I do not *serenade*, harlequin, you fool. Get on with it!'

'Yes, I shall tell you an expurgated version right this minute, your lowestness. I do love a short story; prose poetry gives just quite enough. Yes, now I must hurry. *That* music you listen to really is not music at all. It's not exactly music AT ALL —'

'Shut up harlequin, in all my life I have never heard a poorer excuse for someone wanting to see me. I must say I am not at all flattered.'

Mr 101 sat back down onto his saffra and lit up a new cigarette which, to the harlequin, looked much like a piece of chalk. The harlequin wanted to steal it and write on all the dripping walls. And if he could write by the miracle of some merciful saint, what would it be? Surely not 101? Yes, it must be! 101 continuously in one line; he would persist to write for an eternity. He was rather entranced by the object when he was awoken by a smoke-infested statement from Mr 101, 'Get out.'

'Sir,' the harlequin shook his head to be rid of the image of him actually having the chance to write on a wall, 'I only ever speak the truth; I swear it. Let me prove it to you right this minute. Right this minute, I will prove it to you.'

'Don't repeat yourself harlequin, just don't repeat yourself,' said Mr 101, quite taken aback by the duration of this conversation which seemed to span for an eternity. He never thought the imbecile could possess this many words in his vocabulary.

Holding his cigarette between two fingers like a boy does with his pebble, he ambled towards the harlequin who had removed the needle from his music box and began playing the record with his long, fang-like fingernails. The song found exit through his oral sphere, the only difference was that the record was played backwards. Mr 101 was astonished as fulsome curses were thrown at him, so much so that he had entirely forgotten about his slowly degrading cigarette. Like a stuffed toy, he stood glass-eyed in disbelief.

Angered by the entire situation, he removed the harlequin's finger from the spinning record and sat him down on the saffra, as it was the only chair in the dusty room. He peered down at him from his height, his face in a thoughtful expression. One could not have predicted the next moment as Mr 101 struck the harlequin with the hand that held the cigarette, and in the next moment there was an explosion of cigarette ashes and glass on the floor. The glass, which had once been the harlequin's head, was shattered and spread out upon the scarred wooden floor; his body remained intact and in the same position as it was before it lost its head. At least now Mr 101 knew the harlequin was not human after all. In fact, he was not quite sure who or what he was or how they had met.

Before he left the room, the butt of his cigarette was pierced into the glass ashtray which resembled a meticulously etched ice sculpture of whose water had been collected from a lake where once a child threw a pebble in its depth secretly hoping that it would float.

The White Horse and the Witch

On foreign land uninhabited, the white horse
had arrived, speeding on dusty, sterile ground.
He was the renewed glowing horse, persistent
and curious at the echoing of another nearby gallop.

From behind a peaked mount, leapt a dark horse
whose coating was that of a stolen night sky.
Gleaming, his eyes lured with essences of old folk lore;
he persuaded the glowing one in his direction to ride.

The dark one began to morph as he journeyed,
once in a translucent cloth, then a crow and at last
a dark figure, a woman, wrapped in shadow couture —
her hands shaking a little as time hurried past.

26. *If I distort my shadow would I remain the same?*

From the clouds, spirals and birds manifested.
She made an apology of some kind in the cold air.
It had been awhile since she had rested.
Beneath cracks of misery, she was graceful and fair.

When her eyes reached the white horse,
he saw what could only have been
The keyholes of a new found world.

Her hands, she'd shown, portrayed no scars of fate —

Above them the birds of war screeched and wrestled.
From afar, beyond the anaemic sky, a jaguar roared.
She bowed before the horse, her long fingers on the land
sensing all the memories the horse had ever hoarded
and finally offered to transport him above the void
by acceptance of her smooth, quaking hands.

He could not trust her, those blank hands
where nothing but nothing dwelt
for she could not keep them still.

From the crystal depth of his heart,
for there was nothing left to do,
he left her on that sterile earth
where the sky was white, rarely blue.

27. *How do we begin to comprehend a world without metaphors?*

Healing the Harlequin

Sometime later into the night, when the fireplace had swallowed its flames and darkness oozed from every crevice like a death-bringing smoke, the only sign of life in the room was the seated harlequin. The remnants of his head scattered on the floor, glittering like little clusters of stars, a nebula of glass on the dark scarred floor from the light of the moon. The moonlight was forcing its way through a previously storm-trodden sky and projecting, beyond the carelessly shut curtains, a streak of silver light onto the floor. Tiny dust particles like ballerinas swivelled and twisted gracefully in the spotlight; some were elevated while others descended.

No-one could have predicted how silent the house would become after the death of a creature whose existence was considered unimportant. Somehow, the muteness was heavy, like a book of lead weighing on a levitating tongue that were both soon to fall in a devastating show of blind destruction.

Entering the room, meddling with this moonshine was the source of Mr 101's nightmare: the woman in the skeletal skirt. She brought with her a shadow which masked the bits of glass, a vial of strong glue, bandages and a collection of colouring pencils that she found lying in dusty, untouched corners of the house.

Patience and meticulous care were important ingredients as she began to work, piecing the harlequin's head back together. If she hadn't been hasty to get on with it, she was sure that a glass-eater would have caught up with the harlequin and would have eaten his head all for its own delight. A violin lamented in her heart and she hummed to it. And a sparrow flitted about her like a bullet in search of a rifle.

When the harlequin's head was glued and held together with bandages, his soul slid back inside him as if it had been outside his body, watching the process of being stuck together all along. He cried as a helpless infant fresh out of the waves of the womb and his sobs swerved their way from his mouth all through the night. Meanwhile the woman, with the help of pastels and colouring pencils, drew facial features on his layering of bandages as best as she could recall them. Regrets were starting to pile up in hills and meadows in the harlequin's mind. A moth of envy for normality flitted away. Maturity was on the verge of discovery and there he would inhabit while always wondering, *what if I hadn't dared?*

Rumours of the harlequin's mishap hurried through like Aphrodite's own winged coursers had done once to respond to the maddening heart of Sappho, along to the highest staircase, sniffing at every corridor for a sign of a lending ear, ruffled the loose floorboards, blew every duvet cover into temporary forts, swung the painting on the walls like lightweight pendulum, caught up with its own breath upon the deserted seat of Mr 101's saffra until it came to halt and glided into Mr Teacup-head's ears which were, in any case, under his armpits.

He had patiently awaited an occasion such as this, when his life would feel the hint of a changing wind, for the mundane was ever such a punisher to the patient. Mr Teacup-head was a complacent devotee of the harlequin. He was not one to notice something as trivial as death — especially as such an event was common under these roofs. But to learn of his own master having befallen such a tragedy hit him like a wet sponge. And his facial features, which were sprinkled on his torso, screwed up naturally into a despairing expression. Should he have clapped his hands as a sign of appreciation at the end of his master's 'show'? Or would it have been wiser to sit down and sulk?

Back to Mr 101

The fog that had dropped from the sky to frolic with the land-laden trees was reminiscent of when the seven heavens obliterated themselves in stages of mass conflagration and had laid the smokes onto Earth and prevented the nasty sun to perform its duty. Of course, this piece of misplaced fantasy only took place inside the sordid mind of Mr 101 who was now viewing this scene with a curious urge to shut the curtains and sew their ends together like Siamese twins so he would never be tempted to ever enquire about the outside world. He believed everything was found on the inside. The universe was ours, it is us! The mind is the moon and the heart is the sun. Since he was heartless, he didn't have a sun. No sun to shine in his life and he was satisfied. Anyone with their doubts may well have enquired elsewhere, for he was an enigma and no one could deny that. One only had to step inside his halls and see what a miracle the house truly was. The sun shone in vain without Mr 101's beauty to widen its gaze upon. Mr 101's grin stretched a little at the thought.

Atrocious as it were, Mr 101 found himself to be in quite a pickle; not so much swimming in it but accurately enough to have been shoved headfirst inside the jar with a slight twist. You see, a problem had arisen in his mind. There was a *problem* — of that there was no doubt. In his solitude, his mind did all the working, walking and talking, that was the only way for now apart from when he dreamt. But since it was now impossible to sleep, he didn't dream. He wondered when he would (although he had what he most yearned for: beauty, money, magic and arrogance) attain his most profound desire to dream.

He would do it. He wanted to talk and digress and shout to sense the core of his Adam's apple about his predicament. But who would he flood his tears upon? The church was rendered useless in his list a long time ago when he found the room carpeted with dust imported from his own severe misuse. Although it was tempting to talk to the undead harlequin, he thought he'd spare himself the embarrassment and (although he was no follower of 'The Time') time. And his unlikely female companion who was now occasionally stalking him would slice an arm for the chance to be spoken to, and so he'd rather not in any case. His conduct knew no standard reasoning but he liked to argue otherwise; he thought most likely the woman would see him to suit her own schedule without a care in the world about him. And sometimes, she would mark her subtle rebellion by not shaking hands with the room before entering. Hence, he deemed her impossible to control; she was the manifestation *and* result of unrelenting chaos. There was, in conclusion, no-one.

In what appeared to be in a different world but was really occurring under the same extraordinary roof, Daffodil had completed her daily deed of collecting a snippet of a photograph from Room 101. She was ever so close to solving her puzzle. On the path to the main door the master of house called her to Room Two, having sensed her.

'Daffodil?' his words came out, a little less threatening than the usual bursting of a jack-in-a-box that leaps out of its enclosure and bounces back to cause a momentary gasp.

Without either a need or expectation of a retort, he beckoned the little creature of a girl, making use of his fang finger-nailed forefinger, into the room. He sat on his precious saffra and her on the nearby sofa which now resembled an arm that had beaten into strawberry jam and bruises. The room was humming with life and the ticking of unseen clocks. It sounded as though there were many people hiding in the room, scratching their backs, arms and faces.

'I smell something, my blossom, I smell something terrible on your part...' he sipped a drop of mulled wine from his teacup which was the microcosm of Mr Teacup-Head without a body, lambently coddled by candlelight.

He sat the cup on the coffee table and Daffodil noticed a couple of jasmine petals afloat, white like lambs drowning in their own ignorant innocence. The steam was awakened from the surface, curling, twisting, unfurling and melting to the sight of Mr 101 whose expression was slightly questioning behind the shockingly white skin and silhouetted lips.

'If it's terrible then it must be from my past no wonder,' he continued. 'I don't wonder as much as I used to...'

Daffodil remained silent knowing that with a single murmur she could excite the most terrible storm.

'What do you think about when you're by yourself, Daffodil?'

'Well...When it's not the photo, I think about chocolate... chocolate. I can smell it everywhere in the house.'

Mr 101 found himself unable to contain his excitement despite his surprisingly calm composure. But what for? One could only wonder...

'You vagarious tulip!' he said. 'Aren't pears enough? You will have to wait for your chocolate. For there will be chocolate for *you*. Chocolate, indeed...now what is this photo you talk about? I see you're deluded, finally deluded. How does it feel?'

Daffodil shrugged. Her eyes were more distant than present and could inspire more acts of suicide than the season of spring. A dreadful season!

Mr 101 waited a few tick-tocks for some sort of elaboration on her part. But after the desired time, it was obvious that the heavy silence and scratching sounds which had begun to become so overbearing, was now beginning to drink the blood on the walls or break them and flood every bit of space in an unnatural disaster. Even if Mr 101's question had been a colourful tea dance, Daffodil would have remained similarly passive.

'Yes, I understand. Leave me now,' croaked Mr 101.

Once Daffodil left him, Mr 101 wished the doorway would step through itself and the window would leap out through the window. If only sleep would show some desperation in reaching him like that damned sparrow tapping the window.

The Horse Plays Chess, Absent of a Knight

Hand-crafted by the divine and speeding along black lustful shores, the white horse arrived on the dangerous land of the mighty Alfinus, who had prepared the game of chess for him to play, not quite for the leisurely way.

A boy watched from afar, a pebble in his hand, peering beyond the fore for a lake, calm like the virtue of the just, to throw it in. The eternal night and the vulnerable sunken sun did not amuse him.

The horse had lost his knight long ago, before this tale began, but his senses remained and he relaxed his four limbs on the square bed. Elephant tusks were not spared for the horse's armour of ivory.

Bishop, spare me this time for I am weak and my destination is far from near.

The game was to be played. Alfinus began. Pawns ended pawns and the horse waited behind, without a knight to direct him. He was hiding with both eyes closed, not willing to take part or descry what has already been inscribed upon the cattle's hide.

And what a fine ruse it was for when all eyes were opened, the horse found he was nearly desolate on endless chequered floors. Positions changed, tides turned and the faithful queen was merely seconds before her destruction. Her helpless king waited. Is he so infatuated with his queen that he makes himself useless when she dies? Sacrifice is the soul of love and along goes the loss of one's ego. Perhaps, this is the entire meaning of love. In the weight of this situation, the dark queen died, crumbled in a hand that can open like an eye. The horse once more succeeded; the Alfinus bowed and departed. Who ever heard of a chess game without a bishop?

After the game, all but one of the players went into the same box; the pawns mixed with the king.

Now the white horse was again on his way, with the might of a Persianist's mystical dream, urging him towards a river and two trees. A vivid fierceness was in his eyes. Now, he was victorious.

28. *All men cherish the notion of being bored, that's how they learn to appreciate it all.*

An Important Meeting

In the wake of the harlequin's death, it seemed impossible not be caught in a pensive state. Days were lost in the depth of an unfamiliar sea and Mr 101 had hardly noticed them flicking away, one by one. Once, he'd been an expert of his own behavioural pattern and known their subtle diversions, now he was almost entirely alien to them, for he came to the realisation that he was absent of identity and he was as much of a fool as the next harlequin.

To his horror, he thought he'd cried when he saw himself in the mirror. When he peered closely he realised that at the balcony of his lower eyelid there stood a boy who was glancing at the edge, dangling a fishing rod to his chin. The boy was tired of waiting and rather wished he could be at the shore fumbling for a suitable rock to chuck to the depths of the lake. At least that's what Mr 101 led himself to believe.

29. *To verbally acknowledge something's beauty is showing one's own former doubt of it having been the opposite.*

Winds like unearthly spirits wooed him to peer from the window so as to satisfy his gaze at the mist that slept while circling their limbs around the masses of branches. This was once his satisfaction, his stability in an ever-changing world, to have the comfort of his own home and stare out and snigger at the sadness which the world harnessed. Now that he was aware that he participated in this very sadness, he grew to hate it. All those sleepless nights were holding on to a piece of string — a red rope that twisted. And soon, very soon, there would be a great deafening fall — a fall of sleep. It was not tragic; the fall of sleep would be nostalgic. It was sought after, desperately needed like an old friend, like the only thing Mr 101 could ever love again.

He retreated to one of the many rooms. This was time for contemplation; there would be no two ways about it. No parties would be held tonight, he was neither hungry nor in the pleasant mood to be amused and being the centrefold of nonsensical talk. Matters were changing.

His appearance in the room was untimely and the lady of Mr 101's nightmares, who sat at the mirror observing herself, let out a short gasp. It caused her arms to horripilate despite the fire crackling comfortably in the corner. It dimmed the walls with an inviting mellow glow which was enough to cause a shudder within Mr 101's being; he sat on the edge of the bed nonetheless.

'You're on my seat,' he claimed finally, to the lady who sat at a French dressing table which was carved preciously with rabbits that glinted with the burning flames.

Indeed she was, for it was Mr 101's most commonplace to express his vanity to the oval mirror she was so fixed upon. But little did she know of this, for she had been attempting in every way to avoid him but their psychic magnetism was soundly improving and soon, the truth will be out...

He watched her attentively behind seemingly careless eyes. His eyes slid to the nude coloured corsage she wore about her bust. The cage had disappeared and she was free. *How dangerous it is for a woman to be free,* he thought. The dress was heavily embroidered in sugar beads of black and silver. Their glassy exterior could challenge Athena's eyes; they glinted at times when they caught the eyes of the flame as stars may do. The wearer was applying black lip-gloss to a masked face in the mirror.

'A fine sight. What a *fine* sight,' Mr 101 whispered, although she could hear every word. 'Why do you cover your face? I have seen you before.'

'You don't understand,' she said, regarding him from the mirror. She was rather flattered that he would want to caress her for once. 'I fear that if you see me for who I am, you will learn the truth...but you must not, for your own good.'

In vain, she struggled to force a tear from her concealed eyes but no such tear ever did surface and she was left stranded on the embarrassment which left Mr 101 so regretful of an anti-climax.

The room's walls were now dripping with the bursts of perfume which hissed as the venom was sprayed out; sandalwood and myrrh.

A blood-diamond, perhaps she could be, thought Mr 101, *exported from a fine quarry, came here to drive me up scent-stained walls.*

She peered at him strangely from the mirror while this thought amused him. In the meantime, the lady was opening the drawer of the French designed boudoir whose handle was carved to its divine detail as a daffodil's head. The inside was lined with dark velvet and shadows which caused great difficulty in seeing the object she took in her hand.

The object in hand, whatever it could be, made the strangest of sounds rather like the cackling of a witch or the faintest sound of the snipping of scissors.

'What are you holding?' asked Mr 101, he was now curious to the point of agitation; somehow it was important. In turn, she was in a panic, clenched her fist around it harder.

'It can't be seen, it must be destroyed.'

'You must tell me what it is!'

Panting, she accepted his request.

'Stand back!' she said. 'You may never have it, at least not in peace.'

She opened her hand slightly and before Mr 101 could catch a real glimpse the fist was closed again. Eyelids or butterflies or flaps or petals or a portal to a void; there was no distinction of whatever it was that he saw. And before he could interrogate the matter further, the lady had disappeared into the oval mirror. The event confirmed his thoughts: *there are yet more riddles to solve.*

30. *Doorknobs would have no use if they were not attached to doors or a device that were to open. A teacup would be rendered useless if it were constantly filled over the brim after each small sip of tea.*

He needed a new obsession. Red like crushed cochineal was the rope that'd been wrung so tightly. He needed to find some sleep. A device to help force himself into the world of dreams; that was going to be his new venture and he will have contact with no-one until his target was reached.

***

Far beyond the incredible dwelling of Mr 101, more specifically in the mountains of which belong to the Kazakh's, exists an age-old tradition. It is that of hunting with eagles. If one could imagine a young boy racing, his guide by his side across a flat mountaintop with a golden eagle perched on his stiffened finger. This creature he will keep by his side for all his life; without the prized possession the possibility of catching the elusive fox is scarce. So for the first time, in anticipation, the boy chases the fox hoping the eagle will finally realise its killer instinct; the boy hoping that he may gain respect from the regional tribes. The neck of the creature gyrates like the needle of a compass, twittering an untranslatable language. Destiny waits to be fulfilled. With the spirit of Kubla-Khan, the boy comes to a stop and releases the eagle with an anxious prayer from above a tilted ridge. The creature dives brilliantly forward, heading for the retreating fox. It is purely the luck and the laws of nature which will determine the outcome and it is with this image in which one can view and grasp how Mr 101 was letting go of his fears and regrets to capture his natural instinct to sleep.

The Removal of Blinking

The girls pounded on the lofty back door but there was no gathering to be held that night or the one following the next, for Mr 101 was comfortably incarcerated in the bedroom he was caught in last. Their rapping, knuckles that hammered in urgency, sounded like the sweet tapping of rain on Mr 101's ceiling, like ripe pears toppling down the many stairs, like hoofs grinding in despair, like a groan of thunder that brings a flood that swallows them all, like drums, drums, drums. They were all in love, not with him but his magic. Love was a drug — one that could fatally harm you. He knew what he knew, not how he knew it! Who had engrained in him such wisdom?

Death Metal Opera played in a farther room; the straining sounds of violins were fought through by the cold, trembling hands of some lost musician. Mr 101, in the meantime, was in no hurry to apply the third layer of black lip-gloss. His own face eclipsed the next in the mirror while the make-up brush glided over his fleshy contours. He glimpsed in dismay at the badly covered bald patch and at his own synthetic eyelashes.

He had struggled through Arabian sands of his own parched patience and filled the drinking bottles of life with sand but now, now was the time. The two glassy globes that were his icy eyes he shut for a moment; a second of peace. He opened them again to an intensely white face and closed them again to complete darkness. They were open, now shut, open, now shut. He would sleep and he would dream. Open, shut, open, shut, open, shut. For a moment, he sat still; two faces, four eyes. He saw himself as strange, perhaps for the first time. Who stared at who? Who was first to blame who? There was a way, there was always a way. He could smell the answer lurking behind the sandalwood and myrrh. The violins had almost sent him into a pleasurable trance but the rapping continued and so he too, must continue. He would sleep and dream.

And so he stared at the other him. A neatly formed gully alongside his cheekbones indicated a prehistoric landmark where many tears had before flowed. The white paint did a horrific job of concealing it in the worst possible way.

The burning fire in the room was almost near its end. He arched his posture towards the glass, eyes protruding until the bitter tears were released as if they had been previously held in a tight embrace. And as he repeated this process it became clearer to him that the longer his eyes were opened the longer he blinked. Could it be? Yes, there it was! And he repeated this process till his eyes could bear it no more and relapsed in a flutter. Tears once again glistened in tiny rivulets; success was nigh. Although he knew the answer, he entertained himself with an overwhelming question: *what if I kept these eyes open for, say, twenty-four hours without so much as a flicker?*

He picked up an eyelash curler and used it to raise his eyelids in order to meet his eyebrow. Again tears began to spill from the sill of his eyelids. Then he tried to force his eyes closed for a while with his thumb but they were too stubborn to be held down for longer than momentary blink. His eyelids were like over-loaded suitcases. Even if one was to force them shut by sitting on top of them, they would not relent, unless there was a removal of some kind, perhaps the removal of blinking altogether.

A mechanical device was needed.

Light-bearers

31. *I'm not the only one to turn a hopeless life into an amusing situation.*

The feeling of yearning, which Mr 101 had disposed of, had travelled rabidly about the house in search of prey to circle and annoy. Eventually it reached an already restless Daffodil. She had collected all the pieces of the photograph like a prized puzzle and all that was left to do was to finally fix the pieces together properly and find out more about the mysterious woman she'd found in the picture. This was by no means a simple task. She no longer slept, and neither did she recollect what the need of it was. It had now become apparent to her that she needed help with the puzzle and that was all she could focus her attention on at this moment. The existence of her father was still a tangible memory but she kept any thoughts of him in a sacred coffin buried beneath the ridiculous debris that was Mr 101 and this endless house.

She was in search of valuable company, anyone that would help her on her perfectly distracting quest, the humdrum which derived from her coming permanent exit from this world. She wanted to meet with Mr 101 again. The house had become silent without the parties, guests and painful outcries. The house was nothing without Mr 101; it existed *because* of him so he must have been lingering about somewhere. If she was lucky she would encounter trails of ashes on the floor but it was difficult to work out whether he was coming or going and it was almost impossible to date these unreliable remnants. No doubt she would fail in any project pertaining to the art of archaeology. But more on this matter later or *never.*

One night after having miraculously fallen asleep under Medusa's gaze, she was awoken by sudden knocks on one of the nearby doors. It seemed strange for a creature to knock on the door of the room they had already been given access to but as she focussed her gaze upon the door, she realised a key was stabbed into the yawning keyhole. Perhaps, whoever it was, had been locked in from the outside when they entered the room. This was the only explanation and no doubt sounded like one of Mr 101's many senseless actions.

She rested her ears upon the door's white-washed surface, not wanting to admit she was fearful of the events that could concur by opening the door, but curiosity gnawed her nerves and she decided she would have to go through with it. A couple more knocks from the other side fed her reason and confidence. She took a deep breath and without thinking any further on the matter turned the key and stepped into the room.

The light-bearers were inside, waiting. Although their anticipation had dried into a scab doesn't mean it couldn't still be picked at and encouraged to bleed again from the fountain of its source. Their souls were, like the sun, bright beyond any other — but tonight they had left them behind as they could cause injury like the arrow which shatters the bone into many pieces. Sure enough, they called only in the night — although in Mr 101's house, night was forever so they came and went as they pleased, sometimes using the space as a gateway between their dimension and ours.

Past the opened door was a curious Daffodil in the usual darkness, save for the intruding moonlight that always chose to show just about enough for sinful, curious eyes, pointed out the ceiling above which trembled with wooden shavings that moved — but no — they were moths with eye motifs on their furry wings. Their antennas at times straightened and stretched like an arm after a long slumber from the halls of dreams.

The light-bearers could sense her questioning in the dark atmosphere they sat in, on plain wooden chairs. A light came on. The moths like a bed sheet in the wind were uplifted in their vast quantities and twisted, threading an invisible cord around the light, they caused a storm of wings in the rooms without so much of a hum. The light was the bearer's head and his body wore a suit. The light was kept inside a glass case, triangular-shaped. A cigarette was held by the creature's fingers, releasing the hypnotic smoke, twirling in sync with the galaxy of fluttering wings. One of the larger sized moths, like a flapping book came and rested on the glass head; the light-bearer hence gained eyes from the creature's wings and sooner than later a mouth became visible underneath it. The other moths gently rattled close by, causing an intricate storm of wings sometimes gently caressing Daffodil on the cheek as if they were eyelashes.

'Hello?' Daffodil was so overwhelmed by the beauty she was close to fearing it.

The light-bearer glanced at his cigarette but didn't smoke.

'Come closer; you wish to ask me something.'

Daffodil gulped. The light-bearer continued.

'Don't fear me. At least, don't fear what you one day *will* become.' He spoke with a decided tone, rather calm and not intrusive so Daffodil began to feel at ease and sat on the floor.

'There's nothing.'

'At the beginning, there was nothing and at the end, there will be nothing but for now I can see you haven't managed to put the pieces together. Time is running short and the end of your days will soon come. Hand me the pieces, quickly now.'

He clicked his fingers at her so that she would hurry up as the moth on his face flew away, rendering him faceless as he was when he first appeared. He scrunched the pieces in his hands, the light grew stronger like the sun expanding and it swallowed the moths that were its stars for a moment. As he unravelled the photograph which was now in one piece, the light began to dim again and the moths fluttered in their trance as if nothing had happened.

'Ha!' he said, handing Daffodil the photograph as another moth, a darker hue of colour from the last, landed on his glass face. His eyes never blinked.

'Is there anything else you need?'

Daffodil glanced at the picture. There was a man, undoubtedly Mr 101, in a shockingly happy smile without make-up, his arm extended around a woman in a wedding dress, holding a bouquet. The house behind them was not this one; it was a small bungalow in the centre of two tall trees. The couple smiled happily in front of the camera. There was a sense of hope in the image; it was hard to accept that Mr 101 could smile without a hint of corruption on his face. The woman beside him was not the lady who haunted the corridors, Daffodil had never seen her before. Her face was rounder, as was her figure. Who could she have been? And who was the lady that persisted to haunt every wall of the house?

'No...' lied Daffodil, for she had been in search for a warm hug for some time now, 'but thank you.'

'I'm not sure who she is,' sighed the light-bearer, having guessed what Daffodil wanted to know; it wasn't hard, even a senseless moth seeking hungrily for light could sense it. 'I recognise her face but I can't remember from where...'

'Is she still alive?'

'Most likely not, whoever rubs shoulders with Mr 101 in the end is killed in the most gruesome manner — that's his custom.' He stated the last part as if it was general knowledge, playing with his cigarette that he wasn't planning on smoking.

It was not an easy concept to explain why the light-bearers held a lit cigarette without consuming them. The laws of nature would need to be unravelled along with the secrets of the skies before one can begin the journey of explanation, like why the grass is not blue and the sky not green.

Back to Wordsworth

In mass grandeur, the hyacinths stood like stained-glass sweets brightened by the shifting sunlight that was flicking through the pages of the clouds like a searching reader. When the sun shone, it turned its vision into diamonds and gold, crystallising the bile that churned in the gall. And the bees closely guarded the garden's beauties with hints of flirtation. But their show of love was fickle, fumbling each plant for a short while.

The sparrow, from the heights of the changing sky, fluttered its wings in swift flight cheerfully and dipped headfirst into the cradled branches of the pear tree and found its destination resting upon Wordsworth's broad shoulder, who was admiring this remarkable scene of nature. Sorrowful were the thoughts that circled his mind. He placed an unusual woodwind instrument to his lips and he blew into as if a human heart was attached to its end and to which he gave life to.

The colony of pastel-coloured hyacinths jerked side to side on the lack-lustre land where the bees were now slowly vanishing in a mysterious world. Autumn was slowly commencing to mark the slight absence of sun — not that the sun was present much this summer. It seemed the island rejected the sun and the sun itself was now beginning to take the hint resentfully. The rock afar, which had once host the migratory destination for many gannets, now stood naked and cold centred by a forever turbulent sea. Before commemorating, Wordsworth altered his gaze at Mr 101's sweatbox house of misery and how it was miraculously constructed. He then turned his gaze at the natural world and saw an exact replica of the idea, except illustrated a little differently. Innocent, one might describe the world of nature, but Wordsworth, a man of vast experience in this world, saw something rather different.

It was a pity of a picture to see Wordsworth in a melancholic daze with the relaxed winds that were his steady wings. Certainly, it was far from one of his heavenly days. His sweet cherub arrived in the puzzling form of Daffodil, who he hadn't seen for many weeks. He resumed his music at once and gave her smile which she returned earnestly and was sat beside him. Neither of them spoke at the beginning as silence was sometimes something to be cherished in a fully-fledged friendship.

A curtain trembled slightly in one of the many windows of the house but neither of them noticed.

'The bees are slowly disappearing from the world,' Wordsworth tore the silence in a slightly hoarse voice.

Daffodil liked to look into his eyes and let rest there for it was pure and offered light in a dark world of fantasy.

'Where do they go?' she asked.

'As far as their delicate wings may take them, I suppose, as far from here as possible; somewhere to be appreciated. Can you imagine a world without bees?'

Daffodil could not find the correct word of consolation to give him and neither did she want to cause any offence of any kind, so she remained quiet for the time being.

'No,' he said finally. 'You should know nothing of death, a child like you.'

Daffodil could not find herself to comment after this statement which held such a soft tone of finality. Death, yes death was on its way just assuredly as the winter was next to autumn yet it seemed impossible to take it seriously in a world of illusion. Without her father, she was misguided, rather like a sheep under a mad shepherd who permitted trespassing in regions she never knew existed. And now that Daffodil had fulfilled her purpose of piecing together the photograph which depicted a black and white composition of a young, smiling woman with Mr 101, she felt herself to be of service to a small thing called indolence.

The image remained in her mind, she would never forget it. The photograph itself impressively captured the essence of a woman in her early twenties who grinned rather flirtatiously in short crimpled hair at the side of her face where happiness took pleasure in residing. It was clear that she had attained this happiness, a kind of joy that didn't fluctuate easily.

Daffodil handed the photograph to a thoughtful Wordsworth. He gave her a peculiar look upon seeing it.

'Where did you find this?' Wordsworth enquired after a long pause of silence; the pebble of his thought had finally sunken into the lovely waters and met the others on the bed of rock. And then, before Daffodil could begin to decry her epic saga, Wordsworth resumed, 'Let me show you something.'

A star glinted in the galaxy of his eyes as he stood up and Daffodil followed him into the mass civilisation of the fragrant cedar trees. It was not long until they were crowded by the large trunks that stood like proud fatherly figures and sheltered them from any hope of natural light. It was here that the seldom violets slept peacefully; spots of purple dreaming in the shadows of forever. Other spaces were occupied by etiolated foliage which was doing the tough work of concealing (and Daffodil had just noticed) a webbed-veiled tombstone on which the naked eye could just about glimpse the engraved, '*My dear wife, Madeleine*'.

As Daffodil approached it, one nervous step at a time, she realised there was no date of passing present. Of course, Daffodil immediately recognised this name from her visit to the shoe cupboard. She was once the owner of horse-printed heeled shoes.

Wordsworth swept the webbed dust and broke off the many clasps of foliage and tendrils to reveal further blankness of the tombstone. Daffodil could not help but assume the most terrible tragedy.

'Did Mr 101 kill her?'

Wordsworth's previous thoughts were conquered by the intensity of the word 'kill'. How could a child assume such horror? Yet, in his silent ways, Wordsworth had learnt the truth many nights ago. Had he not watched Mr 101 build the derelict box of loneliness? And had he not witnessed the clamorous gangs of ladies flooding the doorway and none coming back out? So the truth was there and there was no need or way for it to be kept from the child.

Wordsworth left silence to reply to Daffodil, for now it was time for her to trust her instincts and to listen to the beatings of her heart. That was indeed truth. His woodwind instrument met his lips again and he left the scene with a melancholic tune with his dutiful sparrow after him. He was seen until the cedars' branches embraced him completely.

The sun fawn-freckled the forest floor for one last time that day, waving goodbye through the passage of dusk.

The Shoe Room

On her adventures, Daffodil discovered all but the shoe room; it was like a drop of wine seized in amethyst that could not be yielded by straightforward extraction. She would not be shocked if it had shrunken to the size of a virus that had been plucked away by Mr 101's flaking fingers. Daffodil climbed the never-ending marble stairs after her meeting with the elusive Wordsworth. The Medusa chandelier looked smaller than the eye of a needle and rather comical from the summit of where Daffodil stood, peering down upon it. Medusa's snakes would never reach this height, she thought while she resumed to orbiting a long series of rooms.

The giddy child assumed that the outside, bedazzling world couldn't harm her from in here, but the inside world would. No doubt it was devising its own lucrative plan of cunning to dismantle her in the most theatrical way it could, without half measures, taking its time because nature is the most patient criminal of all (amongst other things it is renowned for).

The house, hosting a piling of stairs upon stairs of tiring despair, gave the traveller an illusory effect of ascension — especially when they were on a steep descent. At the genesis of this encyclopaedia of stairs, Mr 101 was inspired by the words of a wise man, 'More often, misfortune is disguised as good fortune and good fortune snares the good with misfortune, so in this way one must learn to live to not be impressed by frivolity and the brevity of joy...', hence the stairs were adapted to this saying. Depending on time and space, it was fair to say the house created impossible space. And if the stairs weren't manifesting from impossible space, they caused their pursuer to scratch their heads at their puzzling form. Some stairs rebelled and refused visitation by being the same width as a strand of hair. If a visitor wasn't prone to be valiant then the stairs could by all means pose to be violent. It would have been like climbing a storm or the serrated edge of a saw. Either way these stairs were threatening, devastating and perhaps serene, for death is always peaceful. Daffodil steered clear from those extremely challenging stairs and stayed on the ones that accepted the patter of feet like the earth receives rain. And it was an exciting game for Daffodil who, after all this time, had opened her eyes to this truth. Sometimes she'd entertain herself with the metal objects that were strewn about in the corners. Many were cast into oddities and strange shapes protruding with spikes and laced with chains to shackle and punish the human body or at least to suspend it until it disbelieved the idea of positive bliss. Time was now expressive of something that should be burnt away like calories.

There was a ball, which she mistook for a maimed foetus that she would accidently run into as it rolled its way up and down the house, and this posed as a distraction from her search. If the house was a cat, this oddball was its fur ball that was stubborn in its throat. She could always smell it from afar like a roll of garbage before it came wheeling past, haunting her imagination. If the walls could talk instead of hissing or making undecipherable sounds, it would tell the tale of the ball which was once a man, a traveller in the house of 101. His biggest mistake was that he hadn't been ludicrous enough to suspect that there was an escape from here, so he found a way to keep busy. He knew he wouldn't be disturbed as he decided to liberate himself by doing the roly-poly. All of his skin had gradually eroded from him over time, after having rolled and been sliced from the menacing stairs. Even if someone cared, it would be hard to conclude if he was still alive or somewhere in between, the purgatory of existing. For, although his motion never ceased, he never once unravelled to pay a visit to his older, saner self. Over time he'd shrunken to the size of a baby's brain, but the stench increased and coated him as a powerful aura. Once, Mr 101 had seen him, even stopped to admire him. Perhaps he was enchanted by this undiscovered type of dedication. In an instant, the former decided that the traveller was chipping himself away to become a tab of paracetamol; in the last stage of the ball's life he would fizzle into the moisture of the air and if someone should walk through this veil of white dust, they would be cured by the natural hangover which comes from being here. Mr 101 nodded agreeably, thinking his efforts were all well and good, and returned to his duties of not really doing much.

So Daffodil walked on, now bored of the ball as she ignored another occurrence of it passing by. She had been secretly anticipating a surprising visit from Mr 101, for he used to spy on her at times and shout at her when the time was needed, but now he was nowhere to be seen. He was never seen shifting tiles to excavate the truth beneath the chequered floor in the glare of Medusa.

The remnants of him were littered in corners in the form of empty black lip-gloss bottles that relentlessly tapped, tapped, tapped their journey down the stairs, and if one was lucky they would reach the destination of the ceiling.

Death Metal Opera would play, spinning on a gramophone in one of the many dark rooms that were only ever occupied by shadows and these enclosures were privy to them and by no means ever allow a single soul to enter. At one time a forgotten musician superfluously lamented a tune with his accordion shaped as a giant millipede. If it was possible, the house had entered into a darker dimension since the harlequin's death; a death which still remained a mystery to Daffodil. Even the stairs were slowly decisive these days; they weren't churning out destinations fast enough. And as the French would mock in jest they all possessed the *l'esprit de l'escalier*[1]. After an infinity of searching, she found herself in the shoe room. It'd procured a high number of shoes that were stacked carelessly on the metal racks, their heels still strangled by paper tags as before.

The horse printed shoes worn by Madeleine were nowhere to be seen. The other shoes were just not comparable in style and elegance to that particular object of desire. The fire of disappointment burned in Daffodil.

1. French saying "Wit of the staircase" — thinking slowly of a suitable retort after the opportunity to make it has been missed.

Where could they be?

The room was dimming slowly; the light bulb had mysteriously manifested into a pear that hung humorously from the ceiling to the moths' dismay that darted from the room as soon as the transformation was complete. Daffodil, in her desperation, had herself caught in the womb of the pile, desperately seeking the shoes she had kept in the safe of her memory. Her motives were elusive even to herself but there was an arcane resolve to separate Madeleine's shoes and protect their value from all the others. It had regained a sentimental value. However, it was clear that for some odd reason, it was missing from the collection. It seemed strange that it would disappear after so long, and just at this specific time when Daffodil had shown keen interest.

Daffodil uttered a sigh of dissatisfaction in the darkness, swallowed inside a dormant volcanic structure of shoes.

Mr 101's Blinking Preventer

> 32. *I lie down dead. I am born daily. I lie down in death. I am born. I become new; I renew my growth every day.*

In the space of the next few days, Mr 101 succumbed to one of his many bedrooms, secluding himself from all the creatures of the house hoping they'd leave him to his own devices. Without sleep, his days and nights were merged and it was an uninterrupted continuum he was unhappy about.

The crescent moon resembled a curved foot that memorable night when Mr 101 had completed the last few touch-ups on his abstract invention. Up until now, this idea was unheard of — ridiculous some may say — but he couldn't care less. It could be implied that this was the desired reaction he was hoping for. Employing the mask of Ridiculism was a man of genuine wit. Although he vented his doubts to the point of overuse so that they were beginning to take a stale air, his determination was unmatched. The persistent voice in his head pleaded him to keep the idea alive. Nothing important was to be forgotten anymore; he would not make that mistake again, not even if he could.

A glass pear-shaped paperweight tamed the piles of dog-eared parchment which flapped helplessly in the plumes of wind and cigarette smoke. His work was done. A giddy fire was lit in the old fireplace in the corner and scented the room with rich cedar. He could have been trapped in there for days but he cared not for it was worth the wait, the deliberation, the darkness and the light. It had been worth the beads of sweat that drained and cooled the white paint on his face like ice. And at times Mr 101 would accidently chance upon a reflection of himself and that ghastly bald patch of missing hair.

The mirror itself was far more superior than him; its sub-frame was wrought in fantastical silver metal-workings underlining the outer, overall frame that was twice as large and thicker, gilt in the rococo style in an attempt to pose a finer appearance than nature. But if this had not yet pleased the eye enough, the mirror itself had been carved at the sides to look like mists drawn by an artistic hand but rough to the touch. This floral decoration was matched with stylized leaves. So in fact, the mirror itself was already ornate without the support of a frame or even a sub-frame for that matter, or a man with a painted face to sit before it and admire his flaws and beauty sporting his own life-altering device.

Behind where Mr 101 was sitting laid the remains of what used to be a panelled bed. One could hope that it had clawed itself to look like this disastrous version of itself so it could leave for a better life elsewhere, far away from Mr 101, but to be truthful, it was clear that Mr 101 had exploited its strong wood to create his Blinking Preventer.

All that was left from what used to be a bed was a mattress, its vases that held ostrich feathers atop the canopy (in pieces), sheets undone and a few wooden shavings. All night (or was it day?) he'd carefully grafted, designed, sanded down and screwed in the nails for the mechanism. Now that his work was done, he sat in silence blowing wisps of smoke — the trail of a good rhythm — with his eyelids lifted by wooden tongs and the whites of his eyes protruding. Those poor muscles, how they clung on to the eyeballs so that the latter did not just roll out onto the ground.

Mr 101 sat and thought. He pondered on the subject of his wife and her death. There were horrifying rumours circling round like an atom of course, but if only he cared for senseless chatter. He knew every single word of gossip concerning him. Some say that Mr 101 murdered his wife in a brutal magical act in front of an intimate audience that included his close acquaintances Mr Wordsworth and Mr Wormwood.

The lamps had been lit and with a bunch of incense scented with frankincense and myrrh; they dropped ashes per stages on a valuable burgundy mantelpiece. The curtains were pulled back like eyelids and the audience applauded.

His wife had been dressed in a tight and sparkling magician's assistant attire; her dainty fingers had wheeled onto the stage a wooden prop she was to be locked inside, save her head and waggling feet. She did what she was told.

33. *The trick in life is to become whatever it is we admire of others. I, myself, admire nobody, so I will become myself.*

Mr 101 had promised her a painless ordeal as he brought out a theatrically gigantic saw (which was appropriate for that sort of ruse). In her most mimicking manner, she screamed and the crowd jeered; couples turned to one another shrugging in giggles. But Mr Wordsworth had lit a cigarette and stared about the crowd suspiciously. The saw tore through the star covered box and ravaged its way through the box and her waist. She uttered screams of genuine horror when blood and pain told her that her dear beloved husband was in fact tearing her to pieces. The audience applauded in a standing ovation, some had truly fainted but they were ignored. Ladies encumbered in mink fur smiled admiringly at Mr 101 as he not only led his wife but also his virtuous self to bleed.

The curtains swiftly met as the trick was done. This was the death of Mr 101's wife and it was a lie. No one had ever speculated or gossiped on such worthless words. However, it was an illusion created by Mr 101 himself to conceal the truth of what really happened, for if he admitted the truth of his wife's death, other truths will have to be unfolded like napkins. And what if the napkins were unclean still after all these years, even after having been washed, starched and folded in the shape of swans?

Calculations for the Blinking Preventer

On average, Mr 101 blinked thirteen times per minute.

A 24 hour day = 18,720 blinks

1 blink = 1 second

1 hour = 3600 seconds

780 blinks per hour

18,720 / 3600 = 5.2

Five hours and twenty minutes of sleep!

Mr 101 lit a smoke-trailing cigarette on the boudoir chair as the lady arrived like he always knew she would, knocking the floorboard with shoes stylised with white horses which leapt over complete darkness. This woman was the lithium in his waters, ready to pop and fizz at any given time. One at a time she brought forth her elegant legs; once upon a time she had worn a birdcage for a skirt. She was holding the thing, whatever it was that could be heard within her firmly shut fist. There was a worrying sound like heads being guillotined simultaneously, in a perfect sequence (what a tremendous way to die!). But what troubled Mr 101 more were those stilettos, for he did not need to see them to realise who they belonged to; he'd heard them countless times before, in the forgotten land of his past which he was now, as always, terrified of.

She walked gently, leading him into the next room where the walls faded to unmask a clouded room where the Death Metal Opera singer, the renowned Lace-Demon, sat singing, ceaselessly fiddling with a grand piano. With those same hands, rumours had flourished that she had slain a 'great beast' because she believed she would be a much better replacement. Her music was renowned in the Ridiculist world. She was now sitting the famous *'Of Lips Where Beauty Spots Lie'* when the lady seated herself on a table close by. Mr 101 approached the Lace-Demon, noticing her gothic lace attire that was exquisitely made to goffer as it created an illusion of endless trails. The dress appeared to have been lightly sugar-dusted with small diamonds, and the train seemed like it was developed in shadow works that swarmed about her as if the dead would rise from its depth and set bodies tumbling down endless stairs, ending up in places only God could guess where. A corset, tightly bound, was fastened with tasselled twisted red ropes. Mr 101 placed a kiss on her soft hand in respect for her music whose words had been his salvation in numerous times of degradation. Rich, thick honey was the thought which was brought forth from his mind instantaneously because she was, indeed, naturally scented in this way. *A rare scent nowadays,* he thought as his Blinking Preventer jittered in agreement. *Don't you dare have a life of your own!* he thought, after his invention which sat on his head.

Her monumental hair too, honeycombed, was a burst of gold resembling the hue of the sticky fluid. The room was a deserted bar (not one that offered desserts) that appeared to have been situated in a moonlit cave for it was darker than one could imagine. He was seated, clunking with the mechanism that was attached to him. And as he did so he realised he'd sat here before.

A lit match lent itself to Mr 101's cigarette.

'Tell me where you came from,' he began in an almost poetic fashion, undoing a napkin and tucking the supple material around his collar like a ruff although he had no intention of eating or of being served. 'Do you come here for unfinished business as ghosts do?'

Laughing would have not been appropriate and there was still time for crying, so the lady remained quiet behind the small round table (the tables were purposely too small to discourage customers to rest their arms on them). His ignorance fed her jealousy, for she held more intellect than him and yet this made her suffer the most. She thought about his hideous appearance and how beautiful it almost made him.

The Lace-Demon was having herself a rather long piano solo of mastery, getting carried away in her own secret world when the lady spoke.

'What does your heart tell you?'

'It tells me that you don't belong here. It tells me that you should put those shoes back to where they belong because you are not my wife!'

'Your wife?!' she was in shock. 'What a terrible thing to conjure up.'

'Then what is your business here?'

'My business rests with you,' she glared at him. 'The girl freed me. Why do you punish her when all she does for you is good?'

'Whatever happens between Daffodil and I, must remain that way without question. Even if I were to explain, there would be no words for it, I can only mimic a proper explanation and I don't ever dare. However, her fate is just. Deep down I see her suffering and as a young, helpless creature that should not be made to suffer if they can enjoy the long sleep of death unscathed, for the penance would be mine to bear. In this way, I am empathetic.'

The lady sighed. Theirs was a tedious arrangement of opposites that never led to a promising place. She saw what was done and he, what remained to be done. Together they brought the wrong ingredients to make a soufflé that was destined to be deflated.

'Give me your name so I may locate you in my memory. Give me something, for all you seem to do is take.' Mr 101 was desperate to know and if she wouldn't tell him, he'd have to let her go.

'Give me yours first — your real name.'

He growled at her stubborn retort. The house belonged to him, not her, and she should be at his mercy in any case. What complicated the matter was that he did not know his true name. Mr 101 was something he put together out of boredom and a desperate yearning to be a great Ridiculist of the theorist kind. Over-exposure to confusion curdled his blood and ordered the bees of order to disappear. Having sensed this, the lady cleared her already cleared throat and interrupted the pungent silence.

'How can you be so desperate for sleep when I happen to be alive?' said the lady, forlorn. She, too, had undone a napkin and placed it on her heavily embroidered skirt so she may dine on this conversation.

'Whatever, in this state of hell, do you mean?'

She sighed again for she was tired and sought to wander the corridors. There was no use in stirring an empty cup when the empty cup was Mr 101's memory in itself.

'I can no longer argue, but if it is sleep that you seek, it is sleep which you will be given — but blame only yourself when you become more delusional than you could possibly ever be.'

Sleeping

34. *If by chance I stumble across the moon whose symbols I am done fretting over in positive aggression, I shall kick it soaring to a hellish place. And from behind the walls of the universe, demons may surrender as I leap into a deadly dance while Death itself dims the light of my soul and takes me in. And by no means should He be in any position to offer me a peaceful slumber, for silence in my pitiful death-in-life existence has tormented me to no end. Bring me pianos and violins.*

Mr 101 discovered the miracle of the yawn just after his daily journal entry was written; he stood up straight in Room 101 in surprise. His stomach churned with excitement — or was it sickness? Whatever it was, he could tell the new beginning was around the corner. He would... *sleep.* In chronological timing, his fingers began to twitch and awoke from the flat surface of the table to meet the stretched skin of eyelid, stroking it slightly. Yes, he had eyes to see, to observe, to judge, blink and roll from a lack of satisfaction, from impatience, from being ungrateful. But if he observed closely, he would see that they had given him everything he ever wanted but now his eyes had ascended to a higher purpose of closing to rest. They would shut the world away, and explore the sacred treasures from within which were hoarding themselves abundantly.

Things Mr 101 Read and Wrote Before he went to Sleep

An excerpt from *The Importance of Shutting Your Eyes Especially If You're Not Planning on Sleeping*, by the leading author on the subject of Ridiculism himself, Alba Tross Doolally:

> *I would not go as far as to call it meditation; it is merely the closure of one's eyes, both of them together in conclusive arrangement. There is an extraordinary phenomenon which has never been previously discussed because of the rise of fear in Ridiculism. Although Ridiculism ridicules fear, there is no way to avoid that it is the most major hindrance in attempting this practice and permitting it to run free towards success. What is the practice you may wonder? Before I begin, may I ask you to leave your preconception, your nature of nurture, any spiritual beliefs of the conforming type before you enter? And now breathe. Read the title of this essay again for the title is the eye to the body of words. Now, let me reveal to you that while you sleep the world is in motion, change is all about us. While the body is asleep, the soul ventures into the hidden subconscious. This is no news for us and if this is the case please reject this piece of writing as jargon for I am not interested in having such a dotard as yourself for a reader for I, too, have a reputation to keep up. For those who are capable of carrying on further in the reading, listen to me closely for I will only say this once unless you're reading this again.*

35. *In dreams, we can live an entire life in five minutes.*

Now the simplest way to explain this is to imagine that all your worldly possessions have legs, invisible ones. I would even go as to say that they have souls, ambitions and the resolve to attain this soul's ambition. I may just have to remind you that your dreams are just as outrageous as reality itself so this may well be the truth. To cut an extremely long explanation short is that it is only when our eyes are closed that the objects of the world become impregnated with life. They move, they skip down the hall, they play their own songs. But we must not doubt their speed for they return to their original position once our eyes are open. You must realise that the world is not yours. There are many entities unheard of that we must share it with. Think outside your own, star-covered box before you attack it with a giant hammer. And remember it is you inside the box; and the one standing on the outside is you, an extended version of yourself, and there are more of you than just the one.

36. *How is it that truth and fate move in opposite directions?*

Our truths are personal and sacred; we dress them in fine petticoats and send them to the void in gilt reigned chariots, one after another, when all it desires is to be by your side, naked as a new born. When you're in a state such as this be sure to know that Death is lurking upstairs, reigning over the skies with a diamond gilt crown weaving your most unexpected cause of death with shuttles of gold. Do not be frightened at this knowledge for we do not die alone, not unless we keep the truth by our side when we are soaring above the clouds.

The Spiritual Symbolism of a Hiccup by Somebody:

Hiccups are not just a minor hiccup in our lives; we must observe them carefully by measuring the duration of their stay and the strength of each hiccup as we experience them.

Mr 101 sighed in anger, almost reaching for a gulp of wine when he changed his mind about the matter as he did not want chance to lend him a reason to complete his reading. He reached for another book from a pile by his side called *How to Expiate One's Own Soul* by Another One. However, his attention flew into another question altogether, *How do I cast my soul into a mould? So that I may see my true nature, converse with him, face-to-face, friend-to-friend and build a lasting foundation with him?*

The Art Critic by Someone Who is Educated Enough to Write a Sentence That Makes Some Sort of Sense:

> *Remember good art never appreciates itself, it receives its praise from the unseen and the meaningless...*

Mr 101 was on his beloved saffra reading this. It was a short article that didn't dare to be a novel for Mr 101 would have chucked it in the fire a long while ago.

> *...of course, it is tricky to comment on a piece of work especially nowadays when abstract art is á la mode to the point where it leaves the abstract and enters the domain of jargon, as many would say (I have heard this with my own ears). But do not despair, it is time to trust our intuition and instincts. If the work is bad, then your feelings of badness must be analysed because the bad can sometimes turn out to be good. For example, the type of art which offends a certain group is so so bad that it becomes good. Let's take the work of...*

Before Mr 101 could finish the verbal garbage, he lunged the book into the gulp of the fire.

'What a pointless read from a droning drunkard!' he said, taking a sip from his crystal glass-encumbered wine.

He eventually retreated to his pages which were the best of all the refuges in the house, they were the windows he could write on, their glass panes opaque to anyone but him, bearably tactile instead of repelling while attempting to catch the blurs of a future that had not yet fully developed its features and faults in the tight uterus of time.

37. *I believe I am a mirror but I don't want to forget what I've reflected, at least what I think I may have grasped. And people come strolling by for truth, for clarity, for doubt, for a reason to find something wrong and an excuse to be right. I'm motionless as a painting, but often too real. I am a mirror with one reflection, escaping the now because I want to live in yesterday and tomorrow.*

Shortly after, Mr 101 fell asleep. Or more elaborately put, he was transported to the world of dreams and nightmares. He gave them names as soon as he was awake, just so if they visited again he would be well acquainted with them rather than treating them as fiends which would only make matters worse on his part. The previously applied face paint cracked on his face as he fought out a half-smile in his sleep. It was sacred, whatever took place behind those white painted eyelids.

The Funeral

Black was the new moon that dared to ooze its black bile to spruce up an even blacker night. The dark curtains that had once been pulled back vigorously now cascaded from its brass bars and hindered any chance of a good view and anything that could ever dare to be new. Someone of significance had died. Her name was Madeleine. It did not matter when exactly, but it was enough to entertain the idea of a funeral and have it materialise at an immense speed, faster than the burgeoning of a spring rose. No one knows how or when the coffin arrived in Room 13, or why was it so heavy that the floor beneath it was beginning to crack from its lack of strength to withhold it. Could the weight of the world be inside? Why shouldn't it be? Didn't our modest milky way compact and arrange itself within man?

Some guests had turned up for the sake of paying tribute to Mr 101's past. Some wished they were in the coffin instead, but this was a typical train of manic thought that assailed throughout the house without apparent cause.

38. *Wipe off the evil grin on the face of narcissism, then wipe off the narcissism completely.*

They were also unusually attired in pristine black garments and did not brave getting into conversation, not that there was anything to say. The lady of Mr 101's great disgust entered with an air of affectation and holding up to the ceiling something she called the Rosy Grail. It was passed around the room to the guests who took one intoxicating sip until eventually, there was not a single drop left. The essence of wild rose, the Rosy Grail, could attack the tongue pleasurably like hummingbird beaks piercing tough balloons with the soft dedication of a scholar's page-flicking research for true light. But who knows what it tasted like after years of putrefaction, of not being close to a wriggling tongue, the cushion of rouged lips or the stamp of a fingerprint on its encasing.

Some of the guests ignored the lady who took her time to saunter around the room like a moist leakage and out of boredom they mistook the white walls for the pages of a colouring book and began to fill the spaces with scribbles of charcoal. The funeral reminded them that their time in life was short and so it inspired them to begin to find the inner child before it was too late. On that very same wall there was a large collection of old photographs held in baroque-style frames which the pseudo-artists avoided from touching.

One picture which looked more like a coffee stain caught the lady's gaze. It was of a young girl standing next to someone who looked like her father. But his face had just missed the frame to discern properly and resolve conjectures. The girl wore slacks with her shirt neatly tucked inside. With one hand she held her father's and with the other she clutched a fishing rod. There was a small boat afloat the surface of a lake behind them.

The lady stood back from the picture as a thunderous bang made the guests gasp and quickly leave the room. When she turned back, the room was quite empty and frighteningly silent. The artists seemed to have melted through the cracks of the floor leaving behind half a blackened wall. Then she discovered the root of their panic. The floor had given in to the coffin, sending it to land on hopefully a stronger surface. It didn't matter where, as long as it wasn't in this room; anywhere but here. The lady was rather glad to see the back of it.

She looked through the hole the coffin had left like a souvenir. It was too big to avoid, to be obscured by, say, a sofa or a bed or another coffin. Inside, she saw a pool of thick back liquid. Like a black mirror, it returned her gaze with an amorphous reflection. A thought pestered her. And she began to helplessly wish that she had an iron rod to stir the dark embers of time in a hope to unfasten it and conjure up its violet-rooted flames.

Awakening

Long after the experience of being awake, Mr 101 pinched a bright green jerkin from the nearby farthingale chair by the side of his bed, slid it on and set off for a stroll about the corridor, having it flouncing about him with every movement. This 16th century jerkin, once a fine example of a traditional Italian embroidery, had been stripped off completely by the fuss of it 'not looking right' and was, as immediately as one could have it, hand-embroidered with a much more tasteful style of the orients.

And so he went on his unexpected expedition; he strolled on in the most lackadaisical, lacklustre, lack-of-anything-but boredom manner about his house. He didn't follow a straight path in any way but rather darted to and fro from one side of the wall to another, muttering a thing or two. He would say, without an inch of denial, he definitely, quite positively dreamt the previous night. The journal would have to know — not now but later! There was all the time in the world for the journal and that cold, cold Room 101, its concrete walls dripping at all given times, sweating from all the fears it had experienced, sweating from the tiresome experience of having to enclose the revolting space, sweating from the condensation of breathing restlessly, sweating from having to *exist* every single day without sun!

Taking a deep breath, Mr 101 burst open a random door in a hasty handshake. It greeted him with a puff of dust as he entered to be confronted with walls consisting of nothing but door handles occupying every bit of space on the walls. It was dusty and deprived of light, as most rooms were. Of course, quite incongruously, stood a mirror in the centre, for there had to be a mirror in every single room or a glass surface so one could always see a familiar face at all times. *Wow,* thought Mr 101, as he began to realise the purpose of this room. He ran his fingers on a rounded brass handle and on to the one next and so on in a sequential movement, gently sweeping away the dust as he drifted back to a time when his memory was freshly gone and he had started his 'no sun, no fun' routine and delved profusely in the art of Ridiculism. This room would have acted as a supply room for doors seeking 'a breath of fresh air' from the old and swap their much-used hands for handles whenever they wished. They would do this while he slept, for doors were shy beings and disliked conversation so they ventured only in the late hours of the night, dragging their enormous weight on the wooden planks. And Mr 101, being a man of compassion at this time, could not be happier than to have doors unhinging themselves from walls, taking strolls and adjusting their handles while he was asleep. But the predicament arose when he could not sleep, not even when forced or sewn his eyelids together or sprayed lavender perfume on him from head to foot. The trauma had destroyed a natural function within him, stirred a restless bane in the pit of his stomach that even the thought of sleep disgusted him till he grew to ridicule and deem the act as primitive and time-wasting. Those were the days before his physical make-up, that voice within howled at the full moon for sleep, howled from the hunger for slumber, for that day when the flesh blinds would shut and reality would begin to dim. All night, he'd sit on his newly imported saffra in front of the pendulum that persisted like a child on a swing and with a cigarette hanging from his mouth he would leaf through books after books while time hung loose. His memory grew weak with his ability to sleep. And so he was angered at any other thing that seemed to hang loose like time itself. Time was inevitable and he could not change that, not even if he destroyed all the clocks and sent them flying out of the window. But he made sure to destroy the harlequin's hosiery of any kind that hung endlessly on drying lines he erected. They hung like emptied intestines and reeked of dust, especially after having been cleaned. He grabbed them and tore them between his teeth, creating ladders, and the material stretched between the gaps in his teeth, denting his bleeding gums. They would then become twisting ropes in red.

It was clear that the period of losing his mind had begun and Ridiculism had arrived bearing a pantyhose-bloodied grin. But he couldn't damage the curtains, not those thick blocks of black which blocked the sun so precisely, those velvety heavens that nobody but himself was allowed to touch. There was never a frequent occasion to do so anyhow and was not needed to be fiddled with. No, they did the job just fine and he supposed the hanging tights did him no harm whatsoever; all in all it had been a hollow rebellion. An apology would be impossible, now that the harlequin was scattered in pieces. After much thought, he walked out of the room leaving the door open. Times had changed. The room was opened for visitation and if the doors wished to slice off their wrists, they were more than welcome to do so.

In one of the many bedrooms, Mr 101 fixed his gaze on his reflection after having applied two layers of thick white paint on his face. By his side awaited the Blinking Preventer for after his make-up was done. He would have another party soon as he was hungry and the ladies, he was sure, shared the same feeling, having been deprived of his chocolate for so long. It was not that he felt an urge in any way to satisfy their addiction. It was rather a big hoo-ha over nothing, but the entertainment never ceased, the joy of watching such austerity on their knees fighting for the taste of chocolate. And it was just as amusing to observe behind curtains of smoke. It was fine entertainment indeed!

The thick putty was dabbed on his face and the mascara applied, having left the best till last, he put on black lip-gloss. It was like having a dangerous shadow in a bottle, one that could not even be destroyed by the intense heat of the sun. He was not sure why his mind chose to think about the shining star in a positive light; after all, hadn't the black lip-gloss given him the look he had always sought after?

Glancing at the Blinking Preventer made him want to

destroy it with the heat of his anger. It was not that he hated it, for it had helped him to achieve his greatest dream. The dream to dream; it had brought him temporary satisfaction until he was awake again. The main worry was how obscene the object made him feel. It was another layer, a cage and a heavy weight upon his shoulders. As much as he hated to admit, the newly bred fears were haunting him, fears of having his eyes popping out of his skull at any instant. But he couldn't lose his eyes, it couldn't happen! It was absurd! And as he sat there perplexed, he realised if any candidate was to be nominated to have their eyes pop out it would be him and why not? He had lived a life of nothing but illusion and darkness. The award would be given to him but, and he thought this through carefully, *what should happen to my eyes?* Should they be put on exhibition as being the eyes that had witnessed the world's finest beauties and therefore its most overwhelming horrors?

'Like pebble to water, you drown in my love,' sang the Death Metal Opera record.

Far beyond the scene, beyond the echoing corridors, from an overwhelming height, a glass bottle of half-used lip-gloss slipped off the edge of a banister and landed in pieces below Medusa's head. The monumental event would remain untouched for an eternity — or until Mr 101 decided to uncover the secrets behind the tiles — but he was much too distracted these days to care. So the likelihood of its remaining there was almost certain and held the potential of attracting a few brave ants that would drink from its lake and then later drown after their drunken endeavour.

Remembering the Unicorns

39. *April hoards blessings and sings from the orifice of the birds, disappears again, stripping the leaves from the trees.*

'You're losing your touch,' said Mr 101 to the lady, grinning (or at least he felt the sensation).

Mr 101 was dreaming vividly, picturing himself and the lady who haunted his corridors. She sat opposite him in a dark room where the eerie silence spoke the most profound truth.

'You're burning out,' she replied.

There was a unicorn's head on her lap and her long, smooth finger traced its icy mane. Straight-faced, she found a mirror beside her and held it up to Mr 101. He saw his head missing from his neck which was dripping with wax, like a candle.

Now he remembered his unicorns and how they were closer to him than he thought, more specifically on the far eastern side of his hyacinthine furrows.

The Carpenter

Preparations for the last ever get-together were underway; the rule was to not make it appear as if it was planned, but that seemed to be the harder part of the task. So, unnaturally, Mr 101 hired a carpenter. It was unnatural for him to singlehandedly decide to pickpocket someone from the ordinary world to enter this magnificently mysterious building — even more so when he hadn't approved of him. For all he knew, this being could be a criminal of some kind or ugly or fat. But he could not *untrust* the carpenter, not until he'd acquired a standard amount of evidence to pursue him. He'd already prepared himself to scrutinise the carpenter's every move.

Mr 101 arranged a boat (or something along the lines of one) to pick up the carpenter from the Cornish harbour, accompanied by Mr Wordsworth who was on hand to take him to Mr 101's island.

They arrived safely greeted by a sweet zephyr and the birdsong of Wordsworth's sparrow. Mr 101, in the meantime, had fixed his bowtie for the hundredth time that afternoon, but each time seemed like the first and somehow it was never quite in place. He wondered whether there was an active term to describe what measured slightly smaller than a millimetre, because that was a close amount in which the bowtie needed to be moved to the left by but his jittery hands would not permit him to do so successfully. Instead, he would nudge the ends by drastic centimetres! In the end, Mr 101 in a fit of anger pulled on the uncooperative bowtie until it was very obviously stiff on a protruding, unseemly angle. The doorbell then rang.

He opened the door to a Mr Wordsworth, whose smile faded at the sight of his pivoted bowtie, and a rather plump-looking carpenter whose face was florid, puffed up with fat and concealed behind a grey walrus moustache matching his backcombed hair. A well-tailored suit and waistcoat expressed that he was prominent in his field; a hard worker, a well-respected man who took control of business matters and gave orders.

'I knew he would be fat,' Mr 101 remarked to himself and ushered the carpenter as any awkward gentleman would.

Mr Wordsworth was cut short of following suit, with the door slamming shut on his face. It was the kind of behaviour he had come to expect from Mr 101 and he smiled as it happened, doffed his hat, bowed at the door with hint of sarcasm and walked off.

'What a house!' grunted the carpenter, taking a deep breath as this slight burst of enthusiasm had been equivalent to him running up a flight of stairs and back down again.

Mr 101 persisted in silence, employing an air of arrogance and led the man, whose eyes were darting to and fro at the décor, to the room where his last performance would take place very soon. He creaked open the door to a dark room where the walls were painted black. It had once been his theatre where he performed magic and showcased silent films, but now the space reeked of loneliness, the curtains were torn and the low stage broken. The space where the chairs once were was now empty, dusty, a place only fit for spiders and their torn veils of webs. A layer of dust covered a chandelier that once illuminated the audiences' wandering eyes and made glimmer Mr 101's crushed pearl face. And as he swept the dust with his prance, he saw the past mystify, fading away into the now. All those faces, lace dresses, long tresses and well-compressed shirts belonged to an ideal past that would only be re-visited for one more night.

And so, he reminisced while the carpenter pondered how it would be best to distract him. It was an awkward situation standing in the dark, waiting to be given orders so he twiddled his buttons with his fingers and drew quick breaths (that speeded up time according to a popular New Age magazine). Then, after running out of his already scarce amount of patience, he cleared his throat despite his oesophagus already being crystal clear and phlegm-free.

The latter in turn concluded his daydream and glanced at the restless man. The situation was no doubt just as discomforting for Mr 101, who was more sociable by himself when he communicated to the pages of his journal or when he would converse to Mr Wordsworth — though more often than not, they spoke in riddles or what was more like rubbish. Their conversations made no sense and that was precisely point. They spoke to buy time and make escape the sounds between their lips, to emancipate the voice box, to make real what was in the mind and what resided in the mind was Ridiculism, jargon and fragmented desires...

So Mr 101 said the first word which came to mind.

'Uranus...'

The man enlarged his eyes profusely with shock, wiping the sweat from his brows. 'My what?!'

'It remains in each zodiac sign for seven years, you know. What a curse...'

'You what?!'

'Not *my* anus, Uranus...'

'What about it, sir?!' panted the carpenter who was obviously not in tune to the general surrealistic nature of Mr 101.

'There's a certain sound it makes at the terminating seventh year. The celestial sound, it is a cause for celebration.'

'Is that why you want the chairs, sir? How many? I'll fix you a good price for tables too.'

'The chairs are for the girls, Uranus can sit on the floor.' Mr 101 smiled but he was not sure what it was for. More so, he was not certain what he meant to say although he was certain Uranus had nothing to do with the matter. And now, come to think of it, he had begun to doubt his need for the carpenter altogether! Had he not built this house with his very bare hands? Had he not woven those stairs by his own magical fingers? 'A good price,' resumed Mr 101.

This confused the carpenter to the point where, like a child who, on his first day at school, missed his cosy home which happened to be his workplace. 'Yes, precisely...'

Mr 101 then looked him directly into his perturbed eyes, 'Can you put a price on *everything*?' Now for sure, it was his turn to be perplexed, 'You must forgive me, carpenter, I had forgotten the use of *adding tags* on objects. I either make my own things or I am given them OR I swap! Now tell me, which one will it be?'

The carpenter was speechless. After a quick deliberation he realised Mr 101 was being serious. But instead of harrowing the man with insults, he took the request in his pompous stride.

'Your magnificent chandelier should cover the costs!' he said finally and, for the last time, wiped his brow with a damp handkerchief.

The carpenter's reply erupted like Chinese firecrackers in front of Mr 101. He could hardly believe it and he didn't know why. It was not the master's most prized possession; it was fair to say he despised it at times. No matter where he stood, Medusa's frozen gaze was upon him. What was the Medusa's head to him? Yes, the fact remained that it was gilded with pure gold. The legends say the gold is a veil over the head of the Goddess herself, but when she chooses to capture one's gaze, one turns to gold. This, Mr 101 could not believe, as he would already be shining like the sun by now. This was not an issue he sought to resolve, the Medusa's head belonged here, with him. The house would not be the same without her; she was its core. She was the perfect sun in his disrupted galaxy...

Mr 101 thought carefully before he chose an appropriate retort in his closet of frilled fancies and frolics, 'Well, aren't you the perfect pawn in the player's pocket?' *That's the ticket*, he thought, *a grand ticket to hell and beyond!*

Perhaps a more comfortable scene would have been to witness the capture of a fish and see it struggling on dry land. But this was not comforting in the least for the carpenter who, now angrier than afraid, thought he would employ a similar tactic and reply.

'So what if I was to put a price on you? How much does a clown like you cost, say, for a show?'

'Carpenter, I purchased myself from myself a very long time ago.'

As Mr 101 lit a cigarette the carpenter walked to the door. 'Fair enough, sir, I think you have wasted my time enough; I wish to leave!'

'Be trapped here, stranger. No sane man enters this house and departs without the experience of death.'

'I don't wish to be here, sir. This is against health and safety laws, not to mention illegal!'

Mr 101, entangled with smoke, pretended that they could also momentarily deafen him so he was unable to hear the words of this now worthless creature. He followed the carpenter to the door and laid his free hand on the carpenter's shoulders and as he used his magical powers to transform him into a wooden chair leg, he wondered whether he should attempt to get some sleep tonight.

40. *I've been as patient as a cancerous cell.*

A DREAM!

A deafening birdsong sounded like kitchen utensils falling all at once and brought the flowers to bloom, one by one, introducing colours to the room. The sun outside baked the church-like stain-glassed windows to the interiors where Mr 101 sat near a hardy cedar table. He was busying himself by crossing out all the people he'd ever been on a dog-eared piece of parchment. It was a long list, and he wondered if he'd had time to learn all their names and cross them out before the dream was over. During this process of discovery and elimination, a throne sauntered its way through the room and sat next to him. The throne had a soul, was wooden and decorated in molten gold.

Mr 101 looked at it, or *him*, in shock that this furniture could have a life entrapped within it.

'Who was the last person to sit on you?' spoke Mr 101, a sense of urgency in his voice. 'Do you remember them all?'

'Before you ask a question, why don't you answer it in your mind? Hence when your answer is confirmed by another, you can then begin to argue against it if you wish, or commend your colleague for giving you the right answer.'

'I'm sure I do this already...' Mr 101 felt uneasy for a moment.

'Right you are!' The throne was gleeful, his emotions reflecting his golden complexion.

Mr 101, having lost interest in the throne, thought he was acting in a far too predictable manner. He crossed out another name on the list as he pronounced it in order to remember it when he woke up.

'She was on her own,' began the throne, not caring in the slightest about Mr 101's efforts to ignore him, 'I believe she was a queen in *her own* right.'

This speech seemed to stir an unknown anger in Mr 101. He began to cough out something which seemed to be stuck inside of him; it had always been there but it was now that he realised its parasitic nature. More than anything he wished to be rid of it. The throne sat watching him as he finally spewed out a small ball of dust onto the table, like a bird's nest, dry as untouched skin. Mr 101 wished he could throw it as a javelin and fit it through the hole in the sky that allowed the sun's light through. Then maybe, he would brave the woods, take a walk in there and get lost inside. It would be an adventure...

'I want some T!' The throne needed to change the subject because, after having tasted the anger of Mr 101, he thought he'd inspire some more sap from his tree of patience or *impatience*.

The dry bird's nest on the table instantly transformed into a teacup where a fountain of tea flowed, spilling over the table and nearly obliterating Mr 101's list which he salvaged as quickly as he could exclaiming, 'You old wretch! Your cup is full of tea. Drink it!'

The throne merely laughed, allowing himself to be soaked in the burning liquid while Mr 101 stood up in an angry panic. 'T you idiot, not TEA.'

Then Mr 101 began to compose himself. He decided to take control of something which was by all means a fabrication of his mind. His memory was at the door but he didn't open it for the dream was beginning to fade.

'What if I were to remove your T from your t-hrone? Then you'd be...'

His eyes were no longer shut. He was fully awake. Mr 101 sat up on his bed, he found his black lips saying the words, '*Her own*, she was on *her own*.'

41. *We nourished numbing putrefaction within the heart when we are building up our grievances so that we may come to one day face them at a suitable time.*

How the Horse Lost His Belief in the Written Word

There was a place which no one thought could exist, and it is for this reason that it does exist even more than it would if it didn't. The horse, white as a clean bandage, had been there when his width matched that of a sewing needle. He was resting as usual inside a falling orb, lips parched from not having spoken for days and eyes glazed from having been astounded by a tremendous event. Descending in that atmosphere, he hoped to burst upon the meeting of absolutely anything. *Why was there nothing rather than something*? he constantly wondered. In his mind he emerged upon an old wardrobe of memories, he enrobed himself into an embroidered jerkin, a prize catch, which he favoured and danced about in serendipity. It was the memory of his death. When he kissed the coffin and progressed on to his death, he had picked up a book that taught him to breathe. The cover was new, as yellow as a daffodil's heart where sunrays loved to dance. The words were blurred as soon as his eyes became acquainted with them. For once, a book couldn't teach him but with his perception he created his own ideas.

From his demanding journey, he landed promptly and softly on an unusual typewriter, like a pile of laundry in a maid's basket. The keytops of the device were tiny Quaich bowls holding raindrops of unusual flavours — some were alcoholic and others holy. A prepared paper-table was there for him to make his mark upon from his journey on the keys. So he dipped his hoofs into every flavour, though not a word was written until he set out onto the page that lay like a vast horizon compared to his size. His legs were then quills of many colours that turned to blood when met with paper. Although he'd never tasted blood the sight of it made him thirsty. So it was beneficial that every full stop of his sentences were marked by an amphora of wine that he would smash open and drink in celebration. The incentive to write grew as much as his intoxication. Sometimes he perceived their shape from afar as curvaceous women, standing and waiting to be taken. Most writers wrote about what they knew, but at best he was guessing, having been influenced by idle suggestions of vague people. Thus he became more and more ridiculously abstract and corrupt.

The Eighth Room

The debris of the past few days had finally made a resolve to settle and Mr 101 was benefited with a clear vision to store every issue and situation into neat sections. He gave himself the privilege of disposing of things he had grown out of. A burden was lifted as he removed the Blinking Preventer from his eyes forever. It was no longer of great importance to dream. He knew a new future would near his doorstep very soon; at the moment the prospect of its arrival seemed to sweeten the air.

42. *I may wear down my knuckles but I won't cease my rapping.*

He halted the sliding of black lip-gloss on his lips and momentarily looked into the mirror in front of him. He thought perhaps he was not special after all, especially if a simple glass could multiply him. This was not a new idea for him as he had perused it before in a random Ridiculism book. It did not stir something inside of him back then. But now that he had taken two steps back to the world of normality and the realm of dreams, he began to accept that he was just like any other ordinary creature on this planet.

Again, he attempted to apply his lip-gloss when he was interrupted by a ghostly air that shook the door behind him. It was a memory. He didn't bother to look back; it was bad enough to sense it than to see it fully realised. Strangely enough, the warm air of the circus caressed the back of his neck bringing with it accents of joy, the gasp and applause of an awestruck audience...

The session of applying his make-up that day (or night) was also delayed on purpose because he was dreading his visit to the Eighth Room. It was a room used to hoard unwanted objects. The act of disposal was quite simple but it was the horror of encountering the other things he had rejected in the past that he would rather not see.

43. *Now that we have total freedom, we are indolent and unadventurous and what's worse is that we are ignorant to make the most of non-restriction, for it is only when we are held down that we feel anything of worth.*

The room should not be mistaken for Room 8, which was nothing more than an ordinary bedroom. For one thing, the Eighth Room's door handle was round and solid brass and whether or not it was used, dust still managed to avoid being magnetised towards it. What could have happened to render this door to succumb to such a brutal nature? Was it caution that shielded the dust and even the tiniest particle of bacteria to caress its brass exterior? Whatever the reason, it has stayed as it has always been — fresh from when it departed the hands of its creator. This may have happened yesterday or perhaps an eternity ago, when light was created. The main entrance door was accompanied by a smaller, slightly jagged door beside it that was always locked, even for Mr 101. There was no debating over the matter; it was easy to see that the higher powers held control over this room. There was no key to access whatever was hiding behind it.

So Mr 101 stood before the main door, holding his Blinking Preventer to be rid of, and with his free hand grabbed the handle before his fears and doubts would send him running, and pushed the door open. It could not be opened as a regular door. It pulled him like a calling, directing him inside its tunnel-like enclosure that was shaped in the number eight. Past the doorway while being transported in this dark place, the smell of money, the buzzing of every single argument he ever had, the clapping of shoes running from an overwhelming scene, applause from a lively audience, a seductive image of moths destroying clothes, the sensation of a churning stomach, arms twisting like maggots from the lack of comfort, the aplomb of banging knives, the twitching of skin under a bead of sweat came to him. He felt all these with his senses, perhaps not all in the same order, perhaps all at once.

He accepted these experiences, sensations or memories with an unwilling gulp as if that could save him. Mr 101 would have rather liked to have had the courage to point and laugh in ridicule as a suitable reaction. But even with ardent attempts, he failed, frowning miserably. His arrogance was weakening and could not falter the power this enclosure held. It served to excite the part of him which sought the invisible, the very thing that would destroy him in the end.

The discomfort derived from these fears should not be underestimated in the slightest for it frightened Mr 101 into yet another sleepless existence.

Grabbing the doorknob still with his sweaty hand he chucked the Blinking Preventer into the darkness which swallowed it whole. And as he did so he instantly found himself on the floor of an endless corridor outside an ordinary door, its doorknob hand open to be shaken and greeted.

***

Sitting in the decorated room, where the Blinking Preventer itself was created, the lady was on her knees to begin a prayer. It was a changed room, empty as a pack of lies. There were woodprints on the wall depicting skeletons playing music to priests, nuns admiring their lovers in between prayers and a monk, fleeing the scene with all his worldly possessions. As soon as she had opened her mouth to bring out a fruitful display of devotion, the candle before her was blown out. Looking back she saw Mr 101 who had just entered, closing the door behind him.

44. *A room finds itself incomplete when its door is open. Fulfil the desire of each room by closing its door after leaving and entering.*

Room 22

What Mr 101 found when he entered Room 22 (which was a room harder to get hold of than a halo of smoke leaving a pair of desirable scarlet lips) for the first time, was a raven perched on a black table, stone-still. What gave him a fright was that the creature faced the faded curtains that marred the windows. He waited for the bird to acknowledge him, to at least utter that hollow sound from its beak. He thought of turning the black table to face him. Was the creature alive? Were the legs of this table nailed so sternly that it would never move? Would the bird have turned to ashes if he so put one feeble foot forward? Due to his lack of effort, he never found the answers. When he closed the door to Room 22 and tore his hand from its leathered hold, he heard the clockwork locks in the door click — and when the room faded away it never came back.

Mr 101 later sat in Room 101, thinking about the parable the room had given him, the bird in particular and how he'd reacted to it, giving the experience a chance to dance on his tongue for a while before he finally introduced the pen and ink to fresh parchment and wrote the following:

> *As much as I like to think we're all precious little keepsakes fallen from heaven, I can't help but jest that some of us exist for absolutely no reason at all, that we have no purpose here but to linger and teeter here and there, dispensing through so called 'precious' time until we're pushed to become Earth food. More than anything, I mean to say this about myself. For I find my own existence taxing to the world, simply a waste of energy,*

insanity, carbon, stardust, space-time, a soul and other things which make up my genetics and spiritual selves. Surely I'm not here merely to write these words that are nothing special to anyone?

The Truth about Doors

A dark hole of potential, a store-hole for objects (the offspring of opportunities and other things that bring) with recondite purposes had once existed. This was before the universe had acknowledged and therefore honed in on itself. It was a *mundus imaginalis* where the seedling of the Earth had been rolled away to keep from performing its forceful bloom too soon. All the stars that were to exist were swept into a corner as a shimmering Everest; beside it something was fluctuating, it was miniscule in comparison, heart-shaped with iridescent emerald-green feathers. It made the sound of water boiling and bubbling to eventually come to release a fizzing frenzy. There were boxes all about and the dust anointed everything, even a bottomless tape measure which had been recently used. In short, it was an ethereal building site, but lacking with resources.

A woman had been discarded there too, and she was flooded with shadows. Troubles resided in her mind. She feared to live in an interminable system that was soon about to make a start. Sitting on a random box with her face in her hand, she pondered until a tear flowed out of her eye. After some time, she rained harder like an indispensable cloud. As soon as they touched the ground, she stamped her foot on the water droplets, taking them for cockroaches that could dissolve. But this action caused her tears to solidify and become square slides that could fit into a magic lantern. They were the first and last solid sonnets, because like a sonnet they were concise, beautiful and could inspire love. But unlike a sonnet, they could be held, smelt and be plucked like the petals of a rose.

She picked one of them after her biological rain had ceased. Her eyes settled on a mossy picture of a white horse. Her hands caressed the image just in case it was a layer of white dust. For a moment, she believed this animal was something she could call her own. Although the horse's Eden-beauty could not be denied, his mane had been cut and because the image was of macro-detail, the brittleness of its deportment was obvious.

In an instant, three beings appeared in white robes, they were curious about this animal that had not yet been invented or thought of by the gods. They introduced themselves as Forculus, Cardea, and Limentinus. They were given a questioning look by the woman, and so they made her an offer: they would give her anything she wanted if she would not speak of the horse to a single soul, as it would seem devastating to their reputation if anyone else knew a mere mortal could be capable of such revelatory innovation.

She agreed to it, not thinking the animal any more special than a tear itself. She wished to be sent away, through a portal, somewhere where time wouldn't disturb her and where she would not need to feel guilt for her actions.

An agreement was made. The three deities looked around them for a way to transport her. All the objects around them were insufficient. So Forculus turned himself into a square plank, Cardea into a set of hinges and Limentinus into a threshold and a gloved hand acting as a handle. The woman sauntered through all three of them. With one last glance at her pile of lantern slides, she began her journey into furthermore darkness.

Wonders!

Marvels!

Miracles!

Room Six

Like a beetle under a leaf, there was much rustling in Room Six and like many of the other rooms, its contents and qualities were a mystery to the owner of the house. But with enquiry and perseverance, it was never too tricky to unlock the doors and experience the whirlwind of the unknown till the 'un' in the unknown was obliterated like a virus being flicked away.

The house was now the host of a beautiful creature with eyes like the clearest morning sky that could look into the deepest desires of your tainted soul. His long fingers were occupied with Mr 101's mountain of junk letters he took from the landing, resolutely folding them into origami swans. Death Metal Opera spiralled on the Victrola by his side and he followed the lyrics to the song with his scarlet lips when he knew them. His black hair met his shoulders and his fringe covered his concentrated face as he scored the paper with his varnish-chipped nails.

In the room, the visitor thought of many things and when he wasn't thinking, his mind was empty and focussed on the task at hand. The lyrics of Death Metal Opera could send the soul on a journey, detaching itself from the body like a pebble summoned from the depth of a lake to ascend to its surface and upwards to meet a cloud in the sky that rolls itself senseless. The song tickled the ears like a raindrop sliding down on the keys of a piano that later takes to solidifying into a priceless diamond, because Death Metal Opera tasted so good:

'I'm here now, sing to me
about the human anatomy...'

At this time, Mr 101 was spending his usual hours in Room Two having a customary mulled wine perusing a lovely little nightmare he'd once received, cross-legged on his saffra. A cigarette rested between his fingers, but he kept from devouring the meal of smoke. Instead, the shapes of smoke warmed him and caused him to flow into a light state of hypnosis. He was soon to close his eyes and run away into meditation when he heard the Death Metal Opera jingles sift through the dusty planks of his floor. What troubled him further was the male voice that followed the lyrics of the songs that Mr 101 kept so close to his butchered old heart.

Soon he followed his instincts to Room Six as quietly as his footsteps could manage as this slight bothered him to no end. To his annoyance, there was now no meditation to be had that night and a brawl was not written off. The door relented to his touch and was easily pushed open.

When he found Mr Six at the kingdom of the table surrounded by piles of paper swans, he was astounded — even quite amused — but then decidedly acted upon his habitual subdued anger. He cleared his throat, knocked on the door as a way to gain attention, banged on the table (which sent the swans into the air and toppling off the table top) but nothing could make Mr Six look at him. Mr Six did, however, verbally acknowledge his presence.

'The defeat in your entireness looks to be glorious, magnifying all the possibilities.'

He was indeed a speaker of eloquence and a genius who solved such obscurity as to why and how our lives go to such dismal places. He'd dwelled between this and the mirror shadow universe where the planets are black emulating their darker properties in a backdrop of black orbs for stars. Unfortunately being a traveller of the universes stunted him from actually making much sense. Indeed he had visited those subtle places and debated the point of their existence until they were finalised but he never uttered a single word of an explanation. The precious diamonds of wisdom were not something to be spread about haphazardly like rain.

'She is more than just an image in a photograph, I'm certain she has more use than just to be merely torn and tossed away,' Mr Six said, to counteract the silence that was itching to be noise.

Mr 101 sighed, opening his lotus lips for the blossoming of words which were about to come, his eyes on the man's crow-black hair as Mr Six busied himself upon the opening of an envelope. 'I have given much thought about it and it's well...quite *unjust*.'

'*That's* exactly what you deserve. You are becoming soft on the matter.'

Mr Six stood up and made his way to the closed curtains; to Mr 101's dismay, he touched them as if to let them open but of course, he did not.

'I sense the white storm coming, in fact I know, brighter than the Apollonian planet, but I guess it's not my business to peruse. To inform you on your bizarre purpose is not the reason why I'm here. I've come to ask you to evaluate this piece I just so happen to come by.'

He pointed to the far side of the room. There was an emerald dish that was being tickled by the candlelight on its side, the one heralded not even in legends but mentioned rarely in myths and its existence always the subject of debate. The profuse green colour reminded Mr 101 of English farmlands in the sunlight and those endlessly long days of trekking through them for salvation and a roof over his head.

'Is this...?' croaked Mr 101, rather bemused. He walked over to it, no longer insulted by the boy's words or unkempt style of hair for which had been previously causing him much offence.

'It is indeed, the emerald dish from very last supper,' replied the boy with pride, and then blinked as he finally met his customer's eyes.

'I suppose you would be after my Medusa for this... rather lovely thing?' asked Mr 101, knowing the latter was requesting more than just a simple evaluation. Masters do not cross the dimensions for worthless evaluations and useless chatter.

'Not quite, no. Not even, exactly.'

45. *Where goes the piano that fades away to the fingers that seek to play it all night?*

'Come on, child, speak up, what is it that you want?' asked Mr 101, now definitely offended and a little tired.

Mr Six's eyes found the curtains again, his free hand slid up in a hiss and the curtains quivered at his touch. He knew the sun was Mr 101's Judas and that he shouldn't tease, but he was Mr Six, he thought, he was enlightened enough to work out there was no-one else like him and neither would there ever be. Therefore he could do anything which pleased him. He was not quite as wise as seven but his number brought him satisfaction nonetheless.

'The child,' he said. 'I don't see why not, you'd be exchanging one green thing for another!'

Mr 101 quitted the plate to its unworthy table. Employing a different tact altogether, he replied, 'What are you anyway? Where have you come from, boy? Speak up! The walls are not getting any younger, you *see*?'

Six spun round in a flash to admire the dripping walls. He was astounded with the place. He would rather like a place like this to live but where does one begin and even much more puzzling, where does it end?

'Venus...?' wondered the master of the house, his eyes protruding, theoretically poking the latter for a response.

'No. Choice,' replied Six, now fiddling with the curtains yearning to spread them open. 'Make the right one, save the girl.'

These words gave Mr 101 the reason to blush to the tips of his tingling lips and also an excuse to think about the delicious potential of Daffodil's nosebleed.

'I shall not listen to an imposter, you are uncordially invited to my house!' was his burst of fury.

With this statement Mr 101 lunged forward to grab his insolent visitor and as he did so Mr Six disappeared in a puff of dry ice and a blanket of echoing laughter, leaving behind the six of diamonds card where he was standing.

In a tick, Mr Six reappeared in one of the Chocolate Rooms. The aroma of chocolate, strawberries and other sweet things filled his nostrils as he stood for moments being engulfed by the pleasurable experience. However he did not stop for long, knowing well that Mr 101 would be scouring the rooms for his presence. He strode past the ovens which were still and the coolers. His eyes followed the state of the room; everything was still apart from the chocolate and peanut butter fountain which never ceased. Then in his peripheral vision something flickered like a bright orb; looking up he saw the harrowing chandelier desperately pulling its weight from side to side.

In an instance, Mr Six vanished to smoke and reappeared at the top of the chandelier, his whole body enveloped around the rope it hung from. His heart began to race like drums in a ritual. The floor was so far below that the even the chequered floor tiles were merged into a grey colour.

He quickly removed a lighter from his pocket. It was the only thing he could think of. Then he held the flame to the rope which, much too slowly but nevertheless, caught fire.

Mr 101 entered in a hurry, the crystal beads on his forehead reflected the blazing fire above. Finally, after searching the floors, he glanced at the ceiling above to witness the inferno.

Mr Six was long gone between the subtle universe before the chandelier fell magnificently like an angel from heaven, crashing into the machines below, missing Mr 101's dazed little face by an inch or so.

What Mr 101 Really Thought about the Incident

- He didn't care too much.
- Destiny was always out to get him.
- Damn it!

Of course, Mr 101 made no effort to amend the mess in the Chocolate Rooms. He would let everything rot — it was beyond his control now. That damned chandelier deserved it; rainbow strips were not *unattainable* in England. Just because something is in high demand doesn't render it rare. Although his techniques were unheard of, using actual rainbow to make sweets, but he decided it was futile to spend time in regret, he was still and always will be wanted by the ladies.

After the Encounter

Late into the night, Mr 101 was practising bibliomancy — the art of using books as a means of divination. He'd randomly pick a page in his lengthy book of quotes and glance at what was written and in some way or other it was a sign. At times he peered upon a page with anticipation for he was frightened of something appearing that could possibly affect his life in a positive way. It was wrong to practise this method excessively until a desired answer was reached but it was this very wrongdoing that strengthened Mr 101's drive.

His finger followed these words on the page:

> *Rhinorrhea is a common symptom to experience when one has something they need to be rid of that is no longer valid in one's life, but has now emerged as a vindictive aspect that could potentially cause harm of all kinds. It must be noted that this illness does not involve rhinos, how disappointing...*

Mr 101 grunted and chucked the book into the fire. Ridiculism bit every last nerve so that even the master of it, Mr 101, grew tired of it. Beside him, from a pile, he flicked the pages of another book that held the scent of a burnt match as antique books sometimes do. The spine of it creaked like an old backbone that was forcing itself upright to open the door of a page.

> *Just living is not enough. One must have sunshine, freedom and a little flower.*

Mr 101 turned the book; it was written by Hans Christian Anderson. He looked at it for some time, frowning and nodding consecutively. Once he lowered the book from his parallel gaze, he saw Daffodil stood before him. The despicable state of her dress missed his attention as he gazed into her eyes; they were even more sunken than they had ever been.

'Come here, sunshine.' He beckoned her forwards with an index finger whose nail was thickly varnished in black and made to curve as an oblique crescent moon. A sunshine-missing window could be seen reflected on the surface. 'Fill me to the brim on your adventures.'

46. *Women are puzzles, but the pieces don't fit well together.*

The Last Evening in Room Two

Madness and thoughts of Madeleine was what *this* particular spectacle seemed to be about, as well as a celebration to mark the beginning of the end. Chandeliers were on the floor of Room Two to show the aftermath of knife-throwers having trespassed these quarters, and their candles retained their flames after their fall. Long, colourful fabrics draping from the ceiling met the floors and flitted menacingly close by, flirting with the candle-light with every sway as the walls began to extend and multiply in a hundredfold. They were rapidly expanding and growing into a room which would soon contain the entire alphabet of what it took to be superbly grandiose and darkly original.

Imaginative, out-of-this-world performers pulled themselves from the cracks and crevices of the walls, floors, door hinges and basically anything which had a gap in between. They wriggled out to contribute to the last ball in Room Two. Some had waited all their lives, in their own dimension, for this event, having only truly existed to expect this fated climax of an occasion. They had arranged this occasion a long time ago, sending invites to Mr 101's lady 'friends' and his two comrades Mr Wordsworth and Mr Wormwood with Mr 101's consent.

As was his custom, Mr 101 was at this precise time troubling himself over his exertions in journal writing, doing his best to keep up his Ridiculist stance. It was reasonable to assume that he was scribbling away a thought he would not be capable of reading the next day. Unlike him, all good writers had their sense of self that was their beneficial downfall which added a unique flavour to their work. He was too worldly, he thought, and his sense of self melting away too quickly to be given the capability to exercise this particular technique. And he'd analysed the world too much in negative-tinted glasses to deem his own work slightly bearable. In the end, perhaps that is why critics will hail him a genius, he thought, or at least regarded as someone who was slightly special enough to heave himself from the gutter.

47. *Any present hope of a later satisfaction helps us to live our lives, even if it is a farce.*

The guests hadn't yet arrived, bursting through the expanding doors, so the performers took it upon themselves to rehearse their acts in order to later give the illusion that they had not cared at all — they rehearsed spontaneity. They embraced the notion that life was wholly contradictory just as, at that moment, the aerialists were embracing the idea of a ceiling.

Birds of the real sky could have been envious of them, if birds could attempt such a humanly vice. Their loosely dressed flexible bodies contorted into strange shapes as they flew from one end of the ceiling to another giving a sense of unhealthy elation, a threatening mood full of joyful panic. Spheres of roses hung all about them like tended jungles instead of light, giving breaths of puffed-up romance. And romance was known to be one of the many things which could not survive in this environment. But still, the roses persisted in their bloom, sending heavenly scent to meat and knife jugglers on the floor. Smiles were placated on their faces but their eyes were blank. Here and there, Sufis twirled in their meditation and show of love for the worlds. Right in the centre of the room an obese man stood, he was the main Impresario, his back straight as a stabbed knife, his arms crossed behind him, as he whistled a popular Death Metal Opera jingle. It happened to be Mr 101's favourite. The music conducted more flowers to miraculously flourish out of the cracks of the walls like nature's bandages healing something that was never to be mended before. Cocoa powder replaced the flower's pollen for guests who suffered from allergies. Any previous stench now vanished, not being able to withstand its power against the natural scent of roses and other flowers.

Mr 101's Art Deco table, old sofas, his beloved saffra and shelves may as well have not existed, for they were nowhere to be seen. Perhaps the drapes concealed them cleverly behind the fine junketing. These fabric hangings created a type of flexible, inoffensive wall from one section to another, rather resembling a labyrinth so that guests may choose their own type of entertainment if they wished.

There was nothing greatly jubilant about this occasion, not when it was the very last night for Mr 101 to enjoy his vice with the ladies. And it certainly wasn't going to end in pleasantry when the Lace-Demon chose to intrude without an invitation, covered from head to toe in the finest handmade lace, playing Death Metal Opera with deadly elegance on a piano made of sickly-sweet white chocolate. She robbed the obese whistling man of his performance instead of kindly collaborating, but his performance was occassionally rescued when she was forced to stop because of the ladder performer. He bounced dangerously on his ladder. Taking huge leaps, he threatened to kill whoever happened to stand in the way. Many times the chocolate piano escaped pulverisation. When he bounced off, he left a permanent stamp on the Persian rug, which was most definitely thin sheets of sugar dusted chewing gum placed side by side. The Lace-Demon would frown but soon lick her fingers and continue.

Far beyond this scene, if one had the courage to walk further past the wavering fabric enclosures, was what resembled a Roman empire-worthy hippodrome to host a chariot race — except there was not a race intended, but rather another performance of the Ridiculist kind which sought to teach a moral lesson to its viewer. Its pivoted tracks were painted in stripes of blue, purple, green, orange and violet. Five horses, in five colours corresponding to their lane, led an empty carriage in full force round each bend, having not stopped since they started. Large boulders of ice littered the paths, obstructing the horses from the completion of a round without immense difficulty. Injury was encouraged, if not compulsory, in this exercise. It was up to the audience to realise what it symbolised.

Further away from this scene, an antique icebox in silver depicting Neptune riding a sea serpent, his strong arms held up a colossal shell. Puce wine was contained within for the guests to indulge as they willed.

Thus the female guests bustled inside the room admiring every detail, in quatrains like a prolonged Rubaiyat on paper as eyes scan them. Their multi-layered eyelids fluttered perpetually to wonder at the renovated Room Two. They were born with silver spoons handles poking out of their mouths and would perhaps die with this luxury. Some leave this world more fortunate than when having entered it, whereas most will never get this opportunity — this is the infallible truth.

Mr 101 could no longer pretend that the music in Room Two was just the furniture having their own private debate from Room 101, so he joined the festivities. Death Metal Opera was the one thing he could not resist or betray by not succumbing to it fully. The respectable empire he'd spent all his career building, block upon block, was subjugated in an instant when the ladies turned to look at him. They all looked like a social unrest, Mona Lisa smiling, their scarlet-fever blusher dappled from their cheeks to their foreheads. Some cried in disgust, others were for once quietened by the shock of such a sight. Mr 101 was no longer the man he used to be. His make-up had crumbled like paint on an old wall of an abandoned house, revealing his pasty old-wallpaper skin. The black faded on his lips from hours of not having applied a fresh layer. His posture was ruined from hours of bending over a journal to finalise a philosophy he did not even understand.

Persistent time had wearied him and engraved him quite pathetically. When he saw his reflection, he'd tell himself it was someone else's, another part of him he never wanted to be. It was more than likely that he perceived his body as an island that his soul, his true body had taken refuge in at the beginning and as time went on, decided to usurp it, enslave its organs and mockingly graffitied on its healthy mind. He was a notorious criminal, to himself most of all. The thousands he'd killed suffered less betrayal than he did to himself.

Mr 101 would later that evening write, '*...there were too many i's on me at the party like the word insignificant.*'

'So girls or...ladies! Tell me, what is the news these days? Has the sun disappeared?'

Mr 101 chuckled dryly; he was not stupid enough to avoid their disgusted glares. He pretended their sniggers were directed elsewhere because no matter what, he needed this last night in Room Two to succeed. Success would pose an applause for the wonderful things he had experienced between these walls. And what was his excuse for this unusually good mood? He had no idea! It was even more bizarre that he would attempt to converse with the opposite sex.

'Oh I wish it would, it just doesn't seem to go away nowadays,' spoke one of the braver women, fiddling with her teacup elegantly.

There was no doubt that Mr 101 was by then, beyond unhinged as many of his doors were. However it was this self-same element which drew others onto him, denigrating themselves to suit his regime. ' "We want the moon back" — that was the newspaper headline the day before the day before. I'm sure I'm not fibbing,' she said.

Mr 101 was truly perplexed; his smile became loose again and he wondered if he should nail it back together. The rest of the ladies went quiet, heightening the tension in the room.

'D-d-do we want the moon back or does the moon want us back? We will never know and neither should we ever *try* to comprehend!'

And this statement overjoyed the crowds and normality was restored. The ladies decided they were excited to see him after all and have him offer them his service for one last time. But it was also an overwhelmingly emotional time. Their distress made them hiccup, sending the contents of their teacups flying into one another's faces. It was a comical affair and Mr Wordsworth certainly had his fair share of laughter underneath his unperturbed exterior. To make this occasion especially *special*, as it were, a heap of shoes were put together to make a shoe sale; seventy-two pairs in total. It was arranged like a Christmas tree, in a perfect cone, each with a price tag attached. It was Mr 101's way of giving something back to the world and his taking part in the recycling hype. The vintage nonsense was all the talk nowadays and the ladies adored him for it. They shifted around the hill of shoes, picking their favourites and collecting them in their arms like babies.

'Now, here comes my snotty little handkerchief...' said Mr 101 to himself (but was heard by everyone) as Daffodil crept into the room, her eyes darting to and fro, from one frock to the other, until she gasped at the mountains of shoes she recognised had been emptied from the shoe cupboard.

Some ladies cried disapprovingly, others pretended they hadn't noticed anything and resumed to stare at an invisible painting on the wall or focussed on a nice pair of shoes that just so happened to have caught their gaze. As ever, the air was intermingled with a profusion of lust, greed and jealousy.

Mr 101 said nothing more as he reached for the gramophone and put on his desired choice of Death Metal Opera. The candle flames danced to the hypnotic aura of the sound of the opera. Daffodil made her way into a dark corner, seeking somewhere to sit where she would not be easily spotted, but at the same time wanting to receive the best view of the most beautiful dresses she had ever seen.

After the sale was over and the mountains of shoes were cleared and shoved into bags, Mr 101 quietened the music into a soft murmur and raised his arms for attention. Silence was achieved in that very moment for the ladies held an unfaltering respect for him.

'As you all know, this is the last...' and he gazed at Daffodil who stared back from the corner, '*ceremony* that will ever take place between these walls and under this roof. I would like to take this time to thank my irreplaceable colleagues, Mr Wordsworth and Mr Wormwood.'

Upon his conclusion the audience applauded and the two men raised their wineglasses. Mr Wormwood, a most graceless creature that ever existed, smashed his wineglass when he held it between his metal fingers. Wine kisses covered his cheeks and he guffawed at himself, reminding Daffodil of a gorilla. Mr 101 continued.

'To those of you who survive tonight's ordeal, I wish you to join me in a week's time when I'll be opening the door of Room 66 for a very special performance. That will be the last you ever see of me, thank you!' He smiled again, it was a ghastly image but it made his entire being feel lighter than the weight of Saturn itself.

Mr Wordsworth and Mr Wormwood sat waiting for Mr 101 to accompany them, and when he did he beckoned Daffodil to join their intimate circle.

'Why don't you sit on the floor?' Mr 101 took a sip of red wine from his fading black lips. 'Mr Wordsworth has a story he wants to tell you.'

Mr Wordsworth gave him a questioning look. 'I do?'

'You do,' replied the monochrome magician. When he saw Mr Wordsworth's look of disapproval, he added, as if having caught on to a thread of his many thoughts, 'I can assure you, she will be the death of me before it is otherwise.'

'How can you be so sure?' said the other almost immediately.

'Are you worried?'

Both exchanged a telling glance of discomfort. The answer was made clearer by the silence.

'Our minds,' said Mr 101, 'are alike. That makes us geniuses.'

'I truly doubt that of you!'

'And so do I, now tell your story or go back to hell. I need something to laugh at.'

Mr Wordsworth's eyes were sullen as he thought on the topic. There was only ever one story in his mind, and that was the story of his life — one he regarded as an utmost tragedy. Once he sipped his whiskey, he began. Mr 101 lit a cigarette as the raconteur cleared his throat.

'When I was young — well, younger, I used to visit the world's largest antique market, an event held by the gypsies situated far beyond the depthless waters of Acheron. I, myself, was a traveller of the realms and I enjoyed it. Anyway, one day upon the pebbled shores of the island, I noticed the sky withdrawn from colour but the clouds still gathered, foretelling of a near future downpour.

'The ferry left me for the lonely pier; I bade goodbye to its light and the folks like me who held a hesitated attitude towards the gypsies, but I had, many years before, released my aptitude to be constricted by any means of a social boundary. You see, at one point in my life, I began to loosen myself from the norm. Somehow, everyday became a Sunday. I lived life as a tourist.

'Once I arrived, past where the paths were scattered with feathers, it seemed the event was already ablaze with magnificent colours and marvels of articles I had yet to encounter: an array of caravans, tents and unsheltered stalls. Rare sights were all about me. There were all manner of sellers that specialised in dream-catchers, dream-machines and others that were popular in the export of crystals including some forms of the dodecahedron; a special sort of organism that grew to the pleasure of its own will. I was able, by some mysterious power, to shift past the verbal hagglers and retorting sellers. No, I snaked my way past the Geomancers who were intent upon fiddling with the fertile soil to tell the future. It's true back then, a long time ago now, they looked upon the future aeon in dismay and fear towards us, the ignorant —'

'Ge' on wiv it, Mr Wordsworf you prat!' spat Mr Wormwood, already losing track of the plot.

In the corner, the Lace-Demon continued to play her chocolate-construed piano which was now beginning to melt into a crisis from the bottom. The ladies were already eyeing the instrument in between snippets of conversation. They deeply wished that Mr Wordsworth would finish his tale so that they could scavenge every last sticky drop. Noticing this, Mr Wordsworth continued at a slower pace.

'The downpour began and to my disappointment, I'd

left my hat on the boat and I didn't have appropriate clothing or even an umbrella. Crowds had begun to disperse to their closest dwelling, some sellers were packing hurriedly in order for their priceless articles to be saved undamaged. In a desperate fluster I hurried into a small candy-striped tent, missing the sign overhead.

'When I entered, bedewed in rainfall, I noticed that I was in the dwelling of a shamanic healer. She was, like one of Rubens' women, clothed carelessly in a shawl and she sat behind a small puppet theatre occupying her curious gaze upon me. So I, in return, focussed my eyes at the handmade theatre that was painted in such a delicate manner as that of cathedrals and fine China plates. No doubt, I was unquestionably amazed. Leaning closer to feast my eyes upon this structure, I noticed on the backdrop was painted seven-pointed stars with liquidized gold on a night-blue fading wall that represented the sky. There was not a bit of sun or even an inch of the moon in sight. Beside the theatre in star-shaped boxes, I guessed was the confinement place for the puppets.

'The quiet Shaman lifted her one-piece piastre veil from her face as I handed her some coins. She nodded at my subtle request before warning me that the tale was not amusing but fused with sorrow, a happy ending was also debatable. The downpour from outside increased with a profusion of urgency so I urged her to commence.

'Upon opening the star-shaped boxes, she chanted a spell. The puppets, rather like humans, stepped freely from their velvet-lined enclosures and ambled upon the stage. They were chiselled to the matching of a human body and painted thus in perfection to meet the resemblance of being human. I was steeped in awe to admire these beings but I was shocked to realise that, as I sat back into the chair, I was in the process of shrinking considerably to their size along with the chair — or had the tent grown larger? I tried to call for help but the sly seer was nowhere to be seen. But I noticed that I, myself, was front-seated in a dusty little theatre. I dared not moved for, among the fear, I was curious to be enclosed in this illusory theatre. And as I waited in twisted trepidation, I wondered how many others had been in my place.

'Into the far end of a heavily weighing shadow played a scratched Victrola which dragged out a psychedelic mockery of Death Metal Opera, I rather wished it wouldn't aid such a wrong representation of the true musical essence of the genre. Somehow as these thoughts circled my mind, the music began to skip and fade. The curtains withdrew then, my eyes focussed to admire the wooden planks of the stage that shared the hue of an autumn-graced Earth.

'Somewhere beyond my enclosure, Earth existed and I was being kept from it, I thought.

'Upon the planked floor was a bed whereupon peacefully slept a girl with the hair of bright auburn; above her was a sky that boasted a plethora of seven-pointed stars. By her side was a man who I learnt must have either been her guardian or father; his wooden mouth twitched as if there were muscles behind the wooden skin. I begged not to learn what type of dark sorcery lingered behind this and so I sat and watched the girl tear open a present the man gave her. He jerked forwards, mouth pecking at her ear to represent whispers that I couldn't decipher from the intentional silence. At this instant, the girl produced an expression of shock as she revealed a toy: a golden lion of which could be wound up and made to move. The ray of spotlight highlighted the gift among all else. It was a brilliantly crafted prop even for today's standards — I admit, I couldn't keep my eyes from it. The lion's eyes were carefully rounded jades with precisely carved slits in the centre. When wound up, the mechanical lion trotted proudly forwards and roared in fearful magnitude opening its golden-gated jaws and shutting them as the rotation of the key ceased.

'The young girl couldn't resist the temptation of turning the key as her father left the scene and the curtains momentarily closed and then were wound back again to reveal the little girl grown into a graceful creature with longer auburn flowing locks. She was shown as taking a promenade within the backdrop of trees which were there to depict a rather dense forest where harsh black trees pervaded. A bulk in her dress pocket was there to show where the lion rested; such details were a feast for the eyes and there really was no need for binoculars. Her expressions furrowed to show confusion. She was lost. But she persisted along her path holding this expression to clearly show her frustrations of being in a muddle among the trees.

'Finally, she halted and observed her surroundings when another character stepped into the scene. He was a magician of well esteem for the top of his hat nearly reached the stage roof. The two characters seemed to be in argument over a bargaining of the precious lion for the magician held out some coins to exchange for the object. Of course, she refused and stormed out of the scene in a fluster.

'The curtains were closed and drawn to reveal the grown up girl in her bed bidding goodnight to her sacred lion. She stirred in her sleep and the stage lights dimmed a little. Like a maggot from a ripe apple, out wriggled the foreseen magician from one of the larger seven-pointed stars and landed on the varnished floor like a splattered egg. Without a sound, he fixed his oblong hat onto his head and brought out a harmonica to meet his protruding lips. The sound made would have been more fitting around a campfire and not this sombre scene where he cozened the toy and beckoned it forward with the music. The lion's key spun uncontrollably as it trotted and then stopped, sat at the magician's feet like a trained dog, ready to be snatched away.

'The curtains were closed and opened in quick timing. This time, I caught the young lady searching for her lion, firstly in her bedroom until the backdrop changed to the forest, and then the trees faded to the mountain but her lion was nowhere to be found. The curtains closed for the final time.

'I began to feel myself growing into my normal height when I found myself shouting towards the stage, "This cannot be the end."

'My own echo retorted back to me as if in mockery as I started to shrink once more. At this point in time, I believe the play was real so I, in this agitated state, leapt onto the stage and jumped into the curtains —'

Said Mr 101 in an utmost tone of sarcasm, wreaths of silver gliding from his blackened lips, 'Always the saviour aren't you, sir?'

'If you had a crystal ball, wouldn't you look inside?' replied Mr Wordsworth bitterly.

Mr 101 sneered at this and Mr Wormwood snored, having fallen asleep with his mouth wide open. Mr Wordsworth ignored them and continued.

'The young lady was puzzled and rather in a state of shock at my sudden appearance. To me, there and then, she was real and I named her Grace. Darkness blanketed us and she disappeared within it. I tried to catch her as she faded but the curtains were drawn open again and fear filled my entire being as the trees sprouted fervently in masses and enclosed around me. I could, with imagination, make out the seven-pointed stars plastered on the walls behind them and even discern the discreet brushstrokes that they were painted with. Somehow, it was a lucid dream aided by some divine help as I knew I could invent certain aspects of this tale to my desired vision.

'As she disappeared, I found myself lost — inevitably so. And so I trailed every inch of the woods, from corner to corner but found nothing not until I reached the backdrop wall. The seven-pointed stars winked where the trees were transforming to become real, black and bleak, the mechanical birds were singing freely. My feet sank slightly into the muddy Earth as it was no longer planks of wood. No doubt, autumn had begun a premature celebration, for the ground was scattered with burnished leaves rather like confetti. An outcry of wind beckoned me to amble further on until I came to a clearing where I caught a magician in the procession of excavating the ground using a spade. This particular magician was dressed in the usual formal attire. However, his suit was all in shades of green and from his earlobes dangled golden hoops on both sides. It was altogether a bohemian appearance and I found myself admiring his confidence to dress this way.

'As I approached him, he said in surprise, "Mr Wordsworth!"

'Lord knows how he could have recognised me but there it was. And I, bemused, replied, '"What on Earth are you doing?" There was no other way about it; I was lost and needed an explanation. As previously mentioned, he appeared to be digging a hole and seeing the curious glance on my face he resumed to begin his explanation.

'"Well, Mr Wordsworth, it's a pleasure to see you too! I'm preparing my home for hibernation. Rumour has it the Earth *breathes* all sorts of inspirational magic at this time of year; its nostrils reaching far beyond the edges of Saturn's rings only to exhale the flowers in the spring. I can only wonder what she would do for *me* —"'

Mr 101 made a sound like one of a pebble having been chucked into a shallow part of a lake where the river bed rises like yeast not too far off. This momentary glitch created a mildly disconcerting atmosphere in the room and a dark cloud of doubt was conjured. Doubt as to whether he would ever find inspiration in this story, doubt as to whether there was any relevance to it, doubt as to whether there existed men who would go to this much length for the false glory of the Sun and the Earth.

Mr Wordsworth, having ignored the untimely interruption, once again persisted to entertain the entranced Daffodil who was sat crossed-legged on the floor, her neck propped up to him for better listening.

'Of course, I never saw him again afterwards, but I had to delay his work further as I needed directions to find Grace.

'"Yes, I believe she climbed up one of these trees to the circus," he said. "She talked briskly about a lion with a golden mane."

'"Where is this circus?" I implored.

'"Look up." He pointed upwards where the branches intertwined thickly apparently to create a solid ground for another world. The sun or some sort of stage light pierced through the holes in some instances. It was then that I began to hear the muffled music, awestruck crowds and the roar of a lion. And so I left the magician, climbing carefully up the closest canopy waving goodbye to my guide.'

Mr Wordsworth paused for a refreshing sip of whisky before he continued.

'When I arrived I was welcomed by a walking Victrola which bowed to me. My vision was filled by an ocean of heads; bulging marquees and smaller candy-floss striped tents; high-rising ticketing baroque booths; the highest stilt performers I had ever encountered whose heads were so high, they were nearly scorched by the illuminating light; performers heavily perfumed with ruby lips; so-called creatures of the air floating from an excess of joy, twirling umbrellas; ladies in pastel gowns and high-rising buns; entranced accordion players; parading elephants and marching horses; lions in cages; clairvoyants in loose shawls; oriental shamans beating drums while chanting; mime artists painted white with beret hats!

'In all of this, Grace was nowhere to be seen.

'And so, I followed my own instinctual direction, taking great care not to stumble upon the knotted branches under my feet.

'It was not long until I found myself swallowed inside the largest marquee where the main circus was held and had apparently already commenced upon my appearance. From the candy-striped roof hung vast shallow bowls of boiling fat where upright wicks stood aflame. Below them encircled by a fascinated crowd were the envied performers, who had their mouths ablaze with fire. Behind them in this stuffy confinement, a dusty piano was being played by a punk-rock pianist —'

At the mention of this, the Lace-Demon missed a note on her heavy jingle, her lace sleeves retired to her long, beautiful fingers, as she too was quietly following the story. She took it as an insult that he should mention punk-rock pianists in her highly esteemed presence.

Mr Wordsworth, subtly shifting his eyes from her dangerous ones, added, '...for Death Metal Opera as mentioned before, being in its earlier stages, required further foundation. As any of us can imagine, Death Metal used to be very much imperfect, but as the saying goes, the blushing on your face becomes you more when it rises to your eyebrows.

'So, in all of this my mind was still intent upon finding Grace but I couldn't focus among the flaring of fire and the blocks of heads. Acrobats and glass-eaters came and went but still no Grace. At last, before the show commemorated, the awe-struck crowds grew quiet yet as the ringleader marched in; the thief magician from before, pulling on a leash a lion whose mane gleamed golden. If there was any beauty in this world, it was this, believe me. Unleashed, the great creature marched forwards to greet the fear-steeped audience. In the corner of my eye, I caught Grace finally. She stood up suddenly from her seat so her lion could notice her among the faceless strangers but in her dismay, he ignored her as the ringleader gave fire to the hoops which the capable great lion was to leap through.

'The crowds cheered and applauded as he leapt from strength to the strength through the rings of fire. When the act was over, I watched the drowning of a sombre Grace from the standing and fainting ovations — a sea of ignorant appreciation. Although fascinated, I couldn't bear it either.

'So night came and I still could not find her, somehow it was important to do so; I had still yet to learn the reasons. I wasted my time in this strange world having my fortune told using dominoes. Of course, I was distracted still by the thoughts of my mission.

'A bright ray appeared after I had spent most of my money, of which bulged in the seer's pockets like a sack of radishes; he jingled away into the forthcoming crowds in a slanted gait. The show had to go on, I told myself and without Grace there was no rest.

'After the tiresome journey through the mazes of faces, I stopped by the glass-eaters' dwelling and was given the whereabouts of the lion who was apparently kept in the menagerie — a jade-green tent with all the other animals. I thought this was a rather vague description but I was assured that it was impossible to miss. With many thanks, I left them. My pace increased with impatience. A horrid storm spun above me as if it was a sadistic theatrical drama. I think a distant part of me had expected it. Glass arrow-like rain darted headlong unto me; the snaking floor became soft by it and made a strange sort of mattress, slowing me down. It was even stranger to have the ground growing under my soles in quick convulsions. Sorrow was the wage to pay. Again, having no other means to express this more eloquently, I was lost. After relentlessly searching, the winds came and I no longer worried about the storm.

'I heard a lion's roar manipulated within the wind and followed its course as there was no other choice. The creatures of the wind, in an adorable performance with umbrellas, guided me to the striking dwelling of the lion that was covered from end to end in jade stones. It shone above all else in the spotlight and jade, as we all know, is the dearest of all gems that can cause any stone-hearted man to fall in love. With this splendid energy I welcomed myself inside the cosy menagerie lit by burning lamps in all corners. A lion roared in the heart of the settlements among caged elephants, horses, flamingos and other brightly coloured exotic birds. I was quick to catch him and Grace was there kneeling before his cage in conversation, so I resulted to conceal myself behind a boxed prop.

'I could make out the tearful sniffs from Grace as the lion spoke. "How can you live with me for your own selfish needs? Can't you see that I now can experience life?" He yawned after he spoke.

'Grace muffled her tearful reply. "You don't care that I love you and care for you as my dearest friend?"

'The lion sighed, his gamey breath stirred the hay-laden floor and travelled past my feet and made me shiver slightly.

'"Leave me, girl. I have a life here, with you I am dead and at your mercy. Lions should be proud and pampered with appreciation."

'"But you were built for the purpose of a toy and nothing else!" Grace was angered.

'"Look at me now, girl," he was, in contrary to Grace, calm and mocking. "I am mightier than all the lions that have been before me."

'There was silence in the air. The implausibility of the situation must have quietened her — or perhaps it was the sadness of it all? She sobbed for some time as I sat listening, for there was nothing I could do, while the lion sighed yet again sending more pungent fumes my way.

'"Come closer, child," the lion muttered eventually. "Now, you must listen to me carefully this time, this is what shall take place and thus you shall not deny me of it. You will run and find the key to open this cage and then find a knife or perhaps a sword from one of the sword swallowers. There are a few who lay their tents close by so this should not be tasking. Now, they are most likely to be asleep at this hour; nevertheless you should be discreet and fast upon your snatching. The key is hidden within the magician's pocket, he, too, should be asleep. He sleeps underground, under a furrow of branches, you will, using the sword, tear the branches from the ground and hence find him. You must believe that you will find him, there is no other way. When you come back to my dwelling you will take out my heart; that you will keep, for the powerful spell instilled within me allows me to breathe without the instrument. And with that, girl, you may leave and begin a new life."

'Grace agreed to it. I believe she loved him then more than ever.

'When she left, I waited for some time and fell asleep where I was and was awakened into an artificial morning. The circus helpers were in the procession of feeding the animals but the mighty lion ate nothing. He was lying in his cage, looking like sunshine itself, nursing a wound about his chest. He licked his claws of pure gold as I made my way into the open air before I was caught.

'I thought this may have been the end of the tale, for I sensed that Grace may have departed, but it was not to be.

'As I would later find, she remained despite the lion's pleas so she could watch him perform to wound her soul further. He, on the other hand, was progressing in the circus arts and crowds from all over this world came to see him and they begged for encores in their plenty. Again, I found her lost among them in a state of tamed agony.

'You may be wondering how I came to know of this. Well, I was there to watch over her whenever it was possible. I would watch her until I myself fell asleep.

'I was desperate to make my leave from this drama one day but I was persuaded by the power of everlasting beauty to remain and watch the golden lion for one final time; there was no denying his hypnotic presence. And so after purchasing my ticket with my last coins, I found that there was time for further exploration and to linger about a nearby accordionist singing a song about purchasing a politician. The lyrics were rather amusing but I was curious to explore the marquees. Ticket booths were constructed deliberately high so customers would be more obliged to leave their change behind. I ambled into the closest one in proximity as the singing died and I found myself in a hall of "mocking mirrors", of which rendered my face and body irregular. It was all rather amusing but I searched around further and came across a closed cubicle with an eyehole for viewing. The sign read "Past-Life Peepshow".

'Having arched my back to peer into the hole, I saw the screening of a tale, a flickering silent film where Grace acted as a traditional tawaif, an Indian dancer, making bird shapes with her delicate fingers as a small gathering of men admired her, cross-legged on the floor, apparently captivated. Cigarette smoke circled all about and obstructed my chances of being completely absorbed. Behind her was a very real moon reflected upon a still pond where one white lotus blossomed.

'As she moved herself in a mesmeric way, a jittery servant, what other men addressed as a "Chai-Wala", was serving a tray of tea in tall glass cups. I found myself instantly connecting with him; the situation caused me to feel like I was experiencing all my vaccinations simultaneously. I brought myself to think that I was him and he was I. We were, as the case was, of similar gait and somewhat like features except for his shoe-brush moustache. He too sat and gazed at Grace for a small while until the men vented him away as they would a pestering fly.

'For Grace, I wanted to curve myself into a hoop so that she may dive through me. These imaginings were going to bother me, I know.

'I had to step away, and so I ran from the peepshow as

I began to hear the commencing music of the circus. Just in time, I was back inside the marquee; the crowds were on their feet and the candlelight caressed each face lambently as I took my seat.

'The famed ringleader and magician entered having tamed and tethered the golden lion to the point of choking him by a leather strap tightly fastened around his thick neck, leading a string of performers including two of his finest knife jugglers, two heavily-tattooed sword swallowers, two fire breathers, two skipping acrobats, two somersaulting glass-eaters, two crying clowns and two decorated elephants, dragging their step along.

'Acts came and acts went while I patiently awaited the lion with the golden mane, whose eyes were jaded. At the brink of the show, having left the best till last, the cunning magician entered the ring with the unleashed lion. The magician, as I then noticed, wore a golden chain belt with the clasp of a seven-pointed star with the heart of an amethyst. He gave the lion free reign and the creature, in turn, proudly marched towards the front row of the audience. He gave out an outrageous roar that resulted in a few fainting ovations, the impuissant marquee trembled like ship sails in a wind-ravaged sea. My heart leapt from its pearly gates — the excitement was astounding. His enjoyment was obvious for his jades twinkled between his furry manes of gold.

'Far beyond from where I was sitting stood a sallow-faced Grace desperate for her lion to face her, but he didn't.

'After the show I caught up with her into the lion's keep, concealed behind a prop again. This time, the lion was cage-less, resting his head upon the hay. When he saw her he roared.

'"Why do you remain here? Go and find yourself a new life."

'Grace was already in tears. "So this is the end? There is really nothing I can do to change your mind?"

'"No! Leave me," said the lion simply.

'And so, in a fluster, she did so and I quickly made to follow her — until I heard the entrance of the sly magician that stopped me dead in my tracks. He chuckled as I scrambled behind the prop in fear; apparently he had been secretly listening to the conversation. Taking a deep breath, he said to the lion, "Nicely done, friend, but yet so foolish."

'"How so, Master?" replied the lion, puzzled. His jade eyes shone brilliantly.

'"Friend, if you remember correctly you were created to be a valuable, stationary product and not for my entertainment."

'"I'm confused, Master I —"

'"To put this simply," interrupted the magician, "after all this time, I was testing you and you failed *terribly*. You were never mine, you belong to the girl." With the finality of his speech, because I could no longer see clearly, I guessed that the magician must have brought out a wand and transformed the lion to its former self: a wind-up toy.

'When I left, I later learnt by an eyewitness, the heart given to Grace by the lion had transformed into a bird and flown away. I found her in a hurry in the woods back on solid ground. She told me it was important that she find the bird but had no idea where to look but it was a distinctly formed bird which resembled a heart.

'As I stood there thinking, a thought flew across my mind that reminded me of the theatrical nature of this play and that I could manipulate the story according to my will. Quickly enough, I grabbed Grace's wrist and we dived into the closest seven-pointed star, which was by chance the largest of them all, and we were inhaled completely therein. We found ourselves in a garden of lush greenery where birds found their sanctuary. A white stallion galloped towards us with grace; he was to be our guide for this land was vast. We marched alongside him as we passed meadow after meadow that sloped near the lazy streams of nectar. Birds of paradise entertained one another with their mating routines, blurry hummingbirds cajoled with the bright asphodels and swallows swallowed each note of song and replied in sweet chippers.

'Grace had been silent throughout our journey — very much unappreciative. I was unsure whether it was right to prod her on the matter as her eyes were doing the meticulous work of scouring every inch of the trees for the air-bound heart.

'We marched on behind our guide. Trees and birds nodded and greeted us; a seven-pointed star watched us as we came to a wide pond where lotus flowers thrived like origami sculptures. In the far end posed a white lotus, one of the moon's gems, and perched upon it was the heart-shaped bird. It could not be mistaken. A more vulgar creature could not be more undeserving of a blessed land such as this; its wrinkled neck retracted its bald head forwards unto the plant in the process of picking it apart. I couldn't stand such a sight so I began to shout some words of blasphemy at this vengeful creature. Our guide, the horse, must have understood my anger as he hurtled forwards into the serene lake, forcing the bird away.

'Grace was more intent upon saving the bird so she ran towards its direction of flight in desperation.

'Her stubbornness angered me slightly but I vented this pointless emotion away swiftly. I chased her into the moor to witness her begin another episode of sobbing. From my pocket, I held out a handkerchief when another idea flew across the skies of my mind. She handed me back the damp the cloth from which I chanted an ancient spell I learnt from my years of training as a magician and produced a cooing dove from beneath it. Now I must admit I was never a great magician —'

'And you never will be!' Mr 101 gave out a congested laugh that brought down one of the wine-filled ladies who was sitting on her fan-chair, for it was much too unexpected. A cluster of ladies emerged around her, surprised and glad it was not one of them.

Mr Wordsworth, a man of humility, shook the comment off him as if it were confetti and continued his tale with a smile.

'I was never a *great* magician, but when I saw the joy on Grace's face I knew that I had done a great thing. I told her she should keep the latter and forget the former. And she received it with a grateful nod. She opened her mouth to speak but before I could make out a word a great light summoned me and I was back on the chair in my usual size under the roof of a candy-striped tent.

'"Better than having your dominoes read, wasn't it?" asked the gypsy with a smirk.

'I, for one, was glad it was over.' And so Mr Wordsworth reached the tail-end of his tale and he gulped the last drop of his whisky, winking at Daffodil.

Daffodil was awe-struck by the enchanting story and she wished he would go on all night, if not forever, but the story had to end somewhere. Mr Wordsworth, having told this story particularly for her amusement, sat her on his lap. He was warm and comfortable enough, the only haven in the house — although he did reek of tobacco and strong cigar paper.

48. *Even my door hinges are decorated!*

'I was never a great magician,' repeated Mr Wordsworth. Mr 101 laughed admiring the remainder of wine in his carved glass. 'No, not great — but I knew my goals. I learnt what was valuable and what should be and shouldn't be explored,' Mr Wordsworth continued.

Daffodil sat perplexed and overwhelmed by his cigar breath as he fiddled into one of his blazer pockets, removing a bulky object wrapped in a handkerchief loosely tied by a thin red rope. He untied this before her, peeled back the layers of the cloth revealing a golden lion wind-up toy. Daffodil recognised it instantly.

After the toy was wound up, he placed it on the nearby mahogany table. Somehow it was much too incredulously life-like for something man-made that no-one would be foolish enough to explain its workings without adding the word 'magic' at some point in their unworthy description. It marched forwards in a forced pride, roared once before it suspended its pose with the dying rotation of the propeller. In the end there was not a worthy word to describe the greatness of the moment and not even Mr 101 made such an attempt.

49. *Love + Trust = Lust.*

Daffodil was ordered out of the room when the ceremony began, though she was requested (by a departing Mr Wordsworth) to visit Room Two by Mr 101 after the ladies and Mr Wordsworth and Mr Wormwood were all gone. It was a rare incident — or even an enigma as it had never happened before — to be needed by Mr 101, rather than being an obligation or like a badly kept secret he needed to hide. No. Daffodil had never felt needed or wanted for that matter. Upon making her first step into the room, she was as still as her name did allude to; a flower belonging to the time of joyful spring of which graces the earth with vivacious vitality and beauty in an environment of constant brevity.

Mr 101, black-lipped, sipped his wine that was as red as a scorpion's heart from his glass and planted himself upon his saffra almost silently as a ghost. At first, there was apprehension in his behaviour as he wondered whether he should stare directly into her eyes or wait, concentrate on his drink while he spoke. The latter seemed to make much more sense. Yes. That was the kind of man he was, an arrogant, obscene —

'Where would you rather be, Dill? Are you afeard?'

Daffodil remained standing in the doorway. Her lips spoke before she could stop them, 'I don't know...'

'Would you rather be asleep, curled around my wrist? Those sunken eyes of yours have seen better days, I'm sure...'

50. *The loss of love brings about an undesired freedom. It is as the removal of a ring that we're used to wearing, then it slips from us to be disregarded as a dried pear having undergone a fall from its branch.*

He expected no reply from her and in return, she did not fail to disappoint. But just because he had expected it doesn't necessarily mean he wanted it to remain as so, and so he employed another tactic.

'Your father wrote to me.'

'Did he?!'

Mr 101 smirked, his lips curled into one giant eyelash. It was sad, he thought, as his smirk returned to its normal pout. 'No, no he did not. Why do you still believe that he will come to save you?'

This was torture for Daffodil; he had her trapped like a moth whose wings were nailed to the table. Of course, she stayed silent, hoping to release her tears to her mattress later.

'No, no,' spoke Mr 101 (Daffodil rather wished he wouldn't) 'you're right; a peacock does not know the meaning of *hideous*. It has eyes in its head and on its feathers, but it cannot see anything but beauty. If it's any consolation I only knew I wanted you when I met you. Was it not through the faults of your own and father that I met you? In all honesty, Dill, would you rather go home?'

There was a pause. The host was smouldering on his seat but his composure was much too relaxed, verging on the uninteresting, to betray him. If he was a photograph, he would have done well. If he was a whale-watcher, he would have done even better, for he was waiting for the truth to swell the surface before it forced itself out in a deafening clamour.

'No.' Her throat was dry as the answer to his question crawled out. 'There's nowhere to go.'

'No, sweetheart, there isn't.' Mr 101 made his way to the curtains and touched them with his free hand. The struggle of his fingers did not prevent him from a deed he so despised. For now, as long as he couldn't see her eyes, he was satisfied.

'Young minds,' he commenced, 'subjected to violence can only grow up to face becoming the leftovers of society through no fault of their own. I'm here because I've been there, you see.' His words gave him the courage to look at her then. 'No-one pities us because we are too strong; we are not convincing enough as victims, and so we're damned onwards to crippling loneliness, to lead a life desperately seeking success to keep us afloat. But all the while you're in the shadow of it, believe me, that's if you're not already imprisoned by it.'

The candles flickered like autumn leaves and in a moment, Mr 101 was gone. The room began to grow darker with the dusk; the candlelight melded into one sunrise and for once the room felt clean. Daffodil wondered if another day had already approached and ripened so quickly. As she issued a breath, she saw him reappear as if nothing had happened. He was neither in this dimension or the next. Barely existing now, he was a glittering vision of the ruthlessly terrible and a blur of the spiritually learnt. And he hulked to a forlorn cupboard, opened one of its drawers which held up the bookshelves and removed a package, wrapped in tissue paper and tied with a thin red rope. He signalled Daffodil to come and collect it.

She did so with cautiousness but it was soft, light and harmless. A gasp escaped her as she fixed her eyes on a simple white dress which sported a bow at the waist.

'You may wear it for my performance next week; I daresay that green ensemble you have on will distract me when I'm performing and that could cause me to show a very bad side of myself in front of the ladies.'

'Thank you!' cried Daffodil, she wondered if it would be appropriate to offer a quick hug. She was elated for the first time in an eternity.

'My dear!' exclaimed Mr 101 as he backed away. 'This is by all means not a kind favour from me; you must understand that I detest the solidified mucus that is your dress! And I am done with the embarrassment you caused me to be in, in front of my friends...this is most certainly, definitely, precisely not a...*gift*.' His eyes widened at the very hideous thought.

Mr 101 was frozen on the spot, his eyes wider still, continuing to ponder the preposterous nature of a gift. He was, if a doctor had been there to give a brief observation, having a minor panic attack. Daffodil stood there silently, patiently and rather clueless as her eyes darted around the room for a remedy, when she spotted a glass of his unfinished wine on the table which she took and waved under his nose. It seems a second later he was recovered as he gulped down the rest of it. Taking a deep breath, he looked back down at Daffodil who stared right back, her eyes an ocean of liquid iron.

With a trembling hand, he covered both her eyelids firmly. He could feel them shut like two tiny warm oven doors. On the other side of her eyelids, Daffodil saw the universe before her; a flurry of stars and planets swirled about her.

After Mr 101 removed his hand from her face, she found herself asking, in a daze, 'What lies under the Earth?'

After a moment's consideration, Mr 101 finally said, 'You will find all the questions our civilization has ever asked about the meaning of our lives, all valid but unanswered.'

The Horse Finds Speed

This was a unique attempt to escape the saving grace of non-reality. The simpler option to achieve its opposite would have been to plunge from reality and remain suspended in a place where time was forbidden to slide its iron tongue on a face of numbers. In a deluge, a black horse barred the sliver of white road; he was larger than a Taj Mahal covered in a wafer-thin layer of soot that any swipe of a finger could begin the restoration of. He was an obvious beauty, and pure, but no-one had ever seen him but the white horse.

The white horse, for hours, had been galloping without cease from Arcadia — all this effort to be later lacerated. He'd tolerated abuse like an anvil under many hammers, though he's witnessed many sparks there which had helped to smooth out his destiny.

Now he was quicker than ever, more so intrepid on his soon-to-end journey. Darkness was never destined to be the harbinger of fear, he realised for he felt comforted by it. The white horse waited by the black creature like a whisper cut-out, glad in his frame which glimmered. Impatience pervaded; it marched on faster than a sprint. He would always remain perfection unfathomable, in two minds like a split river that sings hymns instead of water.

The black horse spread himself on the ground more expertly than the sea, so the other could drink up all his legs until he had eight and ecstasy. The white horse grew four more legs. He didn't need wings as he journeyed his way on a carpet now damp with blood. Now he was able to pick up further speed, because the hovering portal that led to a lengthy reality was beginning to shut so that it may never open again. His heart was, as it always will be, in a constant battle for survival.

51. *We don't follow religion. Religion outlines the moral constructs of the mind that some may conveniently forget from time to time...*

A Diary Entry

52. *We can never be truly original, exempt from the past.*

The master was scouring his mind for any morsel of unexplored ideas while his pen scuffled away at something inside the deadly Room 101. It could have been something between revolutionary and a scribble, who knows? It was from the seed of determination that these futile lines were awakened, of which only a learned few would understand and the rest would dare to criticise. This is the edited version of what was written in a space of two hours. Sweat, scratching, pinching and excessive touching rendered his face an inconceivable mess.

53. *When you're at the bottom of the food chain, it is inevitable that you will be eaten or else you risk the humiliation of being left behind.*

Everything you love, hate and know was created in the first few minutes of creation, even the people that come in our lives to destroy our livelihood. Creation itself happened wherever it is you dwell, not in a space far, far away, not under your bed where darkness pervades, not in an enclosed box. Everywhere about you once occupied the stars all huddled together to make the very essence of you. What a tiresome party and gathering of souls life is...
No, there is an end. There must be.
What is it in nature that forces the trees into such deadly postures? Pleading almost, with branches outstretched

like a many-armed Hindu deities?'

Mr 101, a distorted complicated product of nature, saw no plausible explanation for viewing himself as one of nature's victims — neither friend nor foe.

A Strange Woman

'One hundred,' Mr 101 read the large, red numbers on the wall aloud as he walked through the room, thinking how it was nearly time to end the little girl. He only needed one more life.

Like an arm resting upon a table graced by a shawl, laid a divan held up by stout wooden legs upon which rested a creature — not a woman to Mr 101: she was a creature until she had properly introduced herself and made it clear she was not in any way threatening. Mr 101 simply stared at her in her distress as she sobbed without tears.

> 54. *First, we plan out our own destiny meticulously and then, we forget about it.*

'Do you think I'm insane for not going through with your procedure?' she was heaving in her weariness. 'I couldn't, I just couldn't.'

He narrowed his eyes at her as one who is about to fall into another bout of thought, but he quickly snatched himself out of it as he said, 'You are sane for allowing it to cause you distress — rather brave. If you like, you can follow me. I'll show you, and *only* you, the way out.'

Down a narrow corridor where nothing could be seen, but the harsh breath of Mr 101 could still be heard, they walked on. Mr 101 walked on ahead of the woman who kept turning her head here and there as if to spot an exit. She heard music behind the walls. She touched them as if to touch the music itself. This was when she felt their dampness which nearly numbed her bones. Eventually, Mr 101 exchanged a hand-shake with a door that was numbered

Room 18 and entered, after gesturing the woman to do the same in his most gentlemanly way. As soon as the door was shut, its hand curled into a fist as if to look unapproachable. Perhaps this gesture was a make-shift 'do not disturb' sign.

There was light in the room but its source could not be found. It was another bedroom that was once lavish but now after years of neglect was much too dusty and reeking of damp to be even given any praise. The number 100 which seemed to have melted on the wall alarmed the woman.

'Where is the exit? Why are we here? Let me out!'

'You're the last,' Mr 101 croaked.

He couldn't bring himself to look at her. In a game of chess, this would have been checkmate; in life, this was death. That no one could escape his house without death was a paramount rule, an ancient mindset that could not be replaced or overruled. The fact that this sort of trickery was involved for this kill saddened Mr 101, but, unfortunately, he was desperate to end this ruse — to end everything. He almost whispered an apology. However the prospect of losing his pride always made him feel tense, even at this point in his life.

'Lie down,' he ordered.

'NO!'

He leapt onto to her like a ferocious mammal and backed her up against the dripping wall.

'Why make it hard for yourself when, either way you look at it, you're going to die?' he hissed, forcing out the ring on her Saturn finger.

When he tossed it away, the ring jittered on the floor before it settled, as if to demonstrate, with immense haste, how the mind works. Its owner reacted with shock as if Mr 101 had separated her from her partner.

'Where are the other two?' she struggled on. 'You can't do this without them, it won't work!'

'Ah no, you are part of *another* experiment, you are the most important, for you are the last. We don't need them. I don't need them! I am more powerful than I've ever been! I don't even need the three-hundred and sixty degree door anymore...'

'What are you talking about? You're mad, do you know that?' Tears were streaming down her cheeks that he would later taste.

'I'm mad? *I'm mad*? I'm not the one who signed her life away to me — a madman!'

'You tricked all of us!' she cried.

Mr 101 inhaled deeply before sending a blow across her face. She ended up on the floor nursing her face, gasping ceaselessly. This was when Mr 101 lifted and threw her onto the bed, with whatever strength he had left. Without a second to waste, he squeezed her neck with one hand and with the other, lifted her to his mouth to take the first of many bites.

***

After the screams died down and the unspeakable took place, Mr 101 closed the door of Room 18 behind him. On his tongue he tasted blood, as if there was a penny coin in his mouth to suck on.

The lady he now neither hated nor loved had been waiting for him. She frowned when she saw him. The two voices spoke very low; they were the light of two lamps dimmed by a cover.

'Are you happy with yourself?' she demanded.

'I don't know what happiness is.' He walked on away from her and she followed on behind.

'What about Daffodil?'

Mr 101 halted on the dusty spot. 'A hundred and one women have died because of and for her. She is ready; she will not age to become one of you, I will not allow it! Let *me* take care of her after the show. She is not your concern, whoever you are.'

He removed a bundle of wet hair from his mouth and dropped it on the floor.

55. *That much I know is true, the darkness plays tricks on you.*

Mr 101 escaped to a room where he could find solace and a mirror to look into and converse with. This mirror, for some odd reason, trembled ceaselessly whether Mr 101 was there or not. This way of being was its true nature.

These eyes have seen, these eyes have known, these eyes have loved, thought Mr 101 to his reflected self which was blurred from the vibration. These eyes have yet to be born again and enlightened many times more.

He was the source of all his reflections, but where in the skies was his origin?

It seems life is a vast hall, walled in mosaics where in the centre rested our true being hidden behind many stages that are cordoned off by screens. These ancient screens are stained glass merging beautiful colours together depicting many of nature's features sullenly caressed by candle flames from the corners of the hall. And as we sift through, we become more aware of the beauty and the sheer pointlessness. We sift in certain scents from the everlasting whirls of incense smoke, emotions as raw as freshly cut meats and we march on in our heavy steps like the shadow of a ghost, having caught the remnants of the smoke and the lingering motives of emotions.

Then we enter a confined circle where, like an arm upon a table rests the creature of our core, pasted in magnificent maharaja jewels. To our horror she speaks: 'I can lie here no longer...' sobbing without tears for it had run scarce in her reservoir after an eternity of waiting.

'And I, like a fool,' muttered Mr 101 to himself, 'I stand there, perplexed without any convincing or any appropriated words, dying to leave this place which starts to choke me.'

Those unjustly undulating jiving jewels sent shivers to Mr 101 as he exited his meditative state. Perhaps there were inclusion marks in his diamond.

'Life is a lie we choose to believe,' he pondered aloud. Madness and woe had now resided in him, never ever to leave. 'We pick it up in its pieces and pretend there are no sharp edges, then after a while we forget. We become comfortable to hold such an object, and then the lie becomes truth. After a little more time, we begin to despise ourselves and adopt another, a shadow, an illusion who is much easier to handle than the truer being we once were. Life is a lie we choose to believe for reasons I've never understood. I have seen men lose their minds and leap off edges high. I have already seen the world where the end is nigh, the repetition of time.'

56. *Tell me, if I scratched hard on the edge of the universe, would it bleed? And if I terminated all life on Earth, is it certain that I will die alone?*

In a silence that brought about the chill of a prison chamber soon to be opportune by the most savage criminal of all, a young boy called out for Mr 101, dousing a fishing rod in the depths of a lake. The boy called out his name. He had been staring, stirring those murky lake waters that were the depths in his eyes for much too long; the bed of pebbles could not be spotted, not even the ones he had deliberately thrown in. There was a lurid question which hovered in his mind. Should he allow the question to form? Dare he say it? Will it *ever* end?

57. *If I were to die and meet my Creator, I would ask him if I had read all the signs correctly.*

The Running Room

As the name correctly implied, the room was created for the sole purpose of running. The floors did not possess legs, nor would they run if they did. Mr 101, before all sense was lost in him, built this so he could and would lose his senses by the means of running, or in his case amble very quickly from one end to the other. It was through the high velocity of the movement of one's feet that one lost control the quickest.

The light which was seldom was very crucial as to make this experience mysterious. The corners which were not obvious to the eye were marred by the thickest veils and drapes of curtain-like structures, gathered to create a ripple effect which sometimes caught the light to aid one to see. And the floors appeared to expand as he ran. It was an impossible experience but only Mr 101 would beg to differ (although he rarely ever begged, begging was for beggars and beggars alone!). It was an illusory experience and if one was not grounded enough, one may just be lost in the way in which the light intertwined with one another merging and repelling against the swirls of dust which always seemed an inevitable factor in this building. They resembled the endless snaking stairs but without steps or foundations or banisters.

58. *What is the outside world?*

And what about the stairs? They seemed so far from Mr 101 at this moment as he stepped his way to the middle of the Running Room, his steps echoing from the unseen walls and ceiling. He wished for a mirror somewhere so he would have something to focus his gaze towards or at least some Death Metal Opera playing in some faraway place to excite his senses and stir the Ridiculism within him.

'Where have you been?' said a voice. 'I've been looking all over...'

Out of the darkness a woman with short, curled jet black hair stepped out in complete wedding attire apart from her bouquet which had withered over time. She appeared to be troubled, lost and confused, but she seemed to recognise Mr 101. Unfortunately he did not recognise her. He was bemused; he wanted to laugh but found he could even force himself to. Her eyes were familiar to him.

All of a sudden, the aroma of a thousand cedar trees came into the Running Room smelling of damp soil, and he began to remember what it was like to stand outside. He looked suspiciously about him as if smell had an appearance.

Not noticing the slight change of air, she said with a slight tone of desperation, 'How could you?! You know I would have never approved, how could I ever love you now?!'

Mr 101, for the first time since he could remember, felt the beatings of his heart beneath the rubble of nonsense he'd stacked up for years. It was at war with itself but there was no way he could understand why.

'Ma'am...?'

Her sobbing face looked like a scrunched up rose.

'Obviously someone's wife...' he muttered to himself. 'I am not the one you're looking for but I am sure whoever it is you're looking for you will find him elsewhere, now I...'

'YOU'RE MAD! You ruined me!'

'I'm pretty sure my madness has ruined myself above all else!'

59. *All mad, fictitious thoughts have been justified merely because of scientific babble.*

And as he said these words, she disappeared into one of the many shadows. Fortunately, she took the smell of cedar with her, as it had started to become quite unbearable. It was as if he had chanted a spell and he thought about the words he uttered. No, he was certainly *not* mad; it was just a case of being intentionally deluded. He peered about him before he took his shoes off and chucked them into the abyss of a shadow. When he threw them they made not even a tap of a sound, which made him think he'd truly thrown them into a hole.

The room was quite still when Mr 101 lost himself inside it; he raced and skidded across the room. Endorphins exploded helplessly like fireworks. His legs were blurred from the speed. Many times he collided with walls and pillars and rested for a moment leaning upon them but then shortly after, he continued. As he got used to the idea, he began to laugh with the freedom he felt; he raised his arms, threw off his pin-striped jacket and his waistcoat into the air, shaking the spotlights above. If he was capable of falling in love, he would have certainly done so without so much as half a thought.

He grew tired but carried on until his legs gave up and he collapsed to the ground, yelping from catching his breath. Even after his legs were normal, he laid there still, thinking about the woman who could have once been his bride, but every time he stepped closer to the truth, a door closed and when it did, the Running Room door opened revealing Daffodil. Mr 101 stood up quickly.

'I'm tired...' she said.

'*You're* tired?' he panted. 'The earth gets tired too, you know, but it never stops spinning! It doesn't just say "I think I will rest here for a moment and have my afternoon tea!" No, it swivels along, always, like a freshly chopped head, sliced momentarily by a mighty sword and left spinning on the floor...'

'Whatever do you mean?'

'I *mean...*' began Mr 101, but he didn't quite know himself and he too was tired to invent anything. 'No matter, no matter,' he said, as if he trying to somehow describe the atmosphere at the very beginning of time. And indeed there was nothing at all in the beginning, no sense of materials, no chocolate, no silks to caress Mr 101's face or structure to hold this damned house together.

A Diary Entry

60. *The waves are always crashing against the rocks outside but I blocked them away, all this time until now. I see the beauty in it. I see heaven in it. Heaven can only be reached in solitude, indoors. In heaven, love, only love resides.*

Mr 101 wrote until the paper drank all the ink. This was escape, this was also a trap. A trap is an escape; an unwilling freedom. He took a great sniff and wiped the rest of the mucus on his sleeve and received the taste of seawater. The sleeves which had held many testimonies to distressing times wiped those eyelids spilling tears in abundance. But in denial, he fancied the notion that he had attempted to drown himself once beneath those crashing waves but somehow survived. Perhaps both were plausible but only Wordsworth would know about the latter.

'*There is a passion within me*,' he wrote, '*One which I cannot decry for certain. It haunts every minute of my life, apart from the time when I'm devouring a young lady*.'

His pages were the windows he could write on and rely on, their glass panes opaque to all but him, tactile instead of repelling.

Wordsworth was, at that very precise point in time, having himself a dream under the pear tree. The clothes on his back, his sparrow and profound wisdom were all the things Wordsworth did ever possess. And he was pleased with what he had been given. A gentle wind glided its soft finger upon his cheek, which was as pale as a steamed scallop, and attempted to flick his sandy hair from his face but failed triumphantly. It succeeded only in producing a beautiful image to the eye. He slept soundly as a child who tires himself from playing all day.

In his sleep, he was racing through a forest in search for something unknown. There was nothing chasing him, no company to be wary of but the crowds of emerald trees which glowed in the sunlight. It was a heavenly sun, not scorching or beaten by a bitter wind. It was silent, as though he was the only being in this world. After hurrying through the many trees, he reached a clearing where he found himself surrounded by a green mist. It was quite still for a moment until it transformed into a flight of stairs which he walked up unquestioningly until he was above the trees, reaching for the clear sky. The stairs terminated precisely where the sky starts; he looked over his shoulder to see a village in the distance. As he hurried towards it, the village backed away, scared as a wild hare. Wordsworth carried on forward and the village retracted further, until it was just a dot, so Wordsworth gave up his venture and turned back to return to the forest. As he did so, the village began to follow him; instead of chasing the village again (because he'd learnt from previous experience that it was unwise), he walked back further towards the green mist of stairs. Yet before he could even catch the stairs in sight, he found himself in the midst of what appeared to be an empty village, but what was really just another forest.

The path he took was beaten and scattered with white feathers; he followed the feathers until he reached a small white cottage where inside there were lighted candles, taller than him and white linen curtains, tickled by a light wind. As he touched the curtains his eyes opened and he was fully awake.

The 360 degree door

'Abhaddha Kedhabhra' in Aramaic means to 'disappear like this word'. The incantation was used to make medicine disappear, cure fevers, make depression disperse like sneeze fluid. Like the disappearing word, this door, the 360 door, held the same sort of definition. It aroused a fevered obsession to the one who knew about its existence, hence the reason for its mild concealment to all those apart from Mr 101. For he and he alone was the sole purpose of its existence, he created the 360 door. It was used for a special sort of divinatory purpose in the same way that the crystal ball and tarot cards were used by the soothsayers. But Mr 101 craved a new exciting venture, clad in an extreme need to cause a calamity which he and he alone knew how to use and something rather eccentric to match his own nature, his way, his Tao.

> 61. *In which temperament and idiosyncrasy of an atmosphere did my woeful mind which experiences sorrow at the greatest impact, came to be, flourish and exist?*

The door wore mirrors like a protective coat in the upper room, the attic, the ceiling, the domed cupola or whatever the doomed higher structure of that house could profess to be! And the door turned full circle, stirring empty space continuously as a silver spoon in the speed of light once it was touched. After so long in solitude, he had the power to empower a meditative state for him to perform this arduous task.

Mr 101 took it to believe that matter was universal; his

substance could be found at any place he wished and all he had to do was become conscious of it. He could have spent his entire life finding all his existences, under the covers, in dusty corners but he was quite content with the one. And this one was by all means valuable to him, for it enabled him to be the closest observer of Titan. Mr 101 was his own star, not yet reached his red dwarf stage and at ease with the fact. He was more than happy to gaze at Titan as his thoughts were profound then, much more than they were in his sunless enclosure but it was impossible to put into plain English — or any other language for that matter — but they stayed with him nonetheless and with him alone.

> 62. *Not one man has ever been able to proclaim the importance of a magician's sleeve, which like the mind can transform thought into reality but the magician's sleeve does this and more with flaming colours, always for the awe of the audience.*

Titan was his closest companion; he held it dear to his soul. He also yearned to catch a glimpse of the white horse he once spotted on a half-sober evening. From afar it had appeared as a crawling moth spreading its angel-white antennae to the surface of a dewdrop a million times its size. The horse belonged to nowhere, but it had a purpose, hence the reason for its disappearance from Titan.

Mr 101 stayed for as long as his patience, space and time could hold him. He grew weary for the search of answers. It was beautiful nonetheless — everything was. He glanced at the worlds of light around him, each a sample version of the sun. It didn't bother him; perhaps it was true that the Running Room had made him much too happy. Happiness stirred awkwardly in him at times of realisation, like vinegar poured in a well to contaminate its contents of spring water, but indeed there was not much difference between the stars and the sun, was there? And just as he was about to change his mind, a firm voice pleaded, 'But you hate the sun, you must always, without a doubt, hate the sun!'

The Last Performance

"Again within the heart there is a heart hidden like a horseman hidden in dust." Rumi.

Mr 101 watched the scene intently, as always, on his precious (but now a very much worn) saffra as he waited nervously behind the satin backdrop while the ladies paraded through the entrance in twos, arms linked in flesh-pretzels. For the last time, they would be his finely arranged instruments that co-existed and partook in the orchestra of his biosphere, and then no more. Their attires were in more magnificent colours than they have ever been. Their clothes were their flamboyant trailing flags that represented and confessed that their dominions were ready to be thrashed and annihilated. Even by the dimming light shining above, they held that undeniable beauty of the birds of paradise that had perhaps grown stale in their wings, for their shades were not inspiring but overwhelming like a gasp of strong perfume. If they lacked anything, it was grace and modesty. However, these things which money couldn't afford were least expected of them, especially from Mr 101, who was rather glad that there was now a high chance for him to steal the show. And of course, it meant a great deal, as it was the last the ladies would ever see of him and he'd certainly made an effort tonight.

Room 66 was revamped, more so, unrecognisable from when the carpenter had paid a visit (and was turned into a chair leg). And the carpenter who was now the leg of a chair was not to go to waste. As ever, there was a purpose to Mr 101's seemingly erratic behaviour and chaotic reality.

A chair was propped on stage, irregular in appearance as the seat was held by just three legs. One of which was the former carpenter, another was a golden sword and the last was a cedar wand.

It was, by all means, the central topic of conversation. As the ladies planted themselves on rows upon rows of church pews covered in snake skins, they began to observe the rest of the room. Some uttered expletives when they realised their garments were being ruined from the carpet's layer of chalk. They would never learn that it was intentional, and owed to Mr 101's unfading mischief. Ancient Chinese bronze mirrors were hung from the ceilings but not a single face could be reflected on their surface. They were as large as round tables, the kind of which kings would meet with their associates and deliberate. The surface was grey and clouded, a clear refusal to reflect — some much more than others — but this did not stop them from being admired. Between these large ornaments, wherever they could be fitted, acetylene lamps dangled like eyes to observe and absorb the beauty of the room. When the ladies were tired of elbowing one another to catch their own futile glimpses through blighted mirrors, they stretched their necks to catch a wholesome view of the stage. The pillars, which held the ceiling, were lacquered with gold. The ladies whispered profusely about the decor but mostly the chair and they gasped in surprise when the orchestra began. *Where was the piano?* they wondered. There was always a piano, even if it wasn't being played.

It was beautifully strange. The members of the band were sitting on the left side of the stage, which was predominately cast with a great shadow before they began playing. It was their faces that awakened an even greater element of surprise. Much like the light-bearers, their heads were lamps aglow from the clusters of fireflies which circled their faces; if one stood close by one of the musicians, they would have sounded like many fingernails being clipped simultaneously. But fortunately the blanket of cymbals, drums, gongs, trumpets and the flute warmly covered that discomforting sound. They played with a

Zen calming notion in front of a thickly embroidered silk hanging where wispy clouds slithered; rain washed the infertile ground and a glowing phoenix rose up to the ceiling above in showing the four elements in harmony. But behind this backdrop lurked Mr 101 who for the first time today (if he could tell the difference between yesterday, today and tomorrow) was feeling a tension inside of him. It was bubbling, a soft magma of desire — the very desire to have Daffodil. She was what brought a twinkle to his eyes, the reverent element he salivated for. Very soon this liquid would erupt, fully fledged and furnished to the heel with the vindictive desperation of a first-rate killer.

Props, costumes, boxes and make-up tables populated with greasepaints and brushes were around him. Tonight, only tonight, he would relive his past in order to bid goodbye to it. At times, he thought perhaps he should have exaggerated with the whole thing. After all, he only had a pole with tassels on its end to symbolise him riding a horse. That is, of course how he planned to enter the stage. It would have been nice to have had the real thing. His adopting of the Chinese theatre tradition had humbled him and allowed him to step down from his shaky stairs and dwell on a stable level. It was somewhat comforting not to be in need of the sense of superiority, to accept another's culture, to accept diversity in this way, to realise the diverse nature *within*. He was going back to a child-like state. He wanted it. He needed it. And he was ready for nature to take its course now that he'd learned to let go. It was a time of rejoice, a coming together of opposites, one of his final deeds in this life. There could have been tears behind those lovely curtains but not a soul would ever know, and neither did it ever matter.

His thoughts were interrupted as applause and cheers broke through, the backdrop shivered. On the other side, the satin banners unfurled revealing waves, the patterns of the sea and fish to depict the setting. The bearded ghost of Mei-Lang Fang[2] from the ceiling appeared and vomited a large mass of mist from his mouth that hugged the dark

2. Renowned Chinese theatre actor.

stage floor, covering most of the orchestra apart from their glowing faces. His robes were all the colours one could imagine, blended together in one controlled chaos. To the crowds, he was nearly as transparent as any ghost would be, though his colours shone him bright, holy as an angel. His eyelids held the blue gems of his eyes and they sent the audience into a relaxed trance. This was to stop the ladies from whispering. Inevitably, an overwhelming sense of silence clasped the room as the Pao Tsen arrived and the music quickened in pace for her dance.

She was a character of many mysteries, a shamanistic traveller between the worlds, a snake trailing wonderfully in heaven. The moon-shaped symbol on her forehead depicted her role in the performance. She was what the Chinese would call 'lily-footed', for her gait was that of an oriental ballerina: full of feminine grace. Sometimes she bowed, other times she twirled sending her satin robes flying like wings with shards of lightning twined within and around them. Her feet were lost in the mist and she was more than beauty; she transcended the word until it was indescribable and could only be grasped by the more intuitive members of the audience. Every sound, every step was momentous, every breath had its own special effect.

63. *We have a tendency to love things that will never last.*

The beautiful but seemingly meaningless introduction to Mr 101's performance was, in fact, crucial, and was filled with the essence of his rejuvenating soul. The Pao Tsen disappeared to wherever she was called to, fading into the mist underneath her feet. And then, silence grew like an overwhelming tree overshadowing the audience into the depths of its darkness. They awaited still, it could have been a second to a century but the audience would have never recognised the difference for they comprehended very little.

Then, there was one character on stage; the one and only, him and him alone — Mr 101. He was the only being of importance in his world. He was the only person whose existence was perfectly known to him; an incredible existence by all means, all the others were clouded with judgement in a world of polarity, overtaking shadows and resonating voices. But there he stood. Having gone through the thickets of malevolence and waged war with his nightmares and returned in one piece, he was now ready to banish this phase for the next and fight his last battle without fear. But even in this state, he had yet more to learn, more to discover.

In perfect timing, Daffodil entered for the first time in decent attire. She glowed in her puffy white dress; it was as if she was held in a bubble of light. Mr Wordsworth signalled her to sit next to him in a comfortable corner with Mr Wormwood at the very end but he was captivated by Mr 101's entrance enough to not notice her being there, and so she ran to Mr Wordsworth without question as she was rather frightened by the overwhelming silence of the audience.

As soon as Mr 101 was on the stage, he felt quite comfortable. He knew now that whatever his performance entailed, the ladies would be impressed because the first two acts had already stolen their attention and any negative opinions they might have had. And true to that, the ladies were fixed upon him and his robe. Like a traditional Chinese emperor, he wore yellow — a type of yellow that was verging on the appearance of gold, liquid gold. And to impress the eye further, most of this golden fountain was usurped with lashings of extraordinary embroidery, sewn on were the many manifestations of nature, all overlapping and intertwined into one whole image of a tempered chaos. Snakes became branches and stars lunged to create birds. Here and there one could spot beaming pearls, golden beads and crystals.

He skulked to his chair, barefooted, his tasselled pole held high to show that he was walking with a horse by his side and planted himself upon the three-legged furniture, dragging his heavily embroidered satin train behind him.

Invoking the gestures of a lady or perhaps a Goddess, he held a blood-stained fan to hide half of his powdered face that were accompanied by two red spots on his cheek to indicate the fake blushing of a maiden. Of course, there was a slight hint of the grotesque but it was undeniably magnetic. No one could be forced to look at anything other than him because of the magical force; perhaps it was also a hint of envy which gave Mr 101's heart the satisfaction it so needed after spending what seemed like an eternity behind the backdrop listing down all the possible factors which could cause this moment to fall apart. His heart was, as he was no longer ashamed to admit, an unpredictable organ which would beat like a drum awakening the shackles, the red ropes that twisted tightening the red chamber within where one dwells, dreams, prays for the horseman covered in dust to come alive.

He removed from his shimmering pocket what was a dollop of mercury in a flask, lifted the opened jar skywards so the audience might see it. The ladies were silent; some recognised the metal, others did not. It was unnecessary for a lady to be intelligent, educated and/or smart, although it did help — especially on occasions such as this.

Mr 101, without hesitation, swallowed the specimen, causing Mr Wordsworth to jump to his feet but he planted himself back to his original position after his senses made him realise that Mr 101 was a madman and there was nothing anyone could do now to save him. He loosened his collar a little as he felt his temperature rising from the pressure of not being able to save his close acquaintance. Beside him, sat Mr Wormwood quietly, not a care on his face, consumed with curiosity.

Mr 101 was quite still as he sat sucking on the metal, his first metal meal in...well for quite some time, as he had forgotten. His old age was rinsing away his memory, or perhaps it was something else; he was not quite sure and he was not sure if he was not sure.

His lips were absent from black lip-gloss, his eyes were open but at the same time absent, innocent and non-judgemental as a baby's. In all the chaos, the expression on Mr 101's face did not disturb his decision to stay as Zen as possible.

He saw Daffodil's little face floating above the sea of heads and blinked twice to greet her. She in return neither smiled nor frowned but was rather surprised he made the effort. His gaze wandered about the room, registering each and every face. And then, unexpectedly, he dropped the tasselled whip that was supposed to represent his horse. A foreign force took over him and he worked with it, trying to manifest, transform the dot of mercury. He leapt onto his chair and crouched, moaning with his mouth still shut. He bent forwards so no-one could see his face and furthermore, he covered his head with the blood-stained fan.

If ever a more deadly thing existed than silence, it was not present, as silence was on everyone's lips. Mr Wordsworth stood up yet again in a panic and was about to run to the stage when he felt Daffodil taking hold of his arm, pulling him back to his seat.

'No, wait!'

And she was right; somehow Mr Wordsworth could not deny her.

On the stage, Mr 101 unfurled himself and removed the lace fan from his face; his lips were coated in silver.

'You're mine,' Mr 101 said finally, looking directly at Daffodil as a bunch of solid golden daffodil flowers slithered from the pit of his mouth. His orifice became a vase of gold flowers, and the veins from under his skin protruded from the pressure of the sudden growth. Where was the line between sanity and insanity? When does it no longer matter? The audience gasped and applauded, Mr Wordsworth wiped the beads of sweat onto his handkerchief and Mr Wormwood chuckled. He was the greatest magician they had ever seen, he excelled his own title. But even so, the show was not over.

From his chair rose Mr 101, arms spread wide as a phoenix. The mist rose about him, covering his robe, and he leapt forward towards the floor with a shout of 'Abhadda Kedhabhra!'

Confetti flew into the air as Mr 101 disappeared, leaving the blood-stained fan and his supposed horse behind. He ended up in a part of the universe that was dark with clouds and known as a pool of potential, closed eyes, in lotus position and had already begun a long journey of meditation.

In Room 66, the orchestra lingered on like strong scented incense as if nothing had taken place. The ladies cried in horror, gossiped and demanded for the appearance of Mr 101 who was nowhere to be found that night, and the ladies left his premises bitterly and rejected all kindness from Mr Wordsworth.

The house was de-cluttered, flooding out the ladies it had swallowed over an hour ago, including a very confused-looking Mr Wormwood who disappeared into the trees. Mr Wordsworth turned to Daffodil with the utmost urgency.

'Now Daffodil, you have to run, run as fast as you can. He will come for you, you know that!' His eyes were darker than the night but the warmth of his voice comforted her.

'Where will I go? Can you come with me, Wordsworth?'

'*Mr* Wordsworth,' he corrected her. 'I will be with you all the way but I can't help.'

'What do you mean?'

'Well, child, the truth is... I am not alive — neither is Wormwood. He doesn't know, he denies it, but I do. I've known for quite some time. The ladies who came tonight have no idea that they were killed by us, they're happy to live Mr 101's lie and he is more than happy to make a mockery of us, play out our fantasies in front of us, ready to lead us into a paradise of illusions. He only invited the dead tonight — and you. Recently, he's been acquiring living women for your sake so after one hundred and one deaths, he could allow himself to have you. But the rest of us are all projections of who we once were, a projection that you can touch and communicate with. I died a long time ago. You know the story I told you, about the circus? *I* was the magician who buried himself. I wish I could have been a great magician but I never was.'

'What? Is *he* alive? Mr 101?'

'101? Why, yes he is, but he chooses to live his life like us. He is a disgrace, a man without a sense of responsibility or care of how much pain he can inflict onto others; that is why he can do what he does and no one else can. It is why he is sought after from all parts of the world.'

'But...you're his friend?'

'Child, I'm a ghost, a lonesome spirit. I am nobody's *friend*! I suppose I do care for him in a strange way —'

'What about Wordsworth?'

Mr Wordsworth looked at her curiously for a moment.

'I'm afraid I have no idea what or who you're talking about. I don't advise imaginary friends around here, they can be dangerous. Now Daffodil, listen to me before it's too late, do not go back into that house. Run away as fast as you can!'

How the Horse Found Freedom

He'd sensed this was a stifling enclosure; this building had been noticeable even from afar, from Saturn and even Mars. This must have been done on purpose by the architect's sordid intentions as if he'd wished his visitor to feel intimidated by the enclosure as soon as they'd begin to question his motives. Even for the excess of chambers in this house, this one was a rare finding. The horse had always known he'd end up here after transpiring through the vicissitudes of time that'd taken its toll on him all the while and, not to mention, his emotions. Though it could not be denied that in every world, whether it'd been self-created or not, he'd been exceptional. He'd always been intent on becoming a more picturesque version of himself, a classic piece re-worked; all the mould incised which is why he was always undergoing these questionable, demeaning trials. Raising his head like the mast of a ship that comes up from underwater, he felt his neck bound to a thread. Just as he instinctively tugged at it, the light came on.

A chandelier bearing slivers of light and endless chains and beads ascended slowly from the floor, signifying the commencement of the unexpected. It revealed what was holding back the horse, or more specifically dragging him forwards but nowhere. The object was a self-driven mourning carriage that looked more like a dome made from old picture frames positioned on wheels. More intricately put, this carriage was a concoction of a wealth of honey, blanketing its golden liquid-glass substance over a selection of faux vintage photo frames, connected by the sides and heaped together. The white horse couldn't help being tempted to gobble up those honey-coated memories in a second to help fortify him, sustain and lengthen his limbs. It was the shrine and synthesis of all his shameful memories, to prove that the mind does build itself these monuments that are worthy of devotion by art connoisseurs and the insane alike.

In this severely complicated meshing, a newly-married couple resided, only their silhouette discernible. They acted and entertained like a moving memoir in one of the much bigger frames which the horse, lying down, observed as a pair of opera glasses (which also gave the opportunity for three dimensional viewing) had descended from above and adjusted to his eyes — perhaps to remind him that the naked eye was not enough. He knew the lines of this scene off by heart; each sentiment was given graciously like a bouquet and was exchanged with more of a visual flair like a cascade of petals.

The couple had their backs to the horse, sitting down facing the front of the carriage. The entire scene was prolonged with silence but the actions could be clearly seen with the accentuated drama of silent cinema. Both characters were amicable at first; the gentleman coiled his arm around his wife, poured her champagne and they laughed and kissed. As time rode on and what seemed like years setting off in an hour, the alcohol in their system faded and arguments sparked as if they were splints scraping together. For the horse, it was like watching a documentation of the worst part of someone's entire life, yet their most precious, having been recorded for the purpose of warning another individual on approaching the matter of love or to warn them of wandering into that unfulfilling department altogether. On his face, he felt the fire-mask of embarrassment envelop him; he was on his hoofs.

His opera glasses turned to granulated sugar, rained down from his eyes, drew two spots of white on the dark floor like a separate pair of eyes that looked up at him. He thought about the songs of a gazelle he'd buried within the echoing walls of his heart, the songs he didn't want dead or to accidently kill by forgetting. The dread which he'd half expected to feel throughout every journey was now immeasurable within him.

The air was thicker than it had ever been, so much so, that if he had the chance he could have carved his name on it, a name he could not remember and had never heard spoken by anyone but his master. But what was the use of a name now? He was beyond a permanent distinction, to be severely Latinized from all else, when he was connected to everything. The horse wished to express his torment in words but only a line of bees flew from his mouth towards the makeshift beehive so he wished to cry a cry that would never end. This sentiment transmuted to his forehead where a blue light created a miniature whirlpool between his brows, the shape of an egg expanded and took form.

When he took a step forward — the carriage moved one pace forward in accordance with him and he felt a sharp tug at his neck. He looked on; the couple were still arguing, and the bride was weeping with her hands on her face, her shoulders in tremors. He attempted to approach the carriage, stepping forward. This time the carriage moved further forwards and dragged him along the floor. Now he was aware of his task. Before the extant horse considered freedom, it was imperative that he should break the bridge between his morass memories and moving on, for both could not sustain effectively in a binary system. The legacy left of his mistake-empire was restraining, dominating his luxurious head. So without hesitation he started to gallop, following the carriage. Although it was dragging him and he had no choice in the matter, he found it as hard to follow as walking behind a line of ants without squashing them.

As he went on, the floor became unstable, rippling like water in a second and then drawing wells causing the horse to climb steeply at one interval and the next slipping on a steep slope. There was no respite for the carriage-drawn horse who was unceasingly being dragged from one end of the room to the other. This was a form of fast-forwarding in a physical and psychological sense, so that the irrelevant could be skipped and the outcome could be more quickly gained. The scene with the couple was still in procession inside the carriage as he mounted an incredibly steep hill which stood like a point, giving him the chance to finally be rid of the carriage. He would reach the top, no matter the arduous work, and come to an abrupt stop at the peak where the descent would provide enough force to send the carriage soaring and the rope to snatch. He was soon approaching the peak, the ceiling was evident and the chandelier was ever so close to his head. The end of the scene was close, he could sense it. His hoofs were blurred like egg whisks at work as he galloped the fastest he had ever done. The carriage tugged hardest at the top, pulling his neck towards the slope downwards. His legs were ready to relent, digging into the mount, but the cord had been restrained for too long and it then split sending the carriage into oblivion. Moments later, he heard the crash of broken plates. The floor straightened as if the ordeal had never happened and the light of the chandelier faded returning the room back to its stuffy old self.

Looking around him for any sign of light or life, the horse began to sob deplorably, as if he'd just bore witness to the defilement of his favourite love song illuminating a false idea. At this pandering time, he longed for childhood comforts, like a parent warming him with a blanket and to be fed the cure with a regular teaspoon, not one that had been decorated to its teeth or been defined as rare by an austere auctioneer! He prayed for a second sun to liberate his world as his tears, which were honey, softened the wooden planks and eventually hollowed out a funnel in the floor that trickled down to the ceiling of Room 101 where Mr 101 was sitting. Hunched over his work, he was too busy scribbling to be bothered by the sound of dripping. In the corner of the room, there was a chair sitting on a chair pretending to be a better chair than the chair it was sitting on.

Daffodil and the White Horse

Cocooned in an intimate arbour of cedar forest, Daffodil found herself a sanctuary. The trees comforted her as if they could exude body warmth; it was a place where she could lay down her burden and run away to act like the child she was. The sun was ominous in the sky and if Daffodil had stopped to look and perhaps damaged her eyesight, she would have witnessed a hasty Venus rolling on its flaming surface: the planet where a single day is a year. The summer had died late that year, as the four seasons had now joined hands to unite and there was no telling them apart. It had been expected that autumn would arrive in a blasted fury, devastating, the trees leafless, but the summer persisted, cement-mixing with the autumn breeze. It seemed the Earth kept on leaning forward for longer, scared to tilt back to witness the horror that resided at the ceiling of the universe again.

The world was so vast around Daffodil it was almost surprising that it didn't engulf her as a recyclable product that can be turned into something needed but altogether useless, like morning dew for example. However, it did not. The forestry became her playground and Daffodil did not hesitate to swing on branches, drink from the fresh springs and run after butterflies that were much too quick for her.

In her exploration, she found a quieter place than before where furrows of nettles and bloomless plants grew. There was a reeking of death and it felt like a place that was specialised for insightful thought and nothing else. There Daffodil discovered buttons lying around, caked with wet earth, white stockings that were a little more soiled than hers and bundles of handkerchiefs half-buried in the mud.

She didn't dare allow her mind to wonder because she knew her thoughts would lead her into an awful place. She was soon to die and she knew it. It could not trouble her, not when she'd known for some time. Her father would not come, that was obvious, so what was there left to do but allow hope to fester if it wanted to and not have a single thing to do with it when and if it did. A surge of adrenaline turned in her stomach; she tried to visualise seeing Mr 101 again and thinking about what he would do to her. But this did not last for long as she was distracted upon seeing a bumblebee. She ran after it as she had done with many creatures of the air that day. She was easily lured by their ability to fly as easily as she would have been beguiled by the music of the pied piper.

The bee had been hovering helplessly without flowers to keep it occupied; it buzzed for attention and then flew away. Daffodil mashed the mud with her feet as she skipped to follow the creature. Through a path where twigs twisted together like hands in divine matrimony, the creature led her to a small pond where lily pads floated serenely upon its glassy surface. On the largest one (which was luxuriously white and glossy and in fact, a thin layer of coconut jelly), the white horse was having a well-deserved rest. He was better and more perfect than the useless things in life, like love, philosophy and most of all, an artistic inclination. This time though, he was neither here nor there, but semi-existed in between two planes as a ghost made of glass but pronounced in distinction. It could be said that he then acted as a semi-colon that is placed to rescue two separate sentences in order to join them together like long-lost soulmates. Cursed gold was arched and attached to his hoofs as a vow that would eventually destroy him, but it glittered in the sunlight that otherwise warmed him and helped him ease into sleep. He used to be an obsessed flame-blower, a light-taker, now a sliver of the sun's corona graced his head as a crown; the sunlight above seemed compelled to glorify him with furthermore shine. Trepidation was far from what he was feeling in the chamber of his heart; the sun was a feebly burning candle in comparison to his inner and exterior light.

The White Lady of Sorrows was once his rider, had loved him and left him for a quest, to go on a walk until her silver shoes would wear out. Until then, she would have already reached the area splayed out in glacier lagoons, the Island of Glass. Her gift to him was song, but the horse dared not use it. She had forced him to pass through a land of sacrifice and snow where the ice-shards were like sharpened clear quartz that could slice straight through the heart. Stops were taken only for when the horse was desperate for water; he would sip from rock-flour water rivulets that were mapped out as intricately as the many paths to God. At any given time, this tale could have escaped his lips as a gold brick. That's if he hadn't given his language away to become this vast forest, which Daffodil now branded as a place of safety that occasionally sent wafts of lemon-thyme whisper.

The horse was chainless and wild as he'd always been, but the overbearing trifles he'd buried himself into in the past was all he could think of when Daffodil came into view. Still, he had time to just take the joys of the first days of autumn, when the air was considerably cooler and stifled no more. She caressed him; he was beautiful and austere in his position like a maharaja on his throne, but one who was on the brink of retiring from existence. The bee had been circling his muzzle but when the horse turned his head to notice Daffodil, it darted to the nearest gathering but shied away from shadows. Daffodil, not having noticed this, began to pluck the mane of the horse as his mane was in fact a collection of fine vermicelli, lightly sugar-dusted. And its roots were different flavoured popcorn that she chewed on. It was a sweet treat for her sour-ball of a situation.

'Tastes good,' she said politely, 'may I have another one?'

The horse who had lain down his head for resting, looked up at her amiably as he was fain to allow her anything she pleased, then his head lowered for another bout of pondering. Daffodil began to inspect his mane before she plucked a bunch of his fine strands as a bouquet and forced the bundle into her mouth. As a mode of gratitude, she planted a kiss on his head, taking care not to break him. She licked her lips; sage was his flavour, but was this also his occupation here? Was he a wise tremor among the ordinary stillness the world had become accustomed to?

The sound of a wine-bottle uncorking was heard. Daffodil shivered, having been reminded of Mr 101. She turned to look; no-one was there. It was in fact the sound of the horse's burp. The insides of his mouth, which Daffodil caught only half a glimpse of, was made of candied papaya — dry and crystallised. His inside fought out a balloon which squeezed out of his mouth and floated skywards. No matter how hard she tried, Daffodil could not get her hold on to it as it was as slippery as the lip of a Venus flytrap. As it edged further up, it was punctured by a branch to release a chemical, which could digest the human body, unto the pond. The liquid was spilled onto the surface but never sank thus rendering the pond into a giant mirror. It was as reflective and wrinkled as the Saturn's own vanity glass, Enceladus.

When Daffodil saw herself, she patted her hair down a little but this could not solve her overall unkempt appearance. Gracefully, her image faded to replace a series of moving images. She saw the sun shining into Mr 101's house. More importantly, she saw daffodils miraculously growing around the house and in the forest, in their millions. She took to think that she would be remembered after she died. This comforted her and even aroused some profound emotions from within. In that moment, a tear formed on her eyelid. The drop of her fallen tear ceased the pond's dreaming as death silences life.

The Truth

In Room 101, the master's journal had been left open. It was the only piece of Mr 101 left in the house, for he had gone out and braved the woods and even the risk of being caught in sunlight for the first time in decades. But it was good that he knew the constant downpour from the last few days was enough to wash the sun away from its own sky.

64. *My slave will set me free.*

In Room 101, there was never any wind to shift such hastily written pages. A glass paper-weight shaped like a pear lingered in the corner, unused as ever. The journal was laid bare, like a dead body found in the bog marshes for inspection.

> *I will now tell of how things are — well, how I see them. I was sitting in a dark room on the floor. Tears were streaming from my eyes due to the emotional intensity of the sound that came from a farther room, but I wouldn't call it crying. This absurd behaviour weighs on me now. I couldn't find myself to understand this pain that came in a deluge, so long overdue. Some tables then appeared, misty white recognised by the waning moon but it was blurred from these teary eyes. My hunger that had been awakened after all these years, persisted and there was nothing more to do. A gust of wind then shook me to my senses and then I laid down with my head to the floor, looking up to the starry night as my tears turned to ice. I knew I couldn't sleep forever here, the sun was near.*

65. *It's as if the entire house weighs on me with all its heavy mystery.*

After some time, I saw something appear. It was a mooncake that I recognised from my years of researching the mysterious realms. This food could help me to purify myself. I knew I had to draw out my own blood and splash the cake with it in order to consume, no matter how much I detested the idea. In this life we must seek to attain whatever it is we need but not particularly what it is we most desire. I can't forget that — I shouldn't.

This tale was not a droplet Mr 101 fabricated from the downpour of his life. He'd left the most important chapter of his biography unfinished so it is up to his memory to recount and continue on.

After this he scrambled to his feet, wiping the sleet from his face and removed a small sharp knife from his trouser pocket, but just before the act of self-mutilation could proceed, he was interrupted by a familiar voice. For the first time it was comforting.

'Wait, no,' said the lady whose skirt was the cage of a bird, lifting her sleeve slightly. 'It won't hurt as much if you hurt me.'

Mr 101 collapsed onto her, embracing her, releasing the stagnant flood of unexpressed emotions. His tears had no words, his agony multiplied with every thought so they both stood in silence until it was all released; she was the polar opposite of him, in a calm state as she was soothed by the knowledge that death was looming for her. It was also nice to know that she would be in charge of it.

'There is not much time left,' she said. 'I have to leave, but first you must take my blood.' She slashed her index finger with the knife, still hugging a sobbing Mr 101. 'Here take it, take it!'

Pulling him away, she held the cake and smeared her blood onto it and held it to his mouth smudged carelessly in black. Like a hungry child, he devoured it. His stomach lurched and was alight with appetite.

'Mmm,' he said, and swallowed the sponge as fast as he

could. 'Thank you.'

In return, she bowed her head slightly, in an impatient manner and turned to leave him.

Mr 101 called after her, 'You can't leave now. Not without telling me who you are, your name and your purpose here, in my house. I have beaten you with the same hands I now wish to caress you with.'

He was not as forceful or unkind as before, but this time he truly wanted to know rather than just for a purpose of causing a brawl. The woman looked at him in surprise, her mouth open in the horror of the situation.

'What? You mean to say that you remain ignorant to the truth still? It's been so long but I can't explain now, I have to go — I *want* to go — and there is no need for me to explain anyhow because you will realise that in the end, you don't need to find out about the past. You live for the outcome and your outcome is near. Don't you sense it?'

He returned her desperate glare with a puzzled expression. 'Where exactly are you going? How do you disappear from here?'

'That's not important! I have to leave!'

He rushed to grab her arm before she disappeared and found himself transported immediately on the tiles where he had previously spent many hours shifting them under the Medusa chandelier. Below her magnificent golden head was placed a gilded guillotine. To his horror, its sharp blade glowed intensely like its own sun. The lady appeared from under the shadow of the banister, dressed in something quite magnificent; a long trailing multi-coloured dress that glimmered in the glorious eyes of Medusa.

66. *The sun seeks a dark place to die.*

An awkward question formed on Mr 101's black lips. 'Are we getting married?' If so, he would have rather hoped she given some sort of notice or at least a hint. He scrambled to his feet clumsily.

She grimaced, hoping she'd have the strength to laugh it off.

'No, absolutely not! It seems you are much too inadequate for your own destiny,' she gave him a detested glare, taking one step back so she was a pace closer to the guillotine and some inches away from him. There was a smugness in her gait and that of the cunning in her gaze. It was an alluring moment. Mr 101 was mesmerised to watch her journeying to the guillotine, up the stairs. She spoke her words as she, with meticulous precision so as not to fall, made her way to the guillotine.

'Life is like a buttoned shirt that we must open, but for some reason we forget the use of our fingers to unbutton the shirt one button at a time so we spoil the shirt by tearing it open. And then, after the deed is done our wits come about us, much too late, we realise that the shirt was our very own precious soul. In your case, memory, and so we spend the rest of eternity wafting through unknown corridors searching for lost buttons with the torn shirt hanging from our arms like a dead corpse. After lifetimes of searching we forget the purpose of our duty and discard the shirt and the search for buttons altogether.' The lady gulped, turned to Mr 101, stretching herself forward to make herself perfectly audible. 'You are me and I am you.'

Her eyes were his and his eyes were hers and somehow they were both one. One and one but not a whole. His earth never met her sky. There had been a separation of one and he began to remember in fragments, just as he was himself, a fragment of another person. Questions multiplied in his mind and she spun on her feet and stepped towards the guillotine, sprightly and unafraid. One step above the previous was the sublime and the step above that was the ridiculous and a step above the ridiculous makes the sublime again. Mr 101 needed her, he needed her to tell him, tell him everything. And so, with the energy the cake had given him, he stepped forwards to chase her, calling after her with all his might but she was all without incertitude. The brilliant embraced the untouched, the untouched embraced the crazy. All in all it was a birth of unity, among many other things.

67. *You lose so much more than it was worth winning.*

'No, wait...! Wait, you have to tell me — wait!'

He begged, pleaded, began to chase her as the stairs themselves multiplied a thousand-fold before him, spilling out more stairs, allowing the lady to complete her task and obscuring him from his path. When she was close, she turned to look into his eyes; he was panting on the floor miles below her with a mixture of shock, disgust and relief. She blew him a kiss before bowing forwards and giving her life to the guillotine. Then Mr 101 closed his eyes as he heard the sound of scissor blades coming together. Her head rolled down the stairs from the bloodied jaws of the guillotine and landed on his lap.

His body was frozen. He was silent. He held her head up high to Medusa's head and shamefully collapsed back onto himself yet again, without the strength to burst into tears.

68. *What and where is my disease to show that my soul is sick?*

Wordsworth's Departure

Not a single soul leaves this world unscarred and in the same way; not a single soul enters the Earth without the effects of having lived another. An old wise soul, ready for departure, Wordsworth stood awaiting the verdict of nature by the shores of the turbulent waves, crashing about him, hissing out scum. The sky was an unfaithful mirror recording the malfunction of the waters below, their grey clouds translating the black waves. Both entities should have been blamed for a catastrophically foreboding setting. He was unaware of the chaos. Having known and experienced chaos first-hand, he had learnt the best behaviour to employ was that of calmness. It was with calmness that he waited, looking over the horizon.

After some time, he was awakened from his mild reverie when an unavoidable spectre, bright as a huge diamond in sunlight appeared. Wordsworth witnessed the light diving into the depth of the sea and left him in the darkness of before.

In the depth of the raging water, the light settled to reveal a horse, ripped to shreds like bits of marshmallow, his flesh as white as his coat. He was a treasure torn apart, but not dead. Creatures of the divine could never die. Nothing enters the Earth unscarred. His heart bled, like an opened inkhorn and lingered there like a drowning flag; brilliant blue flames of sulphur burst from him as a divine shield of protection.

Wordsworth, miles away from him where the wind was most ferocious, waited in vain for the light to be resurrected in his gaze but, when nothing stirred, he realised that he must fetch the light himself, for he had hands, feet and the mind, whereas the light did not.

Quickly, he was on his knees performing an act of

benevolence; it was a miracle he had known for some time, something he had acquired from the long days of solitude. His lips touched the water as he surely sucked in the water from the sea. The waves entered him in consistent whirls. He knew the water would be his poison but he persisted as the effects brightened his throat in blue, slowly absorbing his life from him. He sensed it with every breath as tides of salty water crept at the brim of his throat. When he had emptied the sea, he swallowed his salty vomit and ambled towards the carcass.

Upon seeing the horse and its parts displayed before him like scattered petals on a honeymoon bed, Wordsworth removed his clothes, his sparrow from his trouser pocket and drifting to and from his face, greeting him in this new day which was unlike any other. In great urgency, avoiding his chirpy companion Wordsworth was on his knees again, carefully in a skilful manner removing the threads which had bound his clothes together laying them beside him and fetching a stone close by to prevent them from escaping with the winds.

He took hold of his sparrow, pressed its beak together and removed it in a pluck from the sparrow's anatomy, as there was no other way. And as he used his companion's beak as a needle to sew the horse's flesh back together, he recited a prayer for his friend to aid his soul to the heavens, tears flooding his vision until they were blinked to slide away. Tears flowed from his blue-robed eyes over the white petticoat of his skin. Nothing leaves this world unscarred.

The wind was all about him, grey and misty as was a bruised sky above him when the deed was done and the horse was erect on four sturdy legs. He bowed to Wordsworth, who in return patted the gentle creature and wished him a successful final journey. And as the horse began yet another journey, Wordsworth, without a sense of trepidation was satisfied and accepted all that had been done, he stepped up to the heavens to dwell as a sylph on his permanent cloud, calm as the eye of the storm.

On land below was a determined horse, although bearing the scars of before was eager to reach his final destination. Yes, he saw his reflection, on a leftover puddle nearby and he realised now that not a single soul enters this world unscarred. He traced the veins of stitching on his body with his caviar black eyes one last time and at once began to race to his twisted tower. Horseshoes beat the sand like knuckles knocking on freshly baked bread in order to determine whether its insides were cooked.

From the empty sea, his pearly speck died with the ferocity of the winds.

***

This harsh wind subsided when it reached the boy by the lake. A boy he was, observing the egg white clouds which folded into multiple forms until they melted to a rather disappointing nothing. He sighed, he denied. The lake in which the pebbles were tossed into was not a lake. To the world and its people that lake could have been its own seven seas, but to the boy's wilful eyes those seven wonders were less than magnificent, drab as a simple puddle, flat as paper.

69. *Is not our planet merely a smudge of glitter among the remnants of an exploded magician's box?*

A lengthy time had passed since the boy, or Mr 101, had arrived; the spot where his head now rested on the pebbled shore was where he caught his first glimpse of the island close-by with the use of his Galilean telescope. He had held it to his eye and spotted a carob tree. It was then that he saw the opportunity to make chocolate from its purple pods and begin his adventure of exploitation. Greed had glimmered in his eyes. With this greed, he began his mysterious renovation of his modest country house. And the next thing he knew, the ladies came pouring in like much sought after rain when the drought had passed. No — he was not a boy, he was Mr 101. He had lived in denial all this time, giving free reign to his fears and paranoia. He became much too afraid to live his life, to take walks outdoors and appreciate the gifts of nature. Somehow, he felt that if he took advantage of things that were not part of his belongings he would have to reimburse it by a painful sacrifice. This included every fresh, fulfilling air he breathed. He felt that every torrential downpour would then come to melt him gelatinous and that the world would deviously plan his death if he stared at it too much. Because, more than anyone, he knew it was rude to stare.

A pebble crunched nearby and Mr 101's attention came alive at the sound. He turned to see Daffodil, who was white-faced to see him.

'Come here,' he found his feet again.

Daffodil swiftly turned to run and soon she was drifting through the mass of Lebanonian cedar. She could hear Mr 101's hurrying footsteps behind her but with all her strength she raced on, panting. The footsteps of Mr 101 soon ceased behind her as her own quickened but she continued on and soon she was close to the house but she stayed in the nearby forestry as she could not hear a single thing. The pear tree was not far from where she was, bringing memories of the note from her father and enjoyable moments with Wordsworth. She wondered where he was now and whether he was ever genuine with his words. She doubted it very much now, as he was nowhere to be seen and had done nothing to help her. The night had come, promising her many hours of darkness. This was both a favour and a curse, as Mr 101 could have been lurking anywhere but there would be no way of telling. There was not even a single rustling of a leaf. Daffodil began to ease herself. For what it was worth, she waited in the hope that Wordsworth would turn up to save her until sleep overtook her.

While she slept, Mr 101 crept close by her as silently as he could; he had been watching her all along but did not harm her, at least not yet. From what he could see, her face lacked all the life it ever acquired in the first place. He had every right to believe that he was doing her a favour in disguise. Exercising his best quality, patience, he scattered some chocolate rabbits, their flavours varying from bubblegum to Turkish delight, on the forest floor, pulling them from his sleeve along with a few pears covered in syrup, lacquered like lip-gloss: sticky and sweet. The footprints he left behind were filled up miraculously with frozen custard as he sauntered quietly from her and into the house. He thought he should have a rest before she made her way to the house; after all, he was patient and adored a good show.

The moon that night was a round sieve filled with flour resting on a white bowl, having been neglected by its baker for something much more enticing, like a life-changing venture; the caraway seeded stars, the culinary symbol of rebirth, were kept on the side, not yet used in the mixture.

Mr 101 lived for those special occurrences, that moment before he cleared his throat to speak, before the knuckles clench to beat the door because there was always hope then that the person would subside from their exertions, remember they had somewhere else to go. There was the hope. But he was least expecting Daffodil to avoid his persuasion because he lacked faith in her; she was a child and so naturally comprehended little in the ways of the world.

She could take as much time as she wished, for he knew she would inevitably succumb to his trick so he took this alone time, the calm before the great storm, to grieve over his losses. And then it would be out of the marzipan and into the marmalade.

He avoided sitting upon his dearest saffra, as he much preferred to drag it across Room Two on its planks of wood as the sound reminded him of the lady's voice, that constant droning, the repetitive sound of a crowd clearing their throats. Lovely, the sound was, now that he was in control of it. The inexplicable thing was she *wasn't* gone — at least not completely. She was him and he was her, but the part of him which belonged to her was gone. As long as he was still alive, she was alive. What a trivial knot in a rope which no strength could untangle this was! There was not a single bit of his life which was not a lie and he, of all people, was the greatest liar of all.

The chair's friction with the wooden planks moaned with his inner voice. And then he stopped dead on his feet still holding the chair like a piece of luggage behind him, neither smiling nor frowning. His legs jittered in excitement for a second but quickly restored themselves to normal sturdiness, just in case any supernatural creature of any kind was watching and was intending to catch him out by spreading the word that Mr 101 was human after all. This information was, of course, absurd and shouldn't have been mentioned. It was the entrance of his lent-lily which triggered this unsightly reaction. She was his stabilising element, his staple diet, a name that lips cannot form. He sensed the vibration of the opening of his front door and the harsh wafer of wind which entered his world.

He quickly quitted his chair and superficial mourning, whispered a quick apology to his darling saffra as he dived into a close cupboard, rummaging madly through it as if all patience had vanished from the world. And who knew what nature of equipment was hidden and mollified behind those dusty mahogany faces? What if they decided to sneeze out every single terrifying invention — should not the eye of the guest at hand be frightened, even those who claim to have seen and experienced it all? Once or twice, one thing or another unexpectedly leapt from the depths of that black hole, springing out like the contents of a mattress torn out. The reason of their placement in that trap was to anyone's guess.

Finally then, he removed a rusty-coloured old saw. To put it simply and in a most subtle manner, Mr 101 placed a saw to his right wrist, as he was left-handed, and began slicing it as he would a piece of bread. In his mind, he assured his protesting mind that *Pain is in the mind, I shall feel no pain, pain is in the mind*, and so forth, 'til he felt himself emancipated from the prison of pain, soaring on the wings of numbness. The sound of the operation could only be compared to that of walls being sanded down from bumps and scratches in order to be freshly licked with paint.

70. *The luck from which you prosper, first come in shadows.*

He sank to his putrid floor, having lost the chalices full of blood from his anatomy, and with what dismal sound he could make with his dried-up black lips, he spoke to the amputated hand and said, 'Find her.'

By the sound of his voice, the hand became possessed with life and traced the floor on its voyage to find Daffodil.

Mr 101 sat there missing — or rather, contemplating — his right hand, doing nothing to stop the blood flow, listening to the harrowing winds, looking at the unhealthy state of the room. *He* began to rest, whereas his right hand marched off out of the door as soon as the order was given. Mr 101 thought it was a nice little trick on his part to perform, he had always loved the theatrical side of life. After all isn't this planet our own empty stage? And didn't his little spot of a rock lost in the mouth of the ocean which looked like a threatening symptom of the Black Death belong to himself so that he should do as he pleased with it? A cup of mulled wine would have been quite appropriate at this moment; his thoughts flowed nicely with the ruby waters but never mind, he would kill Daffodil first.

***

Daffodil was beyond a withered flower, with brown smudges of chocolate around her lips, but with whatever measure of life was left in her she decided she wanted to make the most of whatever time she had left and perhaps, if she was lucky, find an escape to the harsh judgement she'd been dealt with. Her stomach bulged unnaturally and felt like it would burst with a prick of a pin. The corridors were as dark (or dark blue; the patriotic blues) as they had ever been, the harlequin was dead so he could neither lead her astray as he used to.

Her little legs tripped her to corridors after corridors of emptiness and where the occasional door was spotted. When she took the chance to shake the fist of the door, she found that it was locked — or had been glued to the wall itself. So she began to pace from one to another, hoping to find a place to hide for some time until the morning came when it would be easier and less frightening to be in the forest. Perhaps she'd spot her dear friend Wordsworth; surely a man who has dwelt for so long in this terrain would know an escape to it. The concept of a successful escape kept her complacent for the moment. Little did she know the creeping hand was around the corner, sensing her every step from the pressure points of its fingertips.

As she turned another corner, she spotted three doors. The first one she touched grabbed her hand and thrust her inside. Was this one of Mr 101's effort to dramatise further the already theatrical killing of a little girl?

So of course, she entered the room, which so happened to slam shut and lock behind her, and the candles lit themselves in a corner miraculously. Of course, such incidents were quite natural in Mr 101's dwelling, as were floorboards, which were in fact enlarged white and black piano keys. Each time Daffodil stepped on one it made a sonorous alarming 'ping!' which vibrated the walls and travelled to Room Two, sending Mr 101's eyebrows to the roof. Mr 101's hand was already outside the door.

Just as soon as the door was opened by the hand, Daffodil felt a sharp jolt of pain in her stomach. The hand approached her, plodding the saddest notes of Death Metal Opera it had ever played as she sat in the corner on a black key anticipating her capture. She began to regret consuming the sweetmeats on the forest floor which weakened her entire body till she could hardly move or protest when the hand began to drag her along the corridor to Room Two, where Mr 101 sat on the floor still, bleeding away and waiting for her.

He did not regret his actions because he wanted Daffodil to seek him and not the reverse. His psychological make-up was complex indeed.

71. *I must let nature take its course and the ridiculous to overtake the serious in any circumstance. That's who I am.*

At last, she reached her final destination to the door of Room Two where the number 101 was written, dripping, in blood. When she stepped inside, the first things she noticed were the many candles that were lit like the stars in the universe. In this sea of dotted light was Mr 101, looking at her with a sly smile. On his beaten saffra, he stretched out his hand to the girl.

'Daffodil, you succeeded. You survived and that's all that matters.'

Mourning

The tear is pear-shaped until it spreads its body on the lips or on the neck. Either way, its journey causes a fatal pain to the heart like the words ushered from a Death Metal Opera song. Mr 101 was helpless and the guilt mounted within him with every second. The taste of Daffodil's blood remained on his tongue, he could hardly speak. If he did speak, he believed he would unleash her taste to the world and he resented the idea. He wished to keep her within him forever. With some leftover energy, he made the effort to take a stroll about his house, taking his time to close all the doors and slicing their hands off with a knife, apart from the eighth room whose handle was sealed with quality brass. With bed linen, he covered all the mirrors. Each one trembled under their covers which resulted in them smashing to pieces; it was as if they couldn't handle the intensity the situation.

Mr 101 slipped a funeral biscuit (his choice of lady's fingers) into each and every one hundred and one rooms of his vast dominion with a note: '*You are bidden to attend the funeral of a flower.*' It was pure folly to expect an empty room or any of its contents to attend a funeral but he always appreciated the notion of 'it's the thought that counts' so he continued. He had never paid so much attention to a single death of any of his victims — but then, in saying so, he had never had himself a companion in this dismal house, unless he counted the ghosts and the lingering ladies he hated beyond the word hate itself. How they laughed, and blinked their layers of eyelashes away, how they thirsted for wine and hungered for chocolate, how impatient they were upon receiving his bizarre treatment.

On the bright side, now that Daffodil was gone, there was space to breathe — it was like breathing underwater, but still, it wasn't as bad as not breathing at all. Mr 101 was now, beyond doubt, ready to shed the mask of hypocrisy. He started from the top and ended up on the ground floor, crouching on the floor as his wandering hand tiptoed its way back onto him. Medusa's head stared down at him and he did the same directly back, seeing his distorted reflection on its dusty gilded surface. His tiled floor beneath him conveyed the image of the sun, flames ablaze on its round surface still in black and white. It was now all coming to fruition, the seeds of before. His mistakes, the cruelty he bestowed between these walls were coming to effect. The phoenix was rising from the putrid ashes. The dust, inextinguishable dust, was all lifting like the evaporation of water holding on to the tail of a kite.

In Room Two, he had charged the fireplace with fire, sensing that his eleventh hour was prowling close by to, at any moment, gormandise him in one go. The flames curled and made a sound like a beast clearing its throat for one last damning speech. In that very orifice, Mr 101 fed that gruelling-monster with his entire collection of books, his knowledge to the claws of chance which will decide on its own accord, which pages it would finish to ashes and embers and thus separate. He fancied the idea that he was burying them so that they may ferment into these species of dust; this idea satisfied him and acted as a euphoric medicine to distract him from what he was actually doing. As each book burned, in that very moment when they were fresh in the fire before, they were completely exhumed memories of the questions they had aroused came to him. He knew exactly what each one was and reciting them again only proved how ridiculous he'd been. If he hadn't killed all those who knew him, they would have surely made a mockery of him — that he knew for certain, without even a single cell of a doubt. People were never to be trusted; they were like landmines, and with a touch of intrigue, they could destroy, whether they wore the mask of evil or not. Even the most compassionate could condemn.

Mr 101 burnt all those books that were his kingdom and source of knowledge, save for his journal. This he placed on his now empty (still dusty) mahogany shelf in a twenty-three degree tilt, for the Earth also tilted to this degree to determine the seasons and keep its inhabitants alive. The journal had been his life-force, that place he succumbed to be alive. The white sheets of paper had been his Egyptian linen; the words he'd written were his darkness that he had appreciated of the night.

The last thing he ever wrote in his journal was a letter of apology to the sun, but it was hardly more than a few sentences:

> *I can bear to see you now. You may come anytime you like and I will not in the least act or even be perturbed. I have come to know the full extent of the violence and brutality I have procured under this roof but I must say I am without regret. You may never change me and neither will I ever dare to change you, so we have no choice but to come to accept one another. That's all I can bring myself to write for now. But one last thing — it must be said that I wish this to be over, the sooner the better.*

As for his saffra, which had stood the test of being baked under his backside and battered, it was hastily decided that it would never be left to rot. In the seldom time left, which was flicking like pages in a brisk wind, Mr 101 performed his last magical act. He was perfervid as he waved his hand before the chair with the eloquence of a matador swishing his cape to enrage a bull. The chair began to vibrate and sweat, as if it had indeed understood that it would assume the role of bull in its furniture form. Dew drops glistened from its faded velveteen colour as it began to shrink, seeming to deflate. More cushions began to grow on the seat and curled back in the process. Soon, it became clear that the chair was fast becoming a flower as its wooden legs began to meld and extend upward into a stem. The crimson rose was pinned to Mr 101's breast pocket; it would never wither, at least not anytime soon.

He departed from Room Two for the final time feeling like a groom for the bride of death. Death! The word was a comical illusion to him. Indeed death was a pleasurable oasis, having captured its glimmerings himself from afar countless times. He wondered why he performed magic at this critical time if he had dejected all he was, scoured every penitence from him, screwed it into a ball and thrown it out into the universe to spray into confetti for his appropriate apocalypse. There was one reason — well, a few. Because magic was his all, the vapour he thirsted for, his kingdom come too soon, the reason for breathing whenever he couldn't hold his breath any longer.

Of course, he could have done more, gone out with a bang, performed atrocities with style and affectation; he was still and never will be above any of the above. However, the line between desire and need was become clearer as the light of day. Yes, it was probable. He could've tied every possession together and pulled them all up his sleeve; his Medusa chandelier was never evaluated but he was sure it would have been worth more than he could ever imagine. The problem of it being ghastly was enough to change his mind. In fact, the plain truth that everything was ghastly in this house was enough to quell his bother. And so came the realisation that he was the first and only Ridiculist. He had initiated himself. No-one told him to, there was no need of reform to any other following. He became a Ridiculist because he insisted it would keep him busy and intellectual. At a crucial moment, when he had gone too far into his pit of inglorious disbelief to look back, he realised the mess was as derisive as it sounded and looked. The experience hadn't left him parched, for he'd always been dry; perhaps now he was dust, awaiting more tragedies to refine him to nothing, something that will in turn define him. And perhaps this very wish lay near, next door, in the next hour or so.

Now, even after all this labouring, there was yet more truth to be faced. The chequered floor beneath him faded into a solid glass and Medusa's head in a moment was aglow with a bright light so he was forced to stop staring at his distorted self and focussed at the change of his floor. At first he viewed beyond the glass with incertitude. Then the shock forced him onto his feet as he came to recognise the atrocities of his past. It all came sinking in an instant, like a thousand knives.

He recognised the equipment he used to change him from a woman to a man, the face of his horrified wife when she learnt the truth on their wedding night. Madeleine... her life could not be spared. So he destroyed their home he'd worked hard to build and in place, with his own scrawny fingers, built this one. Being married was like being trapped in a kiss forever; his muscles ached in tight embraces, the fun suffocated him, and love assaulted him instead of effusing him with limitless passion. Who was *he* to marry when he was far from ever *being* a he? Yes, he lived the part, his acting was prize-worthy, his clothes masked the lie perfectly, but his heart would always be in the same place.

It is impossible to move the heart to the head and the head to the heart — dismal science does not allow it, and magic thoroughly advised against it. But in his emotional heart, which up till now he hardly took time to care about, was very much beating. He realised that his feelings for Daffodil would be secreted in his heart forever and even after that. No-one, not even if they dared to approach or stand so close to him, would ever be able to calculate his motives or what went on behind those rightfully closed doors of his eyes. Nothing would be shown or sensed, not a clue given or hidden to later be seen, not even for the most clairvoyant of all to guess.

As he sat on that floor perplexed, exhausted from all the trickery and the chasing and the perusing and everything which added up to this lie, the Medusa chandelier toppled from its hanging and rolled like a giant ball of spiky ribbons down the stairs, leapt over the head of Mr 101 and smashed into the thin layer of the glassy floor to where Mr 101's shame lay. The massive hole it punctured like a wound began to heal, and surely the chequered floor resumed to its normal state.

However, the ordeal had just begun. The roof above the

swindling stairs, like the blooming of a lotus, unfurled, and, to his awestruck horror, the light of the sun poured into his neglected realm. His eyes were in wonder at the sight. To him, it was simply enlightenment. He had always known this change would come. The benevolent light caressed the corners and dried the bloody walls, shone its light upon the lip-gloss scattered stairs, his chequered floor and Mr 101's chalk-white face which eclipsed his shadow on the floor. He could not bring himself to protest against it so he closed his eyes while he concentrated on the sound of the beating hoofs becoming clearer and clearer, approaching him with every beat of the heart. He was not a man of the sun but the sun was a man of him. What could this ever mean?

An acidic stench of film deteriorating gassed the house; it was undergoing a serious case of vinegar syndrome. Every room was going by deliquescing into black paper blood, mirrors grating their shards into dust; some small and irrelevant objects vanished and the precious became a botanical version of itself. Everything, everything, everything, Mr 101's everythings eventually became gelatinous until they splashed onto the floor as black water.

72. *These imprisoning walls have all the liberty.*

Mr 101's totem animal, the white horse of unfaltering vivacity, a Pacolet, drifted swiftly along the hilltop where the trees were clotheshorses for the leaves, speeding on to rescue his master's soul through the tusks of cedar. Around the horse's silver neck, an ankh appeared from orbs of light, a tool for resurrection, as he was assuredly diminishing the distance between himself and Mr 101. Bursting from between the fresh green of grass were daffodils, crocus and hyacinths, cloaked with dew releasing thin shafts of gold. A scene of love it came to represent, as if two lovers had met here, made love on that fine carpet, and retreated to build a home. The white horse, triumphant, neared the pear tree. Mr 101 was quite still and in a daze (much passed the look of haggard by now), nearly cadaverous in colour, as if sitting for a painting, a masterpiece, an oeuvre that was nearing completion. And in this way his horse, which in every way was nature's Lazarus, come back from the dead as a sturdy message that even the most dejected could be saved, was the self-performing paintbrush. This painting would most of all result in hoof-tracks on the forest floor. It would not describe Mr 101's features; it would, however, be more useful as a portrait of his experiences, his Psalterian sort of salvation, an action painting that told a tale of a life lived scant of zeal, but rather to serve desire and complexity.

73. *Now I know who I am, and who I've always been — a slave to my own empty words.*

Meanwhile, on Titan

As if to justify an act so bizarre and uncommon, or simply to commemorate something which took much too long an interval to come to play to an epicure of pleasures, the raindrops which had so found slumber in Titan's clouds now decidedly found release by a helpless force and in their millions, descended. It rained to quench the chocolate lands that thirsted, that waited, that would soon be a testament to the erosive power of methane tears, sculpting its mountain faces gaunt. As if to respond to the touch of a cold finger, every sapphire raindrop quivered in the atmosphere; their slow descent was a tribute to all that could be said to be hypnotic about Titan, Earth's significant other. And in a moment's bother, one drop did touch the ground with a tranquil kiss, heralding many to follow on, more persuasive and more powerful an enchanter than Time.

Author Profile

Z. R. Ghani was born in 1990 and began writing at the age of sixteen after reading *Jane Eyre*. She studied Creative Writing and Art at Bath Spa University and graduated in 2012. She now lives in London. Aside from her usual nine-to-five job and pondering life's mysteries (why is a raven like a writing desk?), she aspires to be a novelist who is able to manipulate abstract thought and perplexing emotions into intriguing, if not peculiar, word play. In her spare time, she likes travelling, engaging in philosophical debates and visiting art galleries for inspiration.

Author of:
Mr 101

Publisher Information

Rowanvale Books provides publishing services to independent authors, writers and poets all over the globe. We deliver a personal, honest and efficient service that allows authors to see their work published, while remaining in control of the process and retaining their creativity. By making publishing services available to authors in a cost-effective and ethical way, we at Rowanvale Books hope to ensure that the local, national and international community benefits from a steady stream of good quality literature.

For more information about us, our authors or our publications, please get in touch.

www.rowanvalebooks.com
info@rowanvalebooks.com

Printed in Great Britain
by Amazon